FAERIE WAR

THE CHANGELING CHRONICLES: BOOK SEVEN

EMMA L. ADAMS

1

When I was thirteen years old, Faerie slammed into my entire world and changed it forever.

Fourteen years later, similar scenes of carnage left imprints on my mind that would never fade. I closed the door on the manor I'd called home for the last few months, and on the bodies that nobody had yet returned to remove. A faerie had killed almost the entire mage council and captured the rest. A Summer faerie, judging by the marks I'd found on the bodies. And here I was, about to step into the Summer Court itself in a desperate gambit to save my lover from the hands of a murderous god, all the while hoping they wouldn't slaughter me on sight for destroying a valuable possession of theirs in the name of thwarting said deity.

I hadn't been known for making great decisions lately.

I hefted my backpack over my shoulders and adjusted the straps so that it wouldn't hinder my ability to carry my sword. I'd packed everything I thought I might need for an impromptu visit to Faerie—spare clothes, food, water and even a sleeping bag—as counting on the Sidhe to provide decent hospitality was an even less wise decision than setting foot in their domain in the first place.

Guilt at abandoning my friends in a time of crisis gnawed at me despite my knowledge that there was little I could do to protect them from here. The mage council members were either dead or missing. The necromancers had no leader and were virtually powerless. The half-bloods had scattered, the survivors of Fionn's latest scheme having been forced to leave their territory, and the last I'd seen of the Chief, he'd fled like a coward in the middle of battle and taken all his allies with him. One reliable leader remained in the whole city: Isabel, my best friend and leader of the largest witch coven in the area. She couldn't single-handedly hold the entire supernatural community together, not with so many people dead or missing, so it was up to me to rescue the prisoners. And, if possible, talk the Sidhe into sending help. No pressure.

"They took Vance," I'd told her over the phone while packing. "Fionn must have sent someone after the mages while he was occupied with the cauldron. I left him there, but I can't guarantee he won't come back while I'm gone. And if I don't make it out—"

"You'll make it back," said Isabel. "We'll be fine. We have hiding places if Fionn launches another attack. You concentrate on getting help from the Sidhe and rescuing Vance."

"Got it." There was another question nagging at me, however. "I worry about crossing between realms after Fionn already damaged the Ley Line. Have the necromancers reported any issues?"

"Yes, but nothing like the invasion," said Isabel. "Rick told me that he and the other necromancers can't cross into Death at all. From what he said, every time someone tries to reach the other side, it's as though they're completely blocked by some invisible barrier."

"Weird." The last time the realms had collided had messed up the spirit lines so badly that the dead had walked alongside the living, but this sounded like the opposite of the last invasion, if anything. Didn't mean we were off the hook, though, and I'd never have left Isabel to deal with the fallout if Vance's life hadn't been at stake.

Fionn had hit me where it hurt the most. I wouldn't leave Vance to die in Faerie. Never.

"You'd better go," Isabel said. "Are you ready?"

"Hell, no, but Vance needs me. I'll see you when I'm back." A promise. I'd get Vance away from Fionn, no matter the cost.

Hmm. That's probably not a good outlook to have if you want to get away from Faerie alive this time.

My nails bit into my palms, and fury rolled through me. My first experience in Faerie as a helpless human imprisoned by a callous Sidhe lord with a liking for torture had stripped away the child I'd been before and left a stranger in her place. Eleven years had passed since I'd escaped, but the scars remained as a constant reminder, and one that had ultimately forged me into someone who wouldn't hesitate to walk back into that hell to save Vance.

Moreover, I had an awful lot to say to the Sidhe, who'd been at least indirectly responsible for all the faerie-related problems in my life. Two of them waited on the manor's lawn, accompanied by Quentin, the brownie who served Vance's family. I'd recently found out that the Coltons weren't his only family—he had another master, in the Seelie Court, to whom he owed allegiance—and while he claimed not to have passed on our secrets to his second family, I didn't trust him in the least. Not that I was in a position to be picky. He, and the two faerie knights waiting outside the manor, were my only route into Faerie.

Lord Raivan and his companion, Lord Burdock, sat

astride their horses, wearing gold and green in the fashion of the Seelie Court. Like most Sidhe, their eerily stunning looks were smoke and mirrors, their inhumanity hidden behind beautiful masks designed to ensnare mortals. Summer might be known as the land of smiles and harmless mischief compared to the brutality of Winter, but I'd be keeping my sword, Helena, close at hand.

Lord Raivan hissed out a breath when his gaze caught on the iron dagger conspicuously attached to my weapons belt. I ignored him. I'd made it quite clear that I was the one risking my neck by going into a realm which was toxic to mortals. I'd take all the weapons I damn well wanted.

"Ready?" I asked. "Let's go."

"This is foolish," said Lord Raivan. "You should have returned our property to us, human."

"I told you," I said, "Summer's ring is gone, thanks to Fionn. You shouldn't have taken your eyes off it in the first place."

"You—"

"She has an audience with Summer," Quentin said in his gravelly voice. "There's no ignoring a direct order from the Court."

Yeah, thanks, Quentin. I just hoped the slippery bastard wasn't leading me into a trap. "How does this work? I just… follow you?"

"Yes," he answered. "You have an invitation, so the faerie realm should let you enter without objection."

"It better." Under normal circumstances, only the Sidhe were able to travel from the mortal realm to Faerie, but I'd become an exception of sorts due to the magic I'd stolen from an exiled Sidhe lord. That magic came with access to the Grey Vale, a segment of Faerie to which the Sidhe sent their exiles, but permission to enter either of the Courts was rarely granted to a non-fae.

Whatever magical quirks I might possess, I was still a hundred percent human, and even a Sidhe lord's magic would only go so far in a realm at odds with my very nature. Despite all I'd learned during my three-year captivity in a Sidhe's castle, the rules that underpinned their realm remained shrouded in mystery.

As had become clear recently, I'd also been oblivious to some glaring secrets concerning the supernatural communities in my *own* realm. Like the fact that there'd been an alliance only a few decades ago between the Sidhe and the other supernaturals in the form of a council whose existence had subsequently been forgotten after most of those council members had died in the invasion. The only survivors had been Quentin, the Hemlock witches, and Lord Frank Sydney, the necromancer Guardian of Death's gates. They'd secured me an entry ticket to Faerie, supposedly to attempt to fix whatever had broken in the invasion. As if rescuing the Mage Lords and persuading the Sidhe to offer a helping hand wasn't enough responsibility to rest on one person's shoulders.

The two Seelie knights turned on their giant horses as a flash of green light enveloped the lawn. Dazzling brightness blanketed my vision. My hand locked onto Helena's hilt, the other gripping the iron dagger. A tingling sensation ran up and down my body like I'd stepped too close to the effects of a particularly powerful witch spell. Then, unfamiliar magic overwhelmed me, pressing against every cell of my skin, my body, my organs. Panic shot through my nerves like I'd plummeted fifty feet off a building, but I held still, focusing on the solidity of the sword in my hand, the familiar press of the hilt to my palm.

The pressure lifted and my vision adjusted, the green light dimming but not vanishing outright. We stood in a clearing of knee-deep grass, brighter than I'd ever seen in the mortal realm, and swaying in a breeze at the perfect temperature for a summer afternoon. Bright flowers bloomed in shades of purple and red so intense they burned my retinas. Wide, thick trees spread out enough to expose the perfect blue sky, the bright sun that bore no relation to the one back home. At once I regretted wearing a leather jacket, though its padded sides would offer some protection if something nasty came after me.

The two knights and their horses glowed even brighter here, surrounded by a green halo that reminded me most humans wouldn't see half of what I did. Carrying a Sidhe's magic had wrought permanent changes, including the ability to see through most glamour, but that didn't change the fact that there were some parts of Faerie that no mortal could look at without losing their mind.

"Nice." I released a breath, my heart racing in my ears. "Pretty. Where are the death traps and the man-eating plants? Do you save those for overly curious tourists?"

Lord Raivan narrowed his eyes down at me. "I would not advise you to speak to all our nobles with such disrespect. Our magic is at its full capacity here."

"Yeah, I know that." I'd hoarded information on the Courts during my captivity, learning from an old man named Gerry who'd been imprisoned in Avalin's castle for much longer than I had. Due to the Grey Vale's destructive nature, the beasts that survived in its dark corners were chiefly Unseelie rather than Seelie, and I didn't have quite as much knowledge of Summer as I did of Winter. I did, however, know enough to be aware that no level of politeness would prevent the Sidhe from turning me into a deer if they so desired. "Is this the Court, then?"

"This is one of the places in Summer's territory closest to the human realm," said Quentin, from somewhere amid the long grass. "Like your human world, the faerie realm itself is extensive and has many parts, not all of which are inhabit-able. We can walk to the Court from here."

The brownie waded through the grass towards a forest of towering oaks and ashes. Each sprawling tree mirrored its counterpart in the mortal realm, albeit brighter, taller, and somehow more solid, more *present*. As though the mortal realm's version was only a pale imitation and not the other way around. If someone tried to take an axe to one of these trees, they'd probably have eaten the would-be woodcutter alive.

The two knights galloped towards the densely packed trees without any fear of collision. The Summer Sidhe held a level of control over nature that was reciprocal, as Summer magic fed on life and fuelled it in turn. At their approach, the trees themselves moved out of the knights' way like subjects stumbling aside to allow royalty to pass by. Quentin and I hurried after, following the riders down a path dappled with sunlight.

I hadn't walked a hundred metres before a vine shot out and grabbed my ankle.

Faerie had tried that same trick so many times that I merely rolled my eyes when the vine flipped me upside down, dangling me over the path. Quentin stopped, alarm flickering across his face, but I'd run out of fucks to give long before I'd left the mortal realm.

"What?" I asked the plant. "If you want to try eating me, be my guest. I have iron in my pockets."

The vine responded by shaking me violently. I gritted my teeth, the blood rushing to my head, and reached for my magic. A faint blue light bloomed at my hands, but nothing as bright as usual. *Dammit, it's still playing hide-and-seek.* My magic had been notably less potent since I'd used it to shatter Fionn's cauldron and prevent him from creating an army of the dead, and being in the Court whose power was diametrically opposed to the source of my talisman's magic likely didn't help matters either.

I inched my hand towards one of my daggers. A second vine locked onto my wrist, but I fought the pull, my fingers closing around the hilt and pulling it free. As the iron brushed against the vine, the plant released my wrist with a violent shudder. I twisted the dagger in my hand and drove it into the thick stem that ensnared my ankle.

The vine emitted a sound almost like a faint scream as the iron pierced the surface. I slid free, landing in a forward roll and coming upright at a crouch. "Nice try."

Lord Raivan, who'd stilled his horse, gave me an appraising look. "Are you certain you're a pure-blooded human?"

"Yes." I rose upright, sheathing my weapon. The dagger was one of a pair Vance had given me, each reinforced with iron and marked with glyphs designed to enable me to find its partner if I lost one. Given my previous experience with using non-fae magic in this realm, I doubted the latter would work here, but the iron alone was a deterrent to most of its inhabitants. "Believe it or not, you tend to make adjustments when you spend years being dangled upside-down, thrown out of windows and beaten up by the fae."

"Then you might survive this trip after all." Lord Raivan's horse resumed trotting after his companion. Quentin looked me over as though searching for injuries and then ran after, his stubby little legs struggling to keep up with the large horse's gallop.

I strode ahead of the brownie, addressing the horse's rider. "Didn't want to use your magic to help me out?"

"I thought you had your own magic." Lord Raivan cast a shrewd look over the back of his horse.

"I do." Defensiveness crept into my tone. "It's from

Winter, and I figured it'd draw unwelcome attention here in Summer. Iron is generally more effective."

"Is it?" Lord Raivan turned back to the road ahead. "Your blade… it's not one I've seen before."

"I'm not here to discuss my talisman." My shoulders tensed. "Not even with the Seelie King, if he wants to lower himself to speak to me. I'm here to learn how to free my partner and stop an invasion of my realm. Everything else is secondary."

Admittedly, I wouldn't have minded learning more of my talisman's capabilities, but I wouldn't find that information here. Summer's Sidhe would be displeased enough to know I carried a blade from Winter without my admitting that the magic it contained was of a different origin. Namely, from one of the very deities the Sidhe had exiled when they'd created the Grey Vale. Given that someone had sent this pair to escort a pair of humans into their home, I was pretty sure they weren't important enough to have high status in the Summer Court and would know nothing of the events that stretched so far back into the past that even most Sidhe hadn't been alive at the time.

The trees thinned out as we emerged from the shade into a wilder area of flowers and bramble thickets. A perfumed fragrance hung in the air, making my eyes water and leaving a bitter taste in my throat that I was sure would linger for the next week. Heat baked the back of my neck and left me cooking in my leather jacket, but I didn't dare remove it. The minor discomfort was nothing on some of the stories I'd heard of humans being cursed to spit flowers whenever they spoke, to grow vines from their ears, to stumble on unwanted hooves.

I'd maintain enough politeness towards my escorts to avoid such a fate, but the sense of being entrapped only intensified when I realised that despite the amount of vegetation, the area was too neat to be called truly wild. Thick trees were lined up carefully, flowers grouped by colour and species, and the sense of order bore little resemblance to the patches of forest that sprang up unpredictably in the mortal world where Summer magic left its traces. The sound of water flowing mingled with birdsong and other animal noises, but I didn't see a single other living being. Perhaps the wilder fae sensed my iron and kept away.

"Does anyone actually live here?" I whispered to Quentin.

"We are currently in the territory of Lord Raivan," Quentin said in his low, gravelly voice. "My own master, Lord Torin, lives on the adjacent estate, and you will not be harmed while you are here."

"Really."

"I admit to a less than perfect understanding of modern human customs, but you and Vance are living together. In the terms of the agreement between the Colton family and mine, you're part of his family. That means not a soul within the other family I serve will raise a weapon to you."

An iron fist clamped over my heart. "That won't do any good if he's—" I couldn't say the words. "Anyway, that doesn't apply to the other faeries, just your family, right?"

"Correct," he growled. "If you wish to know the truth, you'll have to go into the centre of the Court."

"And you'll take me there?" My sense of geography wasn't terrible, but Faerie defied all normal logic, and nobody had offered me a map.

"I will," he confirmed. "I requested an audience for you. It's up to them whether they decide to listen."

"It's in their interests to, or else Fionn and his pals won't stop with our realm. All this is in danger, too." I gestured ahead at a path that diverged into two halves, one which vanished into deeper woodland while the other skirted around a large, pleasant-looking house reminiscent of the mages' manor. A reminder that, like the mages, the Sidhe families were long-lived and cultivated their wealth over many generations. Potentially infinite ones, given their immortality. Yet despite its display of perfect flowers and evergreen trees, I'd seen proof that nothing, no matter how ancient, was immune to decay. Even the Sidhe, unchanging and unyielding though they might be, would be reduced to dust and ashes if Fionn had his way.

The knights veered down the left-hand path, their horses' hooves gliding amid the trees. As Quentin and I hurried to catch up, an odd shimmering overlaid my vision and reduced the surrounding forest to a blur of vibrant green light. A tingling sensation racked my body from head to toe, and when my vision restored itself, the trees had gone. In their place, huge leafy plants flanked an elaborately carved gate that appeared to be made entirely of intertwining thorns. I halted, my spine stiffening, as did Quentin.

"This is the Court of Summer," said the brownie.

My heart gave a shudder. *This is it.* Beyond the gate, vibrant gardens stretched ahead to a palace so large it defied description. Its gold sheen glittered under the sunlight, bearing no resemblance to the castles I'd seen in the Vale yet triggering the same reflex inside me all the same. A trickle of cold sweat ran down my back.

Welcome to your new home, Avalin's voice whispered in my ear. *I've made it comfortable for you.*

I clenched my jaw, averted my eyes from the thorns, and waited for the gates to open. Lord Raivan and Lord Burdock rode through, and I kept a hand clenched on my dagger as I trod behind Quentin. Though the two Sidhe continued to ride towards the palace, the brownie halted at a fast-flowing river, near which stood another horse bearing a golden-skinned noble. The male Sidhe was dressed in finery patterned to match the red and purple flowers blooming amid the grass, and his green eyes surveyed me with marked disdain.

"Human." That single word carried enough contempt to level a building. "You're the one who wishes to speak to the Seelie Court?"

"Yes." I lifted my chin. "I'm Ivy Lane."

"Lynn?" said the newcomer. "I thought I told you not to disturb the Court unless it's an emergency."

"Lane," I corrected. Who in hell did he think I was? "I've been granted an audience with your Court, according to Quentin. Besides, it *is* an emergency."

What had Quentin even told the Court about me? If he'd stuck to his agreement to keep the mages' business confidential, he wouldn't have been able to tell the Sidhe much that wouldn't implicate both of us in severe crimes, most of which involved me breaking their property.

"She is correct," Quentin told him. "You agreed to speak to her."

"The Court has agreed to speak with one human," the Sidhe corrected. "She claims to have information on the whereabouts of the Erlking's missing ring. Is that correct?"

"Good enough." *That fucking ring.* Never mind humanity's near-extinction. In the end, the only thing that had caught the Sidhe's attention was the reappearance of a valuable talisman they'd carelessly lost a long while ago, and that I'd thrown into an abyss from which there would be no retrieval. I'd been trying to prevent the ring's destructive magic from setting a rampaging god loose in the city at the time, but the Sidhe didn't care for such technicalities.

"Very well," he said. "Lord Kerien is currently taking all petitions from mortals."

"It's not a petition, it's a warning."

One I hoped they'd take seriously. My most recent act of vandalism had been the result of Fionn's attempt to use

Summer's ring to wreak havoc in my realm, but the Sidhe had an irritating tendency to slither out of taking responsibility for their notorious criminals. Usually, they dumped them in the Vale. Fionn, being the overly ambitious sort, had wanted more than to rule over part of a dismal corner of Faerie left to ruin, perhaps because he'd once been employed by the Courts to ferry the dead to be reborn into new bodies using the Sidhe's prized cauldron of resurrection. His attempt to use that magic to create an army of immortal servants had come to an end when I'd shattered said cauldron into pieces using an Invocation. My second act of vandalism, and possibly the most serious of the two, since I was pretty sure the cauldron had also been the main source of the Sidhe's immortality.

Luckily, nobody in the Courts knew yet. I hadn't even had time to tell my allies, and I'd keep that secret nestled close to my chest for as long as it took me to see this mission through.

That was the sole advantage I possessed. Pure faeries, Sidhe or not, couldn't utter a single untruth.

I, however, could lie my arse off if necessary. And I'd happily do so if it got me closer to rescuing Vance.

It's on, Faerie.

2

At a wave of the Sidhe's hand, the riverside became a wide entryway decked out in opulence that resembled a bizarre combination of a decadent castle and an indoor garden. We'd landed inside the palace without taking a step. Shaking off the brief disorientation, I took in the splendour. Golden flowers shone like gems in the walls and ceiling, while pink and purple blooms framed the tall glass windows. Vines threaded along the walls and climbed the ceiling and doorways, studded with thorns worthy of the Thorn Princess herself.

Birds and piskies flew overhead, while a deer bounded past, giving me what I swore was a disdainful look before galloping away. My heart jumped. *Hope that wasn't the last human who visited the Court.*

How many humans had ever set foot in here? Few, if any, and fewer still would have walked out. Some Summer Sidhe shared the same fondness for collecting pretty humans as their Winter counterparts, though they tended to prefer to keep their captives alive, in contrast to the Winter Sidhe's habit of freezing humans they liked into ice until they suffocated. Summer Sidhe were more likely to turn me into a tree and use me as a coatrack while I remained conscious of every torturous second of my captivity.

Why did I think this was a good idea again?

As the thought crossed my mind, a tall warrior stepped out of thin air, as though part of the world had peeled itself away to let him through. Visceral fear froze my bones. I'd never seen a Sidhe in their natural habitat before, and now I knew beyond any shadow of a doubt that even the magic contained within half-blood territory had been a shallow reflection of that which existed here. The beings that commanded that power weren't human, not by any stretch of anyone's imagination. My first attempt to look directly at the Sidhe resulted in my vision sliding sideways, my mind tripping over itself in an effort to comprehend the being in front of me. After a few seconds of struggle, I settled on the image of a tall man in medieval-style armour with golden skin and bright-green eyes, yet the sense of uncanniness remained. The man was undeniably solid, but at the same time, looking at him brought to mind the experience of watching a ghost materialise in the human realm. Except infinitely more terrifying. I forgot to breathe for several seconds. I had the distinct impression that every person who looked at the Sidhe would see someone slightly different, depending on how their brain decided to comprehend the ethereal, majestic, and scary as fuck.

"Human." His voice was lightly accented, melodious and deep at the same time. He waved a hand, and the hall disappeared as swiftly as it had arrived, depositing us inside a cave-like room with domed walls shaped like the inside of a hill.

"The hell?" My fear dimmed somewhat as indignation

took over my mouth. "Can you stop yanking me around? I prefer for the walls to stay in one place when I'm talking to someone, thanks."

The Sidhe tilted his head on one side. "What are you doing here alone, human?"

Heart plunging, I looked over my shoulder to see that Quentin had vanished and so had everyone else. Thorny plants sprouted at the edges of the cave, forming a bristling wall that prevented me from taking another step away from the Sidhe lord.

"Stop doing that!" Yelling at a Sidhe hadn't been on my plan, but my body's reaction to being entrapped by thorns reared up inside me, and it was all I could do to suppress the primal urge to scream.

"Doing what?" he enquired.

I ground my teeth. Evidently, like teleporting came naturally to Vance, creepily rearranging the universe at will came as easily as breathing to the Sidhe. Nothing in the Vale had prepared me for this. Avalin and Velkas had been powerful, but their own magic had been stripped away when they'd been exiled, leaving them shells of their former selves. Even knowing that this Sidhe was bound to follow the rules of his Court didn't ease my nerves in the least. No law prevented him from harming humans. To the Sidhe, we were lower than animals, and I was playing with fire by antagonising him, I knew.

I sucked in air and kept my attention on his green eyes, which shone clearer than the rest of his flickering form. "You're Lord Kerien, right?"

"Correct."

"Please." I pushed on. "My partner and several of my friends were taken captive into Faerie and my realm is under attack—"

He raised a hand, and my body shuddered, my legs locking together. I glanced down and caught a glimpse of bark spreading from my feet to my ankles. Oh, no. I was *not* going to spend an eternity sitting in a Sidhe's palace as an ornamental tree.

I whipped my blade out of the sheath, and the glyphs on the side lit up in vibrancy that halted the Sidhe's spell in its tracks. The bark disappeared as Lord Kerien edged closer to me, tilting his head like a human studying an unusual animal. His gaze was fixed on my sword, his eyes tracing the gleaming runes on the hilt.

"You stole this from the Sidhe?"

"Won it," I corrected. "From Lord Avalin of Winter, when I escaped from the castle in the Grey Vale he built to store his human captives."

"You're a human changeling?" His gaze slid down the blade, following the swirling glyphs as though mesmerised.

"Yes." I replied. "If you turn me into a tree, you won't get my story."

"A human could never have won a talisman without cheating," said Lord Kerien.

"Avalin stole the talisman himself." If he refused to listen to my pleas, I'd start with the reason Summer had granted me an audience in the first place. "Didn't Quentin tell you I had information on Summer's ring? It seems in poor form for you to put me under a spell preventing me from telling you what I came to share, doesn't it?"

"Go on, then." His attention slid from the sword back to my face, his manner expectant.

"Fionn—the person who originally stole the ring—managed to lose it again," I explained. "This time, permanently. And now he's looking to kill every human on Earth and conquer your Court."

"You mean to tell me you came all this way to admit you *lost* our talisman?" The prickling sensation in my legs resumed and a warning glint grew in his eyes.

"I didn't lose it. Fionn did." I spoke faster, tripping over the words. "You might know him as the Huntsman. I'm not sure how much you know of his attempt to invade the mortal realm over two decades ago—"

"If you speak true, you'll know that we played our part in ensuring that the Huntsman could not awaken again."

At least he knows that much.

"He did wake up, nine *months* ago," I said impatiently. "Long enough for word to make it back here." Unless Quentin hadn't told his other family. If he'd kept his word to Vance and held his silence on matters that he'd deemed to be confidential, not a soul here in Faerie knew the extent of the threat Fionn presented. "Your exiles convinced Avalin's half-human son that the only way to gain immortality was to wake up the Huntsman. Did you ever know Lord Velkas?"

"Lord Velkas?" he echoed. "For a human, you certainly seem to have encountered a number of Sidhe."

"Because I was *kidnapped* by one of you," I ground out. "Anyway, the ring's gone, because the first thing Fionn did when he woke up was to attempt to rip open the boundaries between realms." Did this guy even know about the gods sleeping between the worlds, the ancient beings that his people had exiled from their own realm? He looked younger than I did, but there was no measurable way to tell age when it came to the Sidhe.

Lord Kerien's eyes flashed a brighter green and my legs locked into place again. "The Huntsman was bound both in body and in spirit, and Sidhe gave up their lives to enact the spell. Nobody should have been able to break it."

"Well, they did," I said. "Ask Quentin if you don't believe me. Or better still, come and judge for yourself. His tomb is empty. I witnessed him walk out with my own eyes. Calder used a spell that involved gathering power from both Summer and Winter and making a sacrifice to summon the Wild Hunt and set Fionn loose in the process."

Bark began to creep up my legs again. Sweat ran down my back. I gripped my talisman, willing my magic to respond, but I couldn't summon up more than a wisp of blue light.

"Just *listen* to me." Dammit, Quentin. Of all the times to disappear. Not that it was his fault. He was one of the lesser fae, and like me, entirely subject to the whims of these beings who started wars over the slightest insult. "Did you think I came here for the sole purpose of winding you up? I'm risking my life to warn you Fionn's plan to conquer your Court is well and truly intact, and this time, there isn't a fully functional council agreement between the realms to stand up to him."

"I was under the impression you intended to return our property," he said. "The Erlking will be most displeased."

The Erlking can get fucked. "Can I talk to *him*?"

"No, you may not. The ring was one of many talismans stolen by the outcasts and the slight has never been forgiven."

"The same outcasts invaded my realm. They killed millions. Billions." Despair crept into my voice. "Fionn was their leader, and he's reawakened. That's the truth."

"Exiles are freed from their bonds to the Courts, and thus their inability to tell untruths. Much like mortals, they can deceive, and if someone is pretending to be the Huntsman—"

"He's not lying about that." Exiles could lie? That explained a lot, though when I'd been with Avalin, I'd been too focused on staying alive to notice if he told the truth or not. Generally, he meant every terrible threat he uttered.

Fionn, though? Liar or not, his intentions were clear, but Lord Kerien might accept nothing short of Fionn himself showing up in the middle of the palace and shattering its finery into a thousand pieces before he believed me.

The Sidhe extended a hand towards my sword, and I snatched it away. "That is a talisman of Winter from one of the earliest eras," he said. "Where would an exile find it? Lord Avalin was stripped of his magic and left to die."

"I don't know where he found it, do I? We weren't exactly friendly. What do you mean by *one of the earliest eras?*"

"The blade is unfamiliar to me, so I assume it came from before my time, more than a thousand years ago."

"Wait, how *old* are you?"

"I stopped counting after the first nine centuries."

Show-off. "How about the oldest Sidhe? I mean, is there anyone who was alive in the time this talisman was forged?"

"No." His jaw tightened. "There are few who endure from that era, and they are not actively involved in the Court at present."

"The ancient Sidhe left you to clear up the mess they left behind?" I spoke without thinking, but this time my legs didn't lock together despite the anger suffusing his face. Possibly, he'd never, not in over a thousand years, had a human come in here and start mouthing off. *Tough shit, mate.* "Let me speak to the leader of the Summer Court. He must be ancient, right?"

"The Erlking is indisposed."

My mouth dropped open a little. "What, he's sick?"

No way. I hadn't thought Sidhe could catch so much as a common cold. Nothing, save for iron poisoning perhaps, had any effect upon their immortal flesh.

"That is no concern of yours, mortal, but he greatly desires the talismans to be returned."

If he was seriously ill… my mind ticked over the implications. To the Sidhe, death wasn't absolute, but with the cauldron gone, would they start dropping like flies from the slightest cause? That was a shitstorm I did *not* want to be a part of, and besides, if I so much as hinted that I'd destroyed the cauldron, Lord Kerien would do far worse than turn me into a tree.

I needed to change the subject. "Well, Fionn is walking free. I even tried an Invocation and it had no effect on him, so—"

"You claim to speak Invocations?"

"I can demonstrate." I hadn't planned to, but my gaze dropped to the glyphs shimmering on my blade and words trickled into my mind, stirring on my tongue.

"No." In a blink, our surroundings changed. We no longer stood inside a cave, but in a forested glade flanked by trees. The words died on my lips as Lord Kerien's blazing green eyes stared into mine. "You're lucky that the action didn't break your fragile human mind. Invocations are the language the first Sidhe once used to communicate with the gods. The words contain so much power that even the Sidhe rarely use them."

"Yet I can say them because I have the magic of a Sidhe," I told him. "Now do you get it? I'm here because I'm the one mortal who can survive this place, and my realm requires assistance in a battle against an enemy originating from Faerie itself. Your people have intervened in our world before, right?"

"Thousands of years ago, and we have learned from our mistakes."

I burst out laughing. "The whole reason Fionn is rampaging around is because of a talisman he stole from *your* Court, and he was freed with the help of one of your outcasts. Do you know of the Lady of the Tree?"

"Caitrina? The Lady of the Great Oak?"

"Wait, that's her name?" I shook off the momentary surprise that he knew of her. "Yeah, she was stranded in the human world during the invasion and then slipped into the realm of the outcasts to steal Velkas's talisman."

"That is enough." His eyes flashed dark green, and vines shot from the ground to bind my hands and feet. I fought, fury and panic writhing inside me at the inhuman gleam in his eyes. "You will not slander us with your poisonous mortal lies."

"I thought you exiled the Lady—Caitrina—yourselves. She tried to kill me." The vines tightened, pain gripping my arms as they climbed higher. "I'm not lying. Stop attacking me."

"It is not I who is attacking you," he said. "Judge for yourself."

I followed his line of sight from the vines to the trees from which they sprang. Two pairs of eyes glared at me from within the branches. Dryads. Oh, *shit*.

"Hey," I said feebly. "What's the deal?"

"They take great insult at your slander towards their own kin," said Lord Kerien. "The dryads will have your blood, mortal."

And to think they had a reputation for being mild-mannered tree spirits. As I squirmed, the trees warped and twisted into tall spindly figures with branches for hands and vines at their fingertips.

"I sense her deceit," growled the dryad. "This human killed our Lady."

Uh-oh. "The Lady killed a bunch of people herself and tried to destroy the mortal realm. Didn't you kick her out of your Court in the first place?"

I directed those words at Lord Kerien, but he made no move to rescue me. "Yes. She was exiled for seeking bloody revenge on those who cut down her tree. However, I did not order her death, and those who wish to avenge her should be allowed to act as they see fit."

He vanished, melting away as swiftly as he'd arrived. Leaving me alone with the two dryads and their murderous vines.

"You bastard!" I wriggled, reaching for my magic, but scarcely a trace answered my call. My vision blackened as the grip on my throat turned sharp and cold. *Shit. I'm going to die.*

3

Cold metal touched my hand. My fingers instinctively closed around the dagger's handle, confusion filtering in. *My dagger? How?*

Comprehension dawned when I glimpsed a small figure out of the corner of my eye, crouched at my side. Quentin.

I swivelled the blade in my hand and angled it towards the vine holding my wrist. The vine retracted, the grip on my neck loosening too. The dryads hissed in fury, but the slightest brush of iron caused the vines to retreat, and in seconds, my body was freed. Sucking in a breath, I looked for Lord Kerien, but the dickhead had seemingly evaporated into thin air.

"This way, human." Quentin indicated a door which had seemingly appeared in the hedge behind me. I wasn't entirely certain there'd been a hedge there at all a moment ago, either. Or that we'd been in a garden. *Oh, for crying out loud, Faerie.* "My family are oath-sworn not to harm you."

"Yeah, right." I cut off a less charitable comment, reminded that he'd saved my life, and that he'd risked injuring himself on my iron dagger when he'd done so. "Thanks for showing up when you did."

I followed him through the door and into a forested glade flanked by trees that I gave a wide berth. I didn't see any glaring eyes or creeping vines, but I kept my iron dagger in one hand and my sword in the other as we walked.

"Bloody faeries," I growled. "I thought the Sidhe would be less like their half-Sidhe counterparts, but they really aren't."

Which made some level of sense, given that the Chief had done his level best to imitate the true Sidhe's disdain for humans, but their complete unwillingness to believe a word I said was a major obstacle when winning them over depended upon a basic level of shared understanding at the very least.

"I hoped for a different outcome," Quentin said quietly. "However, you should have minded your tongue."

"Lord Kerien tried to turn me into a tree and the Lady's friends nearly strangled me." I breathed out, trying to rein in my temper. "And they didn't even bloody believe me."

"The Sidhe have little desire to face the possibility that Lord Fionn escaped their control after the sacrifices they made to ensure his imprisonment. It's likely that you reminded them of their losses."

"How the hell was I supposed to know they even lifted a finger to help? For all I knew, they were sitting around playing chess instead, or whatever bored immortals do in their spare time."

Fionn's claim that the Sidhe refused to entertain the possibility of change came to mind, and maybe he had a point. For all its pretty decor, Seelie was stuck in a time warp. They refused to even acknowledge the possibility of an enemy smashing through their perfect façade and drenching the bright trees in blood and horror.

I took in a breath. "How about Winter, then? Might *they* listen?"

"The Unseelie Court is unknown to me," said Quentin. "Going there would be a foolish decision, Ivy, and one that won't help the mages, either."

"Then what will?" I asked desperately. "I thought I'd find answers here, Quentin. Don't tell me I risked my life for nothing."

"It wasn't for nothing. The information you gained might prove valuable."

"Not enough." If anything, they'd killed my last hope. All thanks to that bloody ring.

"You'll have to make up your mind, Ivy," said Quentin. "I suspect that the longer Vance is in their company, the lower the odds of you being able to rescue him."

I thought so. Oh, Vance.

"Then I have to go alone." If Fionn himself hadn't been the one to capture Vance, the odds of my success were marginally higher, but not much. I didn't know how to get to the Vale from here either, but there must be a way. The Sidhe of the Courts had created the Vale themselves, after all.

Quentin came to a halt. "Someone else is here."

I tried to stop, too, but my feet kept moving of their own accord. Music rose in the background, soft, caressing, wrapping my body in its embrace. My feet swayed in time with the music, and I tensed, willing them to slow down. "Quentin, what's going on?"

No reply. The path sloped upward and still my feet continued to move, even as the brightness faded and became fog, a thick grey haze that smothered the world.

When I emerged, the forest had gone, replaced by a field smothered in thick greyness. Where in hell was I? This didn't look like Summer territory. But I'd know if I'd wandered into Winter, wouldn't I? Or even the Vale...

The fog shifted around me, turning into a cloud-like substance which clung to me like cobwebs, smothering my hair, my mouth. I screamed, the sound snatched away as the tendrils closed over my nostrils and teeth, and even my eyes.

Come on, *magic!*

I lifted my talisman, using my free hand to tear at the clouds stuck to my face. My breath escaped as I freed my mouth, gulping in wet, thick air.

Lord Burdock appeared in a halo of green light that made his pale features look even more alien than beforehand. A similar halo circled the sword in his hand, and tendrils of fog coiled around the blade. His talisman. *Is this his magic?* "You shouldn't have interfered, human."

"I don't know what you're talking about." Was this some kind of bizarre vengeance for insulting Lord Kerien? "Let me go."

"The pact was broken thanks to you."

"Still don't get it." What pact? He'd barely spoken a word to me before, content to leave the talking to Lord Raivan. Unless... "Do you mean the pact between our realms? The one that ended at the invasion?"

The Sidhe lifted his blade to point at my ribcage. The sharp edge pierced through fabric, sending blood seeping down my front. Fog swirled from the blade, threads reaching for my neck like grasping tentacles.

"Why in hell is it *my* fault? Whatever it is I did?" I leaned back. "If you're going to skewer me to death, I'd prefer to know which crime I've actually committed first."

"You made a mockery of our sacrifice when you allowed the Huntsman to awaken."

"Sacrifice?" I echoed. "I thought your people didn't fight in the invasion."

"Incorrect," he said softly. "One Sidhe from Summer and one from Winter were chosen to be part of the council that encompassed both our realm and yours. We were told it was an honour, that we would be rewarded for lowering ourselves to allying with humans."

"Someone you knew was the Summer ambassador?" Quentin had told me most of the original Council of Twelve had lost their lives in the invasion, but I hadn't realised the other Sidhe had been aware.

"My wife." His voice became an echoing boom that rocked the ground under my feet. My teeth rattled in my jaw. The blood seeping down my chest thickened.

"I'm sorry," I choked out, acutely aware of the blade's proximity to my heart. "But I really had nothing to do with it. I wasn't even in the mortal realm at the time. I was a prisoner in the Grey Vale. I was a child."

"Your realm is to blame." His sword shimmered, radiating pure green Summer magic. "And as the one who awakened the Huntsman and rendered our sacrifice meaningless, I will take your life in recompense."

I raised my sword to catch the end of his blade. My magic might not be as functional as before, but a talisman was a talisman. As I pushed back, the tendrils of his magic licked at my skin as though to draw out the very life force inside me. I'd seen this side of Summer magic before, but only amongst exiles, when the thirst for life became the desire to feast upon the living. I'd heard the Sidhe didn't look favourably upon this misuse of their magic, but if Lord Burdock had his way, he'd bleed me dry before the Court ever knew of his transgression.

Not if I can help it.

I pushed his blade back, concentrating hard. The faint blue glow told me my magic hadn't vanished outright, and a promising tingling sensation in my chest indicated my healing power sealing the cut he'd opened.

"You don't have to do this," I said. "I'm not the enemy here."

"Wrong." His magic swarmed around my blade, the threads of green-grey light creeping across my wrists and reaching for my neck. Closing around my throat.

"Let me go," I gasped. "Was it you who sent those dryads, too?"

If my magic was at full power, I'd be able to break his grip, but weak puffs of blue light were all I could conjure to my hands and my iron left no impact on the smoke-like threads of magic wrapping around me. I gasped as they burned my skin like stinging nettles, and my vision doubled.

"You will perish here, human," said Lord Burdock, "and you will disappear."

Shit. If I died here, what would happen to me? Unlike the Vale, the inhabitants of the Courts didn't linger when they died. They moved on, but where to? There was no route to the mortals' Death in here. Except, perhaps, through the Grey Vale.

Gripping my sword handle so tight my fingers burned, I closed my eyes and willed myself to slide out of true Faerie and into the realm that I knew lay beneath. In this place of fog, with Death's touch on my throat, it was easy to imagine slipping from my body and passing through the boundaries between realms.

Lord Burdock uttered a scream of incoherent rage. The threads released my throat, and all sensation abruptly cut off in a torrent of grey. I squeezed my eyes tighter shut as I tumbled out of the world and into a dark tunnel.

The fall ceased a heartbeat later. Leaves cushioned my back, and my eyes flickered open to a familiar canopy of silver and grey.

I guess you were right when you said I'd disappear, Lord

Burdock, I thought as I rolled onto my side, sucking in air, my heart pounding. *Just not in the way you expected.*

Blue light bloomed at my fingertips, a promising sign. Already my magic stirred to life as though pleased to be among the Vale's winding paths and silver-leafed trees. Stillness permeated the air as I rose shakily to my feet and took in my surroundings. The Vale didn't obey normal maps, and everywhere looked more or less the same unless someone uttered a conscious command. People with faerie magic—specifically, pure-blooded Sidhe, and whatever the hell Fionn and I were—could alter the Vale's paths, up to a point. If there was another Sidhe here, I wouldn't be able to find them until they wanted me to. Including whoever had taken Vance.

"Okay, magic," I murmured. "Take me to Vance."

Coming straight here from the Court hadn't been on my plan, but maybe it was for the best that I'd left Quentin behind. It'd only been hours ago at most that I'd broken Fionn's cauldron and left him frothing at the mouth in rage, but the slippery way in which time passed in Faerie meant I didn't know for sure how long Vance had been gone. Nor who had taken him.

My energy was flagging now the threat of imminent death had lifted, and I took a moment to rummage in my rucksack and take a drink of water and a snack bar. I couldn't remember when I'd last eaten a proper meal, but I'd need some fortifying energy if I wanted to beat—*the Morrigan? A Sidhe lord?* Surely not Fionn himself; he wouldn't have had time to return here after I'd destroyed the cauldron and then escaped his castle. Besides, someone with Summer magic had killed the other mages and captured Vance. Someone who carried the life-drinker sword.

I began to walk. The Vale was never completely silent, but the lively noises of Summer were absent here. Instead, Faerie would throw a spontaneous howl, scream or cry out every couple of minutes. Sometimes there was a real threat, some-times the Vale was just screwing with me. I'd grown wise to the usual threats—kelpies lurking in ponds and rivers, will o' the wisps floating through the trees, the occasional wraith imitating a dead loved one—but as long as I stayed on the path and ignored distractions, I'd be all right. At least until I reached the first inevitable trap.

Sure enough, after a couple of minutes, the ground gave way underneath my feet—not in a sinkhole kind of way, more like the area underneath my feet simply stopped exist-ing. I fell, choking on a scream, as the silvery leaves beneath my feet vanished into a yawning black pit.

Air whipped around me. I gripped my sword's hilt with both hands and then tumbled out onto another path. This one was bare of leaves and boxed in by sheer cliffs on either side in the place of towering trees. The area otherwise resembled the Vale's regular setting, so I resumed walking. A chill wind drifted down from the cliffs, biting at my skin. I wrapped my arms around myself, glad I'd worn my leather jacket through the heat of Summer.

The path ended at a tower-shaped construction formed of what looked like random pieces of rock roughly slotted together in a way that should have made it impossible to stay upright. That was faerie logic for you.

As I approached, a ghost drifted into my path. I lifted my blade despite knowing this was a regular ghost and not a wraith.

Someone I knew. Someone who couldn't possibly be here.

Gerry, the man who'd saved my life when I'd been a pris-oner of Lord Avalin.

4

"You." I didn't lower my blade. Faerie had thrown similar tricks at me before a dozen times, but Gerry—whatever he really was—made no move to attack me.

"Ivy." Gerry's ghost spoke with a Scottish accent which I'd forgotten he had. He looked younger, too, with brown hair instead of grey. "I knew I picked you for a reason."

"What are you doing here?" My hands curled into fists. "Where's Fionn? And Vance? The Vale was supposed to bring me to him."

"This realm does as it pleases, Ivy Lynn. You should know that."

"Lynn?" My eyes narrowed. "You're the third person who's called me that. You know my name perfectly well, if you're really Gerry, which I doubt."

"Another has called you by that name?"

I blinked. "Yes. So what?"

"Interesting." He surveyed me, his ghostly outline flickering until I could see right through him to the teetering tower on the other side. "This might mean nothing at all, but when we were first imprisoned here in the Vale, I initially took interest in you because I know a certain family by the name of Lynn who have been linked to the faeries for generations. Your name is similar enough that I wondered if you were descended from one of the offshoots of that family."

My mouth parted. "You thought I was… wait, you mean a *human* family connected to the faeries?"

"That's right," he said. "I was initially taken along with a few others from the same area of Scotland, and the name came up frequently from those who knew them personally. The Lynns are known allies of the Sidhe, and I gather they're peacekeepers of a sort."

"I thought the Sidhe hated humans." I frowned. "Clearly I don't belong to that family, if you're even telling the truth, so I don't know why it matters."

"It might not," he said. "The name might be a coincidence, but the Lynns' descendants are known to have spread across the country, and at least one used the name *Lane*."

"What are you implying?" Wait. "Is that why Avalin took me?"

"No," he said. "I doubt he ever knew the Lynns existed, and you aren't the only person I've encountered with potential ties to their family. They've been around for hundreds of years."

"Damn." The Sidhe who'd welcomed me into the Court had used the name, I recalled, and his reaction had implied he'd interacted with members of that family. Hadn't he said, *I thought I told you not to disturb the Court unless it's an emergency?* "How'd a family of humans get entangled with Faerie? This started before the invasion, I take it?"

"A long time before," he said, "but I cannot speak to the circumstances, and it became clear when I met you that you weren't connected to that line of the family. You had no magic until you claimed that talisman."

"They have *magic?*" If he was right, and this wasn't some bizarre hallucination conjured up by the Vale, that would mean I wasn't the only human who'd gained possession of the Sidhe's power, intentionally or otherwise. "You said they were in Scotland? Are they still there?"

"To my knowledge," he said. "It's been a long time since I was taken, Ivy, and longer still has likely passed in the mortal realm while I have been trapped in this state."

"I didn't know you'd stayed." Others had, too, and the longer I interacted with him, the more I was inclined to believe he was genuine. "The other captives... some of them moved on. I saw."

"I know," he said. "In truth, there's very little of me left, but I decided to remain long enough to offer the truth I owed you."

"You don't owe me anything. I got you killed." If anything, I owed *him* for giving me the tools and training to defeat Avalin without expecting anything in return, and for taking the brunt of Avalin's wrath so that I was able to deal the killing blow.

"I chose to make the sacrifice for you," said Gerry. "I knew I'd never leave that castle. I came to peace with that a long time ago."

"Still." My eyes stung. "I'm sorry. I can help you move on, but there's something else I have to do, too. I don't suppose you've been inside that tower?"

"No." He glanced behind him. "However, I saw a Sidhe enter, some hours ago."

"Did... did this Sidhe have anyone with them?" Dread coiled in my gut. "Fionn—I suppose you wouldn't know who he is, but he's captured some of my allies. He's also the one who started the invasion."

"The Sidhe I saw was alone." Gerry's ghostly face went

paler than before. "Fionn… if he has truly returned, then I understand why it was so urgent that I speak to you."

"Someone told you to find me?" My suspicions returned. "Who's giving you orders?"

"During the recent disturbance with the veil, a spirit confronted me when I was momentarily taken into Death, true Death, where I might have had the opportunity to move on through the gates into the afterlife," he said. "Upon learning where I had come from, he told me to go back and speak with you before I moved on."

"Frank?" It had to be him. There weren't too many ghosts who could order other spirits around and who had any knowledge of Fionn at all, let alone his recent return. "Why'd he want you to speak to me?"

"To convey my knowledge of the impostor calling himself the Huntsman."

"The impostor?" My heart thudded. "What do you mean? He claims to be a god, and whether that's true or not, he's immune to my magic and practically invincible. His only weakness was a ring—Summer's ring—but I had to destroy to keep it from sucking my own realm into the void. Now he has no weaknesses, and he's going to—to—"

Gerry held up a hand for silence. "Calm, Ivy. This Fionn sounds very much like someone I heard about during my early years of captivity. Avalin used to think highly of him, and the two of them conspired together to steal the magic of the true Huntsman for their own ends. Avalin had hoped to use that magic to escape back into Faerie, but Fionn betrayed him, leaving him in the Vale while he assumed the Huntsman's title for himself."

"Fionn isn't the real leader of the Wild Hunt?" He'd *stolen* the Huntsman's title and his magic? And he'd betrayed Avalin in order to do so? "Damn. Is that why my magic hates Fionn so much? I figured something happened between them."

No wonder my magic wanted to wrap itself around Fionn's throat and strangle him whenever we ran into one another. In fact, if Fionn hadn't been the Wild Hunt's original leader, it explained why his hellhounds had shifted allegiances to me after Fionn had come back from the not-quite-dead.

"I suspect you're right," he said. "The ghost also mentioned Lord Avalin had a son, whom you encountered."

"*He's* dead, and good riddance. He's the one who awakened Fionn and started all this shit."

Gerry nodded. "That's the connection. I was there, years ago, when Avalin claimed a mortal woman as his own. There were rumours of a child they had living in their quarters, but none of us ever saw him."

Anger rose inside me. "Of course. Calder was a kid when Avalin abandoned him, but that's no excuse. Who was his mother? Is she still alive?"

Probably not. I'd heard many stories of humans who'd been chosen by faerie lords as their lovers, only to be cast aside when the mood changed. Invariably, their fate was to die alone and heartbroken, haunted by the memory of a love that had never existed.

"Her name was Wilhemina Yarrow," Gerry told me. "That's all I know. I cannot say if she survived Avalin's demise, nor if she made it back to the mortal realm."

"She must have, if she ditched Calder in the human world." I committed her name to memory in case I needed it. "Is there anything else you can tell me before I leave? You only saw one Sidhe enter the tower? No humans?"

"That's right, but earlier today, a huge bird flew over the trees, too. A monstrous creature, holding what appeared to be a child in her claws."

"The Morrigan. Fuck. The child is hers." Was the twisted

old crow still using her unwilling offspring for her own ends? What was she doing in the Vale?

"The Morrigan?" Gerry blanched. "The harbinger? She and Fionn are working together?"

"They made a deal," I explained. "She helped him in exchange for a bunch of human souls to feed on. I screwed things up before their deal was complete, so I don't know if their deal is still intact." Nor what would be the fate of her daughter, Roseanne, who Fionn had corrupted and enslaved against her will, forcing her to kill the human father who'd sacrificed a life with his only child in order to keep Roseanne safe from her monstrous mother.

"The Morrigan belongs to Winter," said Gerry. "That she would make a deal with the Huntsman suggests he's taken his first step towards conquering the Courts."

My heart lurched. If he'd already made a move on the Courts and met no resistance, the situation looked dire for the mortal realm. "That's… shit, I can't even deal with that now. I need to find my friends."

He'd given me a lot to think about, but if anything, my list of questions had only widened, and the odds of my perishing before I found answers remained firmly stacked against me.

"Then I wish you the best of luck, Ivy. I've told you everything I know. If I don't see you again…" His gaze went to my sword, lingering on its soft blue glow. "I heard a rumour that you can put the dead to rest."

"Yeah. I can." I swallowed, an unexpected current of emotion rising inside me. "I did it for Helena. Or I thought I did. I'm still not sure she was real, or if she knew who I was."

"If you think you saw her, you probably did," Gerry said. "Sometimes we ghosts are able to endure, to hold onto our true selves for the sake of fulfilling a last desire. This was mine."

I lifted the blade to point at him. "Then I'll help you move on."

Gerry closed his eyes. "Thank you, Ivy."

Blue light flared up around the blade's edge. Gerry's spirit glowed, and then vanished into a pillar of light. My hands vibrated on the sword's handle as the remnants of his fear and loneliness dissipated, becoming one with my blade.

The promising blue glow told me my magic was back in working order. Good, because if the life-drinker awaited me in the hands of Vance's captors, I'd need it.

I allowed myself one moment of quiet sadness for those Avalin had taken and then pushed the emotions down, hardening my heart and facing the tower. I had hostages to save. And then, the world.

5

The tower door creaked open at my touch, revealing an empty room dominated by a towering staircase. I'd scarcely taken a step onto the first uneven stone slab before it vanished and I pitched forward, hastily withdrawing my foot before I tumbled into empty air. In a blink, the tower had vanished and thick fog obscured my surroundings.

"That wasn't even a convincing illusion." Shaking my head, I walked into the fog, using the residual blue glow around my sword as a guiding light to keep from tripping over. I hoped I'd find the Sidhe alone and not the Morrigan, as it didn't sound like she'd stuck around. She usually dwelt in some dark corner of Winter reserved for the death fae, who held a reputation almost as unsavoury as the outcasts.

The Vale itself was a dead end in a very literal sense, one that the Sidhe did their best to forget even existed. While its inhabitants were chiefly outcasts from the Courts, the Sidhe had originally created this realm as a prison for their own exiled gods. Or so I'd been told. I knew nothing of why they'd taken such a drastic measure against the beings that had supposedly shaped Faerie itself, but if my talisman only contained a fraction of a god's power, I wasn't sure I wanted to meet its originator.

A god, however, might be exactly what I needed to beat Fionn.

An impostor, is he? What had he done to the real Huntsman? Killed him brutally, I assumed, and then stolen his face. That was useful information to have in my pocket, though I fervently hoped Fionn himself would not be waiting on the other side of this trap.

My sword ignited in blue, a warning that another faerie was close. I lifted the blade, squinting through the fog. Trees filtered into view on either side of me, framing a much larger shape formed of grey stone.

"Why is it always castles?" For beings capable of conjuring up whatever they wanted with the wave of a hand, the Sidhe's imaginations were woefully limited, if you asked me.

I approached the castle slowly, using the trees and fog for cover in case there were guards lurking outside. My sword's glow would be a dead giveaway regardless, glowing brighter with each step as the hilt vibrated against my fingers. I'd rather sneak in through a window than rush in all guns blazing and make things worse for everyone, but my sword's light was the only way to see where I was going, and its humming glow indicated a source of powerful energy nearby. Like another Sidhe.

I slowed my pace when a tower loomed out of the fog, and a faint scream echoed from within. *This is his place, all right.*

My sword vibrated so hard my teeth chattered, its humming carrying echoes of the scream I'd heard. Fear gripped me. Many had perished here, and their collective misery fed into the dazzling blue glow emanating from my talisman. Its light shone on a wooden door in the tower's side, suspiciously unguarded. A trap, surely, but the lingering screams banished my caution. Blue light streamed from my palms, knocking the door into a hulking ogre on the other side.

The guard grunted, blinking in the sudden glow. "Intruder—"

I decapitated the ogre in one strike and sank my blade into the chest of a second guard. All pretence of a subtle entrance slipped away, but stealth was impossible when you carried a giant glowing sword, and with my magic back in full working order, I was itching for a fight.

With the guards down, I followed a short corridor to a spiralling staircase. Drawing in a breath, I began to climb. My footsteps echoed hollowly, mingling with the growing sound of someone sobbing from somewhere above. Gritting my teeth, I kept climbing until I came to a door.

A transparent form rose upward, reaching for me with cold grasping fingers. *Wraith.* Evidently, the guards weren't all of the corporeal variety. I swung my blade through the human-shaped patch of grey and the wraith recoiled. Blue light exploded outward and its ghostly form shattered like glass.

So did the door. The resounding crack of splintering wood echoed up the tower, and I winced at the noise despite knowing I'd already alerted everyone in the tower of my arrival.

"You'll have to do better than that." I stepped over the ruined door. The room on the other side looked like a standard prison cell but contained no captives.

As I backed out, a small figure zipped past the side of my head. I grabbed the stone wall for balance and found myself nose to nose with a winged piskie. Shrieking, it landed on my head, mewling like a kitten. "Help me, human!"

"Quiet," I hissed. "Were you the only prisoner in there?"

The creature tugged at my hair and howled. "Yes, human, yes!"

"Shut *up*." I lifted my free hand to my head, loosening the creature's grip on me. "You'll get us both killed. Where are they keeping the other prisoners?"

"Up the tower. Won't go up there! Won't!"

"You don't have to." I swatted the piskie off my head. "Go on, wait for me outside. I'll get you out of here."

Why Fionn had locked up a piskie was beyond me, but at least I knew I was going the right way. The spiralling staircase continued past several doors that turned out to lead into empty rooms. Partway up, a pair of redcaps leaped at me, brandishing curved knives.

"A loose human in the castle?" one of them crowed. "Come and play with us!"

"Yeah, no thanks." I decapitated both of them, letting their heads bounce down the stairs behind me.

Another door waited ahead. One blast of magic took care of the lock, and I was in.

This cell was pitch black, but a groan came from the back. I shone my sword's light across the floor, illuminating the shape of a person chained to the wall. Someone very pale with coppery hair hanging over a face soaked in blood.

"Drake." I ran to him, my heart plunging. The whole right-hand side of his face was a flayed mess, as though someone had attacked him with sharp nails or claws. "Hang on. I'll get you down."

My sword easily cut through the solid cuffs around his hands, and he fell against me, almost toppling us both over. "Sorry. I have a healing spell somewhere. Hang on—"

My sword glowed a warning and a pack of redcaps ran in. Six of them this time. I pushed Drake off me as gently as I could and ran to confront the redcaps. They weren't the toughest creatures in Faerie, but I had no doubt Vance would be under tighter security. Maybe in worse condition. Rage blacked out my vision, and light exploded from my blade. In seconds, I was surrounded by bloody pieces of dead redcap.

"Holy fuck." Drake groaned again. "Please do that to the dickhead who brought me in here, too."

"Who?" I hefted my blade again but didn't see anyone behind him.

"Sidhe bastard with a big sword." He staggered forward a few steps, his gaze unfocused. "I think he left."

"He'd better stay gone. For his own sake." I reached into my rucksack and pulled out a healing spell. "This should work, but it's less effective if the wound's been untreated for too long."

"Worth a try." The healing spell's blue light ignited, and he closed his eyes against the glare. "I kept winding him up, trying to keep him distracted so he wouldn't hurt the others. I don't know what he did with Vance, but as long as he kept his mouth shut, he should be fine. Vance is a tough bastard, and he isn't stupid like I am."

"You aren't stupid. Did the Sidhe mention a name?"

"No, we aren't worthy of the honour, or some shit like that." He stood up a little straighter as the healing spell kicked in, but a deep cut still bisected one cheek, and he'd likely need to put a salve on it before the wound got infected. "Got a weapon I can borrow?"

"Yeah, but if the Sidhe is around, let me handle him myself." I handed him one of the twin daggers Vance had given me, figuring that iron enchanted with witch runes would give him the best chance of survival. "Do you know where they took him?"

"Top of the tower, I heard." Drake wiped his bloody face on his sleeve. "I heard voices downstairs. Did you find anyone else?"

"No. Not human, anyway. I did find a piskie."

He grunted. "I guess Vance and I were the only ones they brought in."

"You were? So—so the other mages didn't..." I couldn't finish the sentence. I wouldn't tell him the rest of the council were dead. That could wait until we'd escaped. "Wanda wasn't at the manor. I thought they might have taken her, too."

"No. She left before we were attacked," said Drake. "I think she was going to find her grandmother."

Hope ignited in my chest. *She might be alive.* "First piece of good news I've heard for a while. Now let's go and save Vance."

Vance. Please be okay. Vance was pragmatic. He'd be massively pissed off at losing his mages, but he'd been in a weakened state and unconscious when they'd taken him. He'd have known, when he woke up, that he couldn't fight his way out of this one.

At the top of the staircase, a corridor shrouded in darkness waited for us, packed with the dead. Rotting bodies stood in a line, a foul stench rolling off them. Behind, a row of half-faerie ghosts hovered, their hands ablaze with icy magic. Ghosts *and* undead?

"Drake, get behind me!" I warned, wishing I'd given him salt instead of a knife. "Never seen undead in the Vale before. This is new."

The ghosts swarmed through the rotting bodies that I strongly suspected had once been their own. I swung my blade, cutting my way through undead and ghosts alike. A hollow sensation grew in my chest as the vibrant blue glow around my talisman built with each raging spirit that fell beneath the sword's edge. *Fionn. This depravity is his work.*

As the dead crumpled, a second wraith rose to block my path to the door. Larger than the first, the spirit resembled a gaping hole, seething emptiness shaped like the person it had once been. Sorrow and anger fed into the rising glow around my blade as I cut a diagonal slash through the ghost.

A high scream rang out as the wraith burst apart, along with the door it guarded.

Inside the cell on the other side, Vance hung from the wall. Like Drake, he'd been chained up with iron cuffs surely designed to use on faeries rather than humans. Blood plastered his dark-brown hair to his forehead, and all the colour had drained from his face.

"Vance." I ran up to him, my sword slicing through the chains, and steadied him against the wall. His grey eyes were half-open, but there was no life in them.

Dread clutched my heart. "Vance?" What had they done to him? I grabbed his hand, relief flooding me when I found a pulse. He was alive, albeit freezing cold, and his unresponsiveness set alarm bells ringing in my skull. "Vance, can you hear me?"

Vance gave a sudden lunge. His hand closed around my throat and squeezed. I gasped, coldness seeping into my skin from his icy touch. *Dammit, Ivy.* With all my experience, it was galling to know that I'd fallen the oldest trick in the faeries' book.

My vision darkened as I flailed, trying to punch him, to do some damage. He certainly looked and felt like Vance, but in Faerie, even my own senses weren't to be trusted.

My foot connected with his knee, knocking his hands away from my throat. I punched him hard in the jaw, but from his lack of reaction, I might as well have been fighting an undead. Except he seemed as solid and strong as ever. Not-Vance grabbed me by the scruff of my neck and threw me into the wall. Stone cracked the back of my head so hard that my vision swam. Grey filtered in, and my bodily sensations disappeared as the veil filled my vision.

Another ghost floated across from me, his grey eyes watching mine.

No. Please, no.

With a cry, I wrenched free from Death and back into my body, dropping to my knees as the horrible truth sank in.

The enemy hadn't harmed Vance's physical body. They'd done worse. His spirit had been ripped out of his body entirely, and whatever controlled his movements wasn't Vance at all.

Shit. Shit. Even if I managed to remove the other spirit without harming him, it might be too late. For most people, when one's spirit and body were separated, that was it.

"No." I forced the word between clenched teeth. The pain in my head receded as my healing power kicked in and my vision returned to normal. "No, I won't let you."

Blue light surged from my hand. Not-Vance dodged, seized my arm, and threw me to the floor. The hard stone took a layer of skin off my elbows and knees, but I managed to keep hold of my weapon. *I can't use it on him. I can't take that risk.* Even my magic might do permanent harm. I couldn't tell if they'd beaten him when he was a prisoner, but if what they'd done to Drake was anything to go by, he'd have a headache and a half when he woke up.

If he woke up.

None of that, Ivy. You'll set him free.

His hands grabbed for my feet as I tried to rise upward, and I kicked him in the face. *Sorry, Vance.* I rolled onto my front and shuddered at the ghostly touch of Vance's hands— or rather, the spirit possessing him. If I squinted, I could see its pale outline overlaying his physical form, guiding his movements.

"Let go of him!" I launched to my feet, holding my blade defensively. He and the ghost were too closely entwined to risk using my blade, but iron wouldn't leave a mark on a ghost either.

Fine. We'll do it this way.

I threw up a magical shield around my body and shifted into Death. Vance appeared in my peripheral vision, but my attention was on the spirit hovering above his earthly body, a dark outline that bore no resemblance to whoever it had been in life.

When I tapped into my magic, intending to draw in the spirit's rage to fuel my power, the ghost raised transparent hands and hit me with a blast of icy energy that sent me flying head over heels, crashing back into my own body. *Ow.* Echoes of the spirit's rage reverberated through me, lingering in the glow around my talisman.

"Spirit," I whispered. "What the hell did they do to you?"

I'd rarely seen a ghost *this* angry before. Teeth chattering, I fell back against the floor again when Vance reached for my throat with hands covered in black scales. *The spirit made him shift. Shit.*

Cursing, I scrambled back across the damp stone floor until I fetched up against the wall. Tendrils of magic streamed out of my blade, reaching for the transparent being behind Vance's body, but I couldn't see the ghost clearly enough to ensure I only hurt the spirit and not Vance himself. I'd have to go back into Death.

This is going to hurt. Bracing myself, I flew out of my body and found the spirit looming over me while Vance reached for my physical form. I extended my glowing hands, dug my fingers into the spirit's raw, angry presence, and *demanded* it let go of Vance.

At the same time, Vance's claws sank into my chest.

I kept shoving, kept pushing against the spirit until I felt its grip break like a rain-swollen cloud releasing a storm. As the wraith rose upward in a ghostly haze, I shifted back into my body again. Pain splintered upward from where Vance's claws pinned me, but I forced my hands to lift my sword, to take aim at the ghostly shape hovering above Vance's motionless body. No longer holding him.

"Whatever chains bind you, I can set you free," I said through bloody lips.

I reached out and swung my blade at the wraith, drawing upon both its rage and mine. The impact sent me flying from my body again as the energy from my sword rent the ghost in two. Its shattered remnants dispersed in a final shriek of rage that echoed through the grey.

In its place hovered Vance, whose blank-eyed ghost looked in horror at his own claws buried in my chest.

I extended a hand towards him, pushing through the resistance as though swimming against a current. "You aren't dead. I won't let you be."

Vance's fingers tightened around mine. I held his gaze with all the fierceness I had in me. "You're alive. You're coming back to me."

He and I shared the same iron will, the same desire to keep living, to keep fighting. For that reason, I refused to believe his connection to life had been severed. I gripped his hand, and using the same force with which I'd torn the intruding spirit out of his body, I urged him to return where he belonged.

Vance's ghostly hand dissolved, and so did I. Sensation returned in a blink, my eyes opening to a new wave of pain. Vance's claws came loose from my body; blood seeped down my front as my knees sagged beneath me.

"Ivy." Vance caught me, his arms cradling me close to his chest. "No. Oh, god. Wake up."

"Don't worry," I croaked. "My healing ability still works. Hang on a second."

The world came back into focus. Vance's face was paler

than usual, marked with a bruise on his cheek where I'd kicked him, but he was awake, alert, and no longer possessed. I took in a breath, averting my eyes from the blood on my chest. It wasn't Vance's fault the spirit had made him attack me, and the sheer miracle of his survival overwrote all other instincts.

"You brought me back."

"You brought yourself back." My magic had been the catalyst, but his desire to live had outweighed all else. "Are you hurt?"

He shook his head. "I don't think so. How did you—"

"I'll tell you later." I wrapped my arms around him, burying my head in his chest for a second. His cool masculine scent soothed my nerves despite the underlying coppery tang of blood. My blood. His skin was ice cold. I squinted at him in the dark. "Are you sure you're okay?" Being separated from your body was disorientating to say the least. I should know, and I'd had enough practise.

"I've been better," he said. "I can't use my ability to get us out of here."

"Don't worry. I've got my own way. Drake's over there—"

My sword ignited as threads of green magic spread across the floor. Vance was thrown back against the wall, the threads wrapping around his feet like vines.

"Hey!" I yelled at the person who appeared silhouetted against the doorway, his shadow projected in green light. Summer magic.

"I've been very interested to meet you, Ivy Lane," said the Sidhe lord.

6

The Sidhe's voice was melodious and soft but unfamiliar. Ashy-blond curls tumbled over his pale face, which was eerily symmetrical with high cheekbones, a straight nose, and full lips. A typical pretty Sidhe with a typical entitled attitude. Green energy streamed from both his palms, and Vance snarled, unable to break free of its hold.

"Let him go," I commanded. "If you want to fight someone, fight me."

"You trespassed on my property, Ivy." My perception shifted as he moved into the light in that peculiar fluid motion common to the Sidhe, as if they were made of something immaterial, something that didn't belong to the physical world. This guy was at full power, more like the Sidhe I'd encountered in my visit to the Summer Court than the other lords I'd met in the Vale. He was no exile.

One glance told me that Drake was in no shape to join in the fight. He'd collapsed against the wall, clutching his arm, his face soaked in fresh blood. He and Vance didn't have the Sight, which meant they'd never see the Sidhe's attacks

50

coming regardless of whether they had the strength to fight back. Icy anger seared my veins. *I'll kill him.*

The Sidhe and I both moved at the same time. Our swords met in a clash of light, blue against green. When the tendrils of his magic reached for my wrists, my body swayed, a current of energy leaking out of me and into his blade. *"You have the life-drinker?"*

If Fionn had handed this guy the talisman, he must have had a reason, but up close, the Sidhe didn't look particularly distinct. He had Generic Evil Sidhe written all over him. Down to the Generic Evil Laugh, which he deployed as he pointed the blade at me. "Yes, and I'll use it to kill you."

"Wrong." I deflected his attack, wary of the rippling threads of green magic attempting to leach the life out of me.

Sweat gathered on my forehead and my legs and arms ached as I blocked each of his strikes. He moved fast and effortlessly as any faerie, but he was clearly new to handling the talisman, and his swordplay wouldn't have passed muster with Gerry. I might not be as physically strong or fast, but I had years of experience behind me.

I dodged threads of vibrant green and his teeth bared in a feral snarl of frustration as I continued to parry his attacks. Perhaps it was the light, and the fact that faeries' unnatural beauty made them look ageless, but he seemed younger than any other Sidhe I'd fought. Still dangerous, but without the experienced edge Avalin or Velkas had.

In a way, he fought like the Lady of the Tree, except he seemed to have more control over the talisman than she did. Blocking his sword's strikes wasn't hard. Stopping his magical attacks was another issue entirely. Every time his magic brushed my skin, a wave of dizziness hit me. I was running on fumes despite the magic flooding my veins, and as my knees threatened to buckle, a stray thread spun Helena loose from my hand. My blade clattered to the floor, and when I reached for the hilt, he threw a blast of magic at me.

I rolled sideways and his attack hit the wall instead, knocking a chunk out of the solid stone. A quake travelled through the tower room, and cold air blew in through the gap in the wall. I caught the sword by my fingertips and ducked a second blast. This one hit the opposite wall and kicked off a vibration that brought a flurry of dust down from above.

Vance yelled a hoarse warning. "Ivy, watch out!"

"The ceiling's gonna come down!" Drake shouted.

I pushed my magic outwards in a shield, not a second too soon. Rock fragments showered down, sliding off the solid barrier I'd conjured, and grey light filtered in from above.

I thrust outward with the shield, aiming the fallen rock shards at the Sidhe, but he conjured a shield of his own. Rocks scattered around me, and my elbows scraped against stone as I rolled forwards to meet him. I brought my sword up in a vicious cut that would have cost him the use of his leg if he hadn't leaped aside with a Sidhe's unnatural grace.

Right into Vance's claws. Blood spurted. The Sidhe screamed and slashed at Vance with the life-drinker; he stumbled back, bleeding from one arm.

Back on my feet, I lifted my own blade. "Don't you fucking touch him again."

"Two against one is unfair," said the Sidhe petulantly.

"Tough shit."

Despite the raw power of the life-drinker, his lack of experience was obvious. Though the draining effect of his magic tugged at my limbs, there was enough darkness and despair flooding the castle to give me a boost of my own. My talisman's glow grew brighter as I tapped into the agony of whoever had been captured and tormented here and launched into another strike.

The draining effect hit as our blades met, and though he staggered, threads of green light caught my legs, locking me in place. My breath came out in gasps as I fought the instinct to close my eyes. Behind me, Vance snarled, caught in the same trap.

The Sidhe laughed. "You've lost, Ivy. I win."

Out of the corner of my eye, I saw Vance on his knees, struggling to rise to his feet. My vision flickered, threatening to fade out. *Don't pass out, Ivy.* "Who the hell even are you?"

"I was chosen to be reborn and carry this talisman. It's mine."

Damn. He talked like a kid because he *was* a kid. One of the half-blood ghosts who'd been given a shiny new body before I'd destroyed the cauldron. If Fionn had given this kid his life-drinker talisman, he must have been lacking in options. Or arrogant enough not to care.

As the Sidhe lifted the blade to deal the final blow, the piskie flew past with a high-pitched screech. "Don't hurt humans!"

I blinked through blurred vision, unable to believe Erwin Junior had decided to come and help after all. The piskie landed on the Sidhe's head, tugging at his hair and uttering loud screams. The Sidhe flailed in anger, trying to grab the piskie, and I used the distraction to thrust my blade into his chest.

His eyes bulged. The piskie let go and shot upward through the collapsed roof like a rocket as the Sidhe dropped to his knees, his chest impaled on my sword.

A green surge of energy swarmed me, and all the remaining fight drained out of my limbs. As I swayed on my feet, my sword came free of his chest, and the wound began to seal before my eyes. *Dammit.*

Vance raised his head—*good, he's alive*—and threw a knife at the Sidhe, who dodged with preternatural grace. I lifted my blade and caught the edge of the life-drinker, more tendrils of green light licking at my wrists. My body trembled, my vision whitening at the edges. A question stirred in the recesses of my mind: *where did Vance get that knife from?*

Drake appeared in a blaze of fire, crashing into the Sidhe from behind. The kid yelled in surprise and pain, and I shook off the threads of magic, regaining my balance.

With a snarl, the Sidhe flung out an arm, a blast of uncontrolled green light rippling outward. I flung a shield in front, but the force still sent all three of us flying back across the stone floor. I'd wondered how he could be that strong, but the life-drinker's magic gained a power boost whenever the sword was used to kill, and the Sidhe had killed at least three Mage Lords. Not to mention any other poor souls who'd been trapped in this tower and had perished here. Their pain lurked beneath the surface, their screaming voices lingering behind the humming energy inside my talisman.

Strong though he might be, he'd made a fatal mistake in forgetting where *my* power came from, if he'd ever known at all.

I tapped into the residual anger and pain lingering in the tower, bolstered my shield, and shifted out of my body. Greyness flooded the room to counter the green light spilling out of his blade, and I sent out a call to any spirits that might still be lurking within the gloom.

"This man killed you." I projected my voice at every spirit within the castle, every death claimed within its walls. "Help me finish him off."

Swiftly I returned to my body and offered him a smile. "You're dead."

"What?" The Sidhe's voice rose high, scared. Had he seen something of what I'd glimpsed on the other side? "No. I have more power than you. I killed—"

"Hundreds, right?" Triumph rushed over me as my shout

was echoed by the spirits I'd called from Death. Their screaming voices rose louder as I tapped into their pain, drawing it all into my own talisman. "My magic comes from the place you sent those suffering souls, and if I were you, I wouldn't want to look at what's on the other side. They're right here in the castle… and you're about to join them."

The Sidhe's eyes bulged, his face milky pale. Like all fae, his fear of mortality would be his undoing. None of them—not even the Sidhe—were truly immortal, and the lie they'd concocted would come crashing down soon enough. With a little luck, I wouldn't be there to see the fallout. I was getting the fuck out of here.

The Sidhe ran for the door. Vance got there first, driving his iron knife into the Sidhe's back. The life-drinker slipped from his hands as he fell to his knees. As I caught up, I grabbed the Sidhe's shoulder and drove my dagger into his back to join its twin.

"Surrender your talisman," I told the Sidhe. I didn't know if this would work, but I'd wielded the life-drinker myself before Fionn had claimed it from me with trickery alone. "If you surrender, I'll spare you further suffering."

"I was supposed… to live forever." Blood trickled from the corner of his mouth.

"Sorry, mate. That dream died before you ever fell for Fionn's tricks." And without the cauldron, he'd be dead for real. Permanently. No reversing it. "Your talisman."

"I… surrender." He coughed, and his eyes slid closed, his body slumping onto his front.

As I took the life-drinker sword, my knees buckled, but Vance caught my arm before I hit the floor. "Ivy?"

"I'm okay." I looked for Drake, who lay in a groaning heap near a pile of shattered rocks. "Come on. We're going home."

"How?" Drake pushed to his knees. "Oh, your weird world-hopping magic tricks. Do I have to hang onto you?"

I reached for the Sidhe first and pulled out the twin knives, grimacing at the trail of blood they left on my jacket as I returned them to my pockets. Then I sheathed Helena and held the life-drinker in my other hand. "Probably best if you do. I'm going to cross the veil. It'll be easier if you close your eyes, keep still, and don't panic."

"Who's panicking?" Drake took my arm, and with the other hand, I reached for Vance.

Then I pulled the three of us out of Faerie.

7

Cold paving stone pressed against my cheek. I lifted my head, taking in the empty road beneath the night sky. Darkness clothed the street, broken only by a single beam of light from a streetlamp. Vance sat up slowly, moonlight from the almost-full moon over our heads throwing the bruises on his face into sharp relief.

"You okay?" I peered at him, concerned. "I didn't want to drag you through Death after what you just went through, but there's no other way out of the Vale. We're home now."

"Don't worry about me," he said. "Do you have both talismans?"

"Yeah." I spied the life-drinker where it'd fallen from my grip on the way out and half-walked, half-shuffled to pick it up. "That fucker never deserved it."

A relieved smile stole onto my face. I'd won back the life-drinker *and* got Vance and Drake back to the mortal realm in one piece. Whatever Fionn threw at me next, I'd take this win.

A few feet away, Drake stirred. "Ouch. Hey, you brought us to the manor. What…?" He trailed off, staring at the dark shape of the mages' headquarters. It hadn't been obvious at first, but the absence of the usual glowing wards rendered the building almost unrecognisable. Not another soul stirred on the street. "Tell me that doesn't mean what I think it does."

"Ivy?" Vance looked at me, desperation and shock wiping all traces of exhaustion from his face.

My throat closed up. "I'm sorry. I wanted to wait until we were home to tell you. If Wanda left beforehand, she might be okay. But the others…"

"No." Drake staggered over to the closed gate. "There's a ward here. A new one."

"Isabel." I got to my feet shakily, drained from both the life-drinker sword and the aftermath of no longer using magic. My body felt like one giant bruise. "I asked her and the coven to set up some wards to stop anyone from getting in, but—you know how time works in the Grey Vale. I'm not sure how long we've been gone."

Vance trod after Drake and studied the fresh ward outside the manor. "Iron?"

"It's all I could do," I said. "I also told Isabel to pass on word to the mages who fled that you were still alive. I'm not sure if they believed her, mind."

"And the rest of the council?" asked Vance.

I shook my head "I'm sorry. He killed them. Lady Penrose, Lord Carlisle. The whole new council, apart from you and Drake."

The raw despair on his face broke my heart. "I need to call the others."

Vance disappeared. *Hope he's okay.* Right before he'd been captured, Vance had transported a group of mages away from a deadly attack by the Morrigan, nearly killing himself in the process. Now he and Drake were the only surviving council members left within the district, and both were exhausted and injured. Not ideal when we expected retaliation from Fionn any second now.

"Fuck." Drake sank to his knees, like he'd been hit by the life-drinker sword again. "Why would they take us and kill the others?"

"I don't know." I swallowed hard. "I think Fionn sent his pet Sidhe to take you hostage while I was trapped in his castle."

He'd be even more pissed off that I'd freed them and taken the life-drinker talisman back, but I couldn't summon up any fucks to give. The cauldron's destruction alone had won me a lifetime membership to his shit list. No going back from there.

Drake shook his head. "I never thought I'd see the mage council fall again."

"Me neither." I'd never met the Mage Lords who'd been killed in the invasion, and I'd spent most of the time since my return from Faerie stewing in resentment of the mages' cushy lifestyles and complete obliviousness to the rampant poverty elsewhere in the city. While some mages undeniably fit that description, the invasion had claimed the lives of an entire generation. Their leaders had fought the Sidhe in defence of this realm and the people in it, supernaturals and non-supernaturals alike. Vance was prepared to do the same —and had nearly done exactly that.

He reappeared at my side, holding a large backpack that clanked when he put it down. "We need to leave. I have all of our most secure documents here. I doubt Fionn knows how to hack into a computer, but if he does, he won't find anything."

"I never thought of that," I said. "He doesn't know your other safe houses?"

"I imagine he doesn't need to," Vance said darkly. "Not when he already thinks he's eliminated the council and thrown the mages into chaos. The manor was equipped for an evacuation, and I'm glad I checked everything was in order beforehand. After Wanda was attacked, I feared something like this might happen." He spoke somewhat calmly, ever the Mage Lord used to dealing with catastrophe, but exhaustion lined his face. "I also haven't heard from Quentin, but he has other means of hiding himself."

"Quentin's okay. He took me to Summer—long story. I'll tell you later. Have you warned the other mages?"

"They're at a safe house. We're going to join them."

"Wait," I said. "You're in no fit state to—"

"Watch out!" Drake yelled from behind us. There was a burst of fire, and a chilling, screeching cry. A hideous seven-foot-long winged creature with black-and-red feathers reeled away from Drake's attack.

Fionn's army's still here?

"Were you waiting to ambush anyone who came back?" I didn't wait for a response, blasting the creature in the chest with magic. My attack came out as more of a wisp than a burst. *Not again.*

The fury lashed at me, its claw catching on my sleeve, but Vance's blade sheared it in the back before it could deal a killing blow. It turned to him next, and I swung my blade, severing its clawed foot. Blood splattered the road and Drake moved to attack, throwing handfuls of fire at the creature. The beast screeched as the flames consumed its body until nothing but burned feathers remained.

"Vance, we need to go," said Drake.

Vance gave a sharp nod. "Yes."

"Wait," I said, realising what he was about to do. "Don't—"

The world tilted sideways as the street vanished. My knees buckled, and once again, cold paving stone pressed against my face. My head spun, and I had to close my eyes for a few seconds to stop the dizziness.

"Vance," Drake groaned. "You really shouldn't have done that."

Vance lay across from me, not moving.

"Hey, Vance." No answer. "Vance?" Shit. I felt for a pulse and found one, barely. "Why did he do that?"

I'd dragged him over the veil when he'd barely recovered from last time and the first thing the fool had done was transport us... where? The terraced houses indicated that we'd landed in the witches' part of town on a road lit with streetlamps that banished the shadows that lurked in other less populated areas. The witches didn't mess about with their security. Every building had some kind of ward on the front, even the ones that belonged to regular humans.

Isabel's flat was close enough to walk, so I looped Vance's arm over my shoulder and pulled him upright. Drake came over to help, picking up the rucksack Vance had brought and slinging it over his back. "Dammit. Couldn't have passed out later, could he?"

"It's okay," I said. "Isabel will help us out."

That we managed to carry Vance between us without anyone keeling over was a testament to our relief to be home after the horrors of Faerie. Drake and I had to stop and rest a couple of times, but we made it to the red brick building that was now both Isabel's flat and our freelance business's new office. The converted Victorian house was much nicer than our old flat, with beds of fragrant herbs in the garden and flowery curtains drawn across the windows.

"Bad faerie!" came a familiar yell as I rang the doorbell.

"Erwin." I leaned on the wall. "You've no idea how glad I am to see you."

The piskie let out a scream and flew around my head. "Bad faerie hurt Ivy!"

"Your friend lives with this thing?" Drake watched the piskie, who resembled an oversized stick insect with wings.

"He's like a really hyperactive guard dog," said Isabel, opening the door. She wore a dressing gown, indicating that it was later than I'd first thought. Her warm brown skin was marked with chalk stains, so I assumed she'd been up drawing spell circles again.

"Hey." I offered a smile. "It's good to see you."

"Hey, Ivy. You're covered in blood and all of you look like you've done ten rounds with a troll. I'm guessing you ran into trouble?"

"Major understatement, but yes." Isabel and I had lived together long enough that nothing surprised her anymore. Isabel's five-foot slender frame might look unassuming, but she was surprisingly strong, and she helped Drake and me haul Vance's unconscious body over the doorstep and into the living room without too much difficulty. Even though I didn't live here, the flat had the comforting smell of candles and witch charms I associated with home. Chalked spell-circles covered the carpet, while every surface was covered in either ingredients or handmade spells shaped like ordinary household objects such as pencils and elastic bands.

"I thought you only made spells in your workshop." I yawned.

"Ran out of space." She moved a stack of pencils off the sofa to make room for Vance.

I hoped he was just tired from the ordeal of the past day or so and that he'd be fine in the morning, but I couldn't imagine any of us being in a fit state to go to war with Fionn anytime soon. Especially with dozens of panicked mages out there who'd lost their whole council and the manor in one fell swoop.

To top it off, the necromancers lacked solid leadership, the half-faeries had already been in disarray thanks to a coup orchestrated on Fionn's behalf, and their former Chief was AWOL. How we were supposed to assemble a defensive force out of this sorry mess was beyond me. I sank into the nearest chair and closed my eyes, the triumph of our victory leaking out of me along with my remaining energy.

"Oh, Ivy." Isabel came over and hugged me. "I'm sorry. Were Vance and Drake the only ones?"

"Yeah. Wanda escaped the manor, but I haven't heard from her yet. Vance called the council, but he…" I looked helplessly at him.

"He's not in pain, don't worry. I think he's just exhausted. Hey—is that the life-drinker?"

"Yeah." I removed my considerably battered rucksack and laid the two swords down on the coffee table. Neither carried their usual glow. Had their power been depleted, or was this some side effect of Fionn screwing around with the veil? "I'd put it in storage, but Fionn broke into the storeroom and probably wiped out the wards in the process."

"Bastard." Drake backed out of the kitchen, a blood-soaked rag in his hand. He'd scrubbed the blood from his face, but the wound remained an angry red slash despite the healing spell he'd used. "Is there anything he didn't fuck up?"

"Have there been any more incidents since I left?" I asked Isabel. "We ran into furies at the manor."

"That's why we couldn't put up any more wards," she said. "We're getting divebombed every time we walk across town. The mercenaries are in a state, too. Larsen's been missing since the battle."

"Oh, shit." I'd forgotten about my old boss, but now I felt bad for the other mercenaries. Most were self-centred wankers, but some of them were decent people just trying to stay alive. "He's probably dead. Are the witches okay?"

"The coven's fine, just shaken up by everything," she replied. "Some of us have been checking in on the mages. I spoke to a couple of apprentices and told them you were looking for Vance, but I think they thought you ran off on them."

"The dicks," I said. "They have so little faith in me after all I've done for them?"

Isabel grimaced. "I set them straight, don't worry. I knew you'd come back, but it's been an ordeal, I won't lie. We've had fury attacks all over the city, and the coven's been actively preparing for the worst. I've been handing out protective wards to anyone I can reach, but the coven can only make them so fast."

I rubbed my forehead. "How long has it been, exactly? Since I fought Fionn?"

"Five days," she said. "It's lucky you prepared me. How long was it for you?"

"Less than three hours," I replied. "I went to Summer first, like I planned."

"Wait, what?" asked Drake. "You never said you went to Faerie. The real Faerie, I mean, not the fucking weird one."

"Yeah, I did," I said. "Quentin took me. Two faeries from Summer arrived at the manor just after I'd got back. I hoped they might help me find you, so I went with them to the Court ."

"And?" Drake said expectantly. "Did you get to speak to whoever rules that place?"

I hated to deflate his hopeful expression, but I shook my head. "No, just a stuck-up Sidhe lord who tried to turn me into a tree and then set a bunch of dryads on me. And to add insult to injury, one of the faeries who took me there decided to try and kill me, so I had to leave. I assume Quentin's still there. He didn't end up in the Grey Vale, at least."

"And you did? Damn." Drake scratched at the cut on his face, an unconscious movement that opened the scab again. "Fucking hell, this thing itches."

"Don't poke that." Isabel tutted. "I'll get a healing salve. Honestly, Ivy, did anyone in Summer *not* try to kill you?"

"Lord Raivan?" I scrunched up my forehead. "He just insulted me a lot and watched while a vine dangled me upside-down, but it's better than turning me into an ornament."

Isabel snorted. "And that was *before* you went into the Vale?"

"I'll tell you the rest when Vance is awake." I pushed to my feet, my legs trembling. "I'm going to make some food and shower, and then we figure out our next move."

"I'll cook," said Isabel. "You look like you're about to keel over, Ivy."

"I feel like it, too, but I want to get that dickhead of a Sidhe's blood off my clothes."

It was lucky the flat was all one floor, because I couldn't have handled climbing stairs. The guest bedroom was mostly free of spells, and I made it to the ensuite bathroom without tripping into a chalk circle and triggering a glitter spell. Even with my ability to heal myself in Faerie, I had a new collection of bruises all over my body which appeared in earnest when I stripped off my bloodied clothes. Isabel had brought some of my clothes from the manor, for which I was grateful, and I showered quickly and changed into pyjamas. I returned to the living room to find Isabel applying a salve to the wound on Drake's face. The strong smell of herbs made my eyes water.

Drake yelped. "That stings."

"Keep still, then," said Isabel. "Oh, fine. Put the salve on yourself and hope you don't poke yourself in the eye."

"It feels like my skin's on fire," Drake groaned.

"Looks like it, too," I said. "Isabel's trying to help."

"I know. Sorry. Ow." He winced, running a hand across the top of his forehead. "It's gonna leave a mark forever, right?" He'd probably had access to healing spells his whole life, but even the best witch-made salve could only do so much if the wound had been left untreated.

"Yeah," I said, deciding to be honest. "On the plus side, you'll look pretty badass."

Isabel snorted. "Can you handle the rest of it yourself? Try not to touch anything while the salve's working its magic."

A groan came from the sofa. I turned to see Vance's eyes were open, looking around in confusion. Blood was smeared across his face, but it wasn't his. I winced a little at the sight of the growing bruise on his jaw. I'd kicked him pretty hard when he'd been possessed.

"You're awake." I leaned over and gave him a quick kiss. His gaze was clear, soft and familiar, and a rush of relief brought tears to my eyes. I didn't want to contemplate what I'd have done if I'd been too late to save him.

"Hey, Ivy," he rasped. "Where...?"

"Isabel's place. Don't move or you'll pass out again. What the hell were you thinking?"

He half sat up, looking at the rucksack he'd brought from the manor, and the two swords I'd laid alongside it. "Is this place secure?"

"All secure!" screeched Erwin, flying overhead. "No bad faeries."

Not yet. I shoved the thought aside. "It's all good. We have wards everywhere, more iron spells than anywhere else in the city, and a security piskie."

Vance gave me a sceptical look and swung his legs over the sofa's side. "I need to get in touch with the mages."

"It's midnight," said Isabel, crossing the room with two bowls of soup. I took one and handed the other to Vance. "You need to recover your strength. You've been gone a week."

"It hasn't been a week for me. Two days at most." I lifted my soup bowl and practically inhaled half of it, even though it was piping hot. Okay, maybe I had skipped a few days. So had Vance. He was too pale and tired-looking, and there was a slightly distant look in his eyes that worried me. I knew how Faerie could get into your head.

"Feels like a week." Drake picked up a pencil-shaped spell from the seat next to him. "What's this do?"

"Don't activate it." Isabel handed him another bowl of soup. "Not unless you want to be covered in glitter."

"Glitter." The faintest trace of a smile crossed Drake's mouth. "Seriously, you should be selling those spells of yours on the side. You could make a fortune."

Isabel ducked her head on the pretext of picking up another stack of spells she'd left on the floor. She'd been busy over the past week, that was for sure. There were enough spells in here to open a small shop.

"He's right," I said, draining the rest of my soup. "Trust me. I knew the city was in safe hands."

Isabel smiled shyly. "You have too much faith in me. Do you need a healing spell?"

"No, but I need about twenty hours of sleep and nobody to try and kill me for a bit. Vance, do you need one?"

I took his silence as a yes and passed one to him.

Vance activated the spell without looking up from his phone screen. "There have been attacks in other districts, too. The furies are widespread."

"I'm not surprised." I went to the kitchen to put my empty bowl in the dishwasher. "Fionn coordinated this. He wanted to scatter our forces, and he must have had his allies carrying out attacks while I was busy dealing with the cauldron." I hadn't told Vance and Drake that part of the story yet, though Isabel knew from before my latest trip to Faerie.

Vance swore at his phone. "I'm going to kill him."

"No, I am," said Drake.

Isabel rolled her eyes. "Honestly. You were imprisoned in Faerie, and none of you are in any condition to go to war."

"Hey," I said, as Vance and Drake voiced similar protests. "We aren't going to war yet. We're going to gather our forces and find Wanda and her grandmother. They weren't at the manor."

Which meant they might still be alive. I didn't dare hope for too much, but Vance and Drake being alive and Isabel being safe had bolstered me. We weren't finished yet.

Isabel watched me return to my seat with her arms folded across her chest. "Not in the middle of the night. See how you feel in the morning."

Drake leaned forward in the armchair and muttered something under his breath.

"What was that?" said Isabel. "Was that a 'thank you for your hospitality and for the healing spell'? It'd be a lot worse if I didn't have the salve ready because I figured Ivy would come back with her usual life-threatening injuries."

"Sorry to disappoint you." I gave Drake a pointed look.

He scrubbed a hand over his newly healed face. "I—I'm sorry, Isabel," he mumbled. "I'm just fucking tired of our people getting killed. I should have been able to stop them. He hit me with that damn sword and my fire... went out."

"It wasn't your fault," Vance said. "If I hadn't been incapacitated—"

"If we're playing the blame game, I kicked off this whole feud in the first place," I interrupted. "He took you both to get at me."

"Ivy—"

"But you know what?" I cut in. "I'm not going to give him the satisfaction. I know how faeries' minds work. They didn't take you solely to torture you or to lure me into a trap. They did it to break all our spirits at once and make us doubt our own ability to take him out. I spent three years as a captive of one of them. I've done this shit before, and whatever Fionn thinks, none of us are finished yet. We're alive, and we'll make him sorry he crossed any of us."

My legs decided to give out, somewhat fizzling the effect, but Drake clapped a couple of times. Vance reached out to steady me as I fell back onto the sofa.

"You're going to sleep first," said Isabel. "He isn't here, and we have a dozen wards set up outside to alert us of any intruders. Get your rest and we'll pick it up tomorrow. Vance and Ivy, you can have the guest room. Drake..."

"It's okay. I'll sleep on the sofa," said Drake.

"Watch out for Erwin," I told him. "He'll try to pull out your hair while you're sleeping if you aren't careful."

Drake groaned. Vance got to his feet and limped to the guest bedroom, discarding his considerably battered mage coat on the bed and then ducking into the ensuite bathroom. I picked up my bag, which had survived the fight with the Sidhe with a few scrapes, and carried it into the bedroom together with my two talismans. Even the life-drinker's light had gone out completely. *But it's mine, right?* I'd claimed it fair and square, and Fionn had tricked me into giving it to him in the first place.

If meeting the true Sidhe had achieved nothing else, it'd been a stark lesson in how far Fionn had slipped away from what I'd once thought of as the rules that governed the fae. Yes, the Sidhe were capricious, but they could be reasoned with to some extent, and their refusal to accept change made them predictable. Fionn, though, was change and chaos rolled into one, and I hadn't a hope of using the faeries' own rules against him as I'd done with Avalin. Not when he was in the habit of adjusting the rules according to his own whims and altering the playing field any time he liked.

He can't change the fact that he didn't start out as the Hunts-

man, and he isn't really a god, I reminded myself. *He's playacting.*

As for the true gods? I sat on the bed and examined the hilt of my talisman, wondering if the only way I might have a fighting chance was to hunt down the origin of its power. The god, whoever that might be. In all the time I'd spent in the Grey Vale, I'd never—

My eyes flew open, all tiredness momentarily pushed aside. I'd imprisoned another god in the Vale myself. The dragon shifter god might know where the others were... though waking an angry god who I'd put into an eternal sleep myself and who might fly over to the enemy's side for all I knew was a hell of a risk. Maybe not, then.

The door to the ensuite bathroom opened. Vance came in, wearing loose jogging trousers and nothing else, beads of water rolling down his bare, muscled chest. It was a sight that would usually cause me to forget everything else, if not for the bruises and scrapes from the fight which remained even after using the healing spell. He'd probably been tortured for hours before I found him.

Anger pulsed through me, but I hugged Vance, burying my head in his shoulder to inhale the scent of him. "Talk to me, Vance. Are you okay?"

He heaved a sigh. "I'm supposed to be their leader, and I let them die."

"You didn't *let* them. Fionn is entirely responsible, and believe me, we'll make him pay for it."

"Yes, we will." His arms came around my back, held me tight. "I don't know how I'll make it up to you for coming to find me."

I leaned into him, savouring his closeness, the reminder that he was *here.* That I'd brought him home. "Considering all the times you've got me out of sticky situations, we're probably even. Oh, and I want to kill the Morrigan, too. Did you see her?"

"Yes." He released me, stepped back. "She's the one who ripped my soul from my body."

"That was her?" I winced. "Don't get me wrong, I'm really glad you're okay, but I'm surprised she didn't finish the job."

"I was unconscious when she showed up." He sat down on the bed and I joined him. "I woke up when she got her claws in me, and it took a bit for me to figure out where I was."

"Maybe she figured you'd die without your body and it wasn't worth the fuss." Had she recognised him from their earlier encounter during the battle with the mages? The Morrigan's agreement with Fionn was unclear to me, and so were her own motives. "The last time I saw her, she tried to throw me into the cauldron, so we both had a narrow escape."

"The cauldron?" His shoulders stiffened. "Yes—what happened with that?"

"I kind of majorly fucked up, but for a good reason."

Vance shook his head at me, but the corner of his mouth twitched. "Ivy, if any phrase encapsulates you, it's that. Tell me." He pulled me into his lap, my head resting against his chest. We didn't both easily fit onto the narrow bed considering Vance's height, but the lack of space didn't seem to bother him. I wanted to lie down at his side and forget we'd ever been apart, but putting off the moment would only make things more difficult in the morning.

I ran through my experiences from the moment Fionn had forced me to follow him into the Grey Vale, my imprisonment and escape, and the cauldron shattering at my command. Then I went through my trip into Summer territory with Quentin again, since he hadn't been awake when I'd told Drake and Isabel, adding in more details of how I'd landed up in the Vale and had come to rescue him.

Vance was silent for a long moment after I'd finished. "There's a traitor in Summer, too?"

"Don't know if I'd call him a traitor. He wanted me dead because his wife was the ambassador for Summer who was killed in the last invasion. Doesn't mean nobody else from Summer will help us, but their one human liaison is a total dick who turned me into a tree and not a single person I met there was of any help. They were massively pissed off with me for losing the ring, so it's a good job I managed to avoid mentioning the cauldron."

"Didn't the cauldron belong to Winter?"

"Both Courts created it, I think. I mean, the Huntsman worked for both, and I never had time to ask for the details." The Hemlock witches had told me, and it hadn't been long after they'd dropped the bombshell on my head that I'd been forced to take out the cauldron with my own hand. "Not only was the cauldron a valuable talisman, the only one of its kind as far as I know, but without it, I'm pretty sure the Sidhe can't be reborn when they die. It sounds like the Erlking, leader of Summer, is in a bad way already, so assuming we survive the battle, the whole of the Summer Court might want my blood."

"Oh." Vance stared at me, his mouth slightly parted. It was rare enough that I managed to astonish him into silence that I was almost tempted to laugh.

"Yeah. We're screwed. I'm really sorry."

"We'd be in a worse position if Fionn had managed to create an army using the cauldron," said Vance. "As it is, it sounds like he was able to create very few new Sidhe before you destroyed it."

"And I killed one of them when I got back the life-drinker." I grimaced. "He was livid, though, when I broke the cauldron. He shapeshifted—did you know he's a shapeshifter, too? If he hated me before, then he's pissed off enough to smite the entire planet now."

When the hit came, it'd be brutal.

Then we'll just have to take as many of them down with us as possible.

"We'll be ready." Steel entered his voice. "I want to take out the Morrigan myself. She owes me a rematch."

"Deal. If I get to kill Fionn." Never mind how impossible that seemed now.

"Yes." Vance cupped my face in his hands and kissed me. He tasted as good as I remembered—better, even. "Vengeful is a good look on you."

"Even in fluffy pyjamas?"

"I like them." He kissed me again, trailing a hand down my face. "I missed you."

"Faeries aren't good company." I straddled him, forgetting the lack of space and bumping my head on the wall. "Oh, for god's sake."

He chuckled and pulled me on top of him. For the first time in what felt like forever, I dared to think everything would be okay.

8

Sun streaming through the window woke me. I rolled over to find Vance was gone, but his side of the bed was still warm, so it hadn't been for long. Isabel had left my spare clothes she'd brought from the manor inside the drawers next to the bed, which was a relief, because the ones in my bag had somehow ended up covered in dirt and blood without me even wearing them. I tugged on jeans and a plain dark-coloured top that would make any bloodstains less obvious. My usual aesthetic, whether I was hunting down rogue faeries or preventing the end of the world as we knew it. I tugged a brush through my hair and swept it back in a ponytail, then picked up the talismans I'd left on the bedside table. Neither responded when I examined them, and the glyphs on the hilts remained dull. Figuring I'd deal with that one later, I left the bedroom.

The open door to Isabel's workshop revealed what looked like the contents of an entire warehouse of witch supplies. She waved at me on my way past, while I found Vance and Drake in the living room, conversing in low voices.

"I've contacted several of our representatives," Vance said

when he saw me. "There's been an uproar. The country's entire Mage Council thinks I'm dead."

"I'm glad you're not." I kissed him on the cheek, wrapping my arms around his warm body.

"Me, too." He ruffled my hair with one hand. "But we have a situation to sort out. I need to show up in person to prove I'm not an impostor. We also need to make arrangements to appoint an interim council, and the manor isn't secure. We'll need new wards—"

"Give me a list of what you need and I'll get it sorted." Isabel entered the room. "The coven will help. I can arrange a delivery whenever you like."

"That would be most welcome," said Vance. "It's mostly the glyphs that'll need redoing, which is a big job, and not one I expect anyone to do while there are furies at large."

"I can do it," Isabel offered. "Just let me know when. The other witches can help, though they've been working over-time for days handing out spells to local residents."

"Wow, you're really on top of things," I said. "You're making me feel like a slacker, and I visited two faerie realms and won a talisman from a Sidhe in the past day."

Isabel snorted. "Hey, some of us have to deal with the practical stuff while you're saving the world."

"It's appreciated, believe me." I grinned.

"Well, I didn't know for sure when you'd be coming back."

Or if we were coming back. I sobered instantly. "Vance, are all the mages in one place?"

"Some of them are," he said. "Others have left to request backup from other regions. It's possible I'll be handling meetings with officials for the next week, and I'd prefer to elect a new council of my own before it gets to that point."

I grimaced. "We might not *have* a week before the war starts."

"Exactly," said Vance. "Drake and I need to speak to the

mages remaining in the city and make a plan. Ivy, you can come, but it might take a while."

"Oh, joy." Drake sighed. A thin scar stretched across his face, a reminder of the close call he and Vance had had.

"I want to come to the first meeting," I said. "Just to set the record straight on Fionn's plans to attack this realm. I can see people like Lady Granville telling everyone I'm making up lies, and I've had enough of that bullshit already."

Vance's mouth tightened. "Yes, I suspect that may be the case. I did make it clear that we were to act on the assumption that a threat as great as the invasion is imminent, and that inaction may cost lives."

"Yeah, the Sidhe didn't get that message," I said. "Even if my warning somehow got through to the leaders of the Seelie Court, it'd probably take another twenty years for them to decide whether to help us or not."

"You're joking," said Drake. "And I thought our cross-country mage council meetings were bad."

"I know," I said. "I have some ideas of what to do next, but if the Sidhe won't help, we'll have to look to our other allies."

After a quick breakfast, we set off for the safe house, which turned out to be located just down the road from the necromancer guild. Perhaps surprisingly, that was one of the city's safest areas, given the sheer level of iron built into the foundations of the necromancers' property. I doubted they'd left their headquarters much lately. They'd lost their own leader a few months ago, and instead of choosing a replacement, they'd ended up keeping his ghost on as an adviser. Isabel's boyfriend, Rick, was the only necromancer I knew of who remotely had his shit together, but the sooty black building was an unexpectedly reassuring sight. There was so much iron in there, even Fionn would have trouble trampling that place.

I had Helena strapped to my weapons belt and the life-drinker sword across my back—the only way I could securely carry both without my movement being impeded in battle—and Drake ran ahead to meet the mage apprentice, who ran out of the large house as we approached. Vance had worn his newly cleaned and mended mage coat so that nobody would doubt who he was.

"Surprise," said Drake, conjuring a handful of fire.

"Mage Lord!" the apprentice shouted.

"Wake the dead, why don't you." I couldn't help smiling, though, as the mages spilled out of the door, all talking over one another and clamouring to speak to Vance.

With his usual efficiency, he swept everyone into the living room of the safe house and asked for their account of the events since Fionn's attack. None of them had been in the manor during the attack and had fled at the first sign of the Sidhe's arrival, and they'd picked this particular safe house because they needed the necromancers' help to safely cremate the bodies of the dead before someone decided to raise them as zombies. A wise move, and surprisingly organised given the state of disarray we'd left them in. According to Bailey, who'd stepped into Drake's shoes in his absence, Lady Harper was working on securing more safe houses with Wanda's assistance.

Unfortunately, the mages' euphoria at Vance's return didn't last long. When he told them that Fionn had returned, together with a proper body, the mages erupted into a panic that Vance had to quell by using his abilities to conjure a cold breeze that knocked all the windows open. His disappearance had brought all their fears of a second invasion screaming to the surface and while I didn't tell them the details of the cauldron or the army he'd tried to build, the mages assumed the worst by default.

"He's not here yet," I snapped for the fifth time. "He also doesn't have the same forces he had during the first invasion, either. But yes, an attack is imminent, and you're going to make it very easy for him if you lie down and accept defeat."

"But he has no weaknesses!" one of the mages objected. "You said so yourself."

"There's no way to win this."

"We're doomed."

"Enough!" Vance raised his voice. "Ivy has a plan, and I'll invite you to remember that while the ring was Fionn's weakness, the Mage Lords during the invasion didn't know it existed. They fought back anyway, even though they expected to die in the process. It's entirely possible that Fionn has another weakness we have yet to discover, and I have absolute faith that Ivy can defeat him."

My cheeks burned. I gave him the evil eye. *Way to put pressure on me, Vance.* But it worked. The others quieted enough to give Vance the opportunity to bring the conversation back around to the matter of electing new council members to replace the ones killed at the manor.

"You don't have to stick around for this part," Drake told me in an undertone. "It'll go on for hours, and likely involve a few duels. You have important stuff to deal with, right?"

"Yeah. I do."

I had no idea where to begin, though. I needed to know if there was another way to beat Fionn—without the ring, and without using my magic—and the Hemlock witches were the obvious people to ask, but the last time I'd tried to get into their forest, I'd been forced to leave my body behind in the process. I wasn't sure if that was even an option with the spirit realm in a state of disarray and my magic glitching out.

"I should probably speak to the necromancers, to start off with. They don't know we're back, unless Isabel's told them."

"Good idea," said Drake. "They weren't on our priority list, obviously."

"I thought not." I waved at Vance, indicating that I was

going outside. He frowned. I pointed across the road, and then he nodded, understanding. "See you soon."

I stepped outside. A cold autumn breeze swept through my leather jacket, a reminder of the changing seasons. A year had passed since I'd first come here with Vance and we'd been attacked by undead in the graveyard next to the necromancers' headquarters. A year, or a lifetime. Behind the gate, overgrown grass filled the gaps between the empty graves marking those killed in the invasion.

On the other side, I heard footsteps. Friendly or unfriendly? Based on my track record, I'd bet my sword on the latter.

I reached out and opened the gate.

9

I drew a canister of salt from my jacket and then lowered my hand. A fair-haired, bedraggled-looking boy scrambled away from my approach, green eyes round and terrified. "You're Ivy. Don't kill us. Please."

"What?" Then my gaze caught on his pointed ears, his too-pretty features hidden underneath a coating of dirt and dried blood. "You're half-blood. Are there others here?"

"There." He pointed to the outdoor mausoleum I sometimes used to contact the dead.

I'd have thought the iron would have put them off, but a closer look revealed at least a dozen half-faeries crowded around a despondent-looking Chief. The former leader of the half-bloods still wore his battered gold crown, though the colour had chipped in places like cheap plastic, and his equally low-budget armour had seen better days. At his side stood Killian, his partner, who held a trident-like weapon in one hand and appeared to be offering him whispered advice.

"Faerie killer!" yelled a silver-haired half-Sidhe who'd once belonged to the Chief's guards.

The faeries all jumped to their feet. I rolled my eyes as a dozen weapons pointed at me. "Lovely to see you, Chief."

"You're a trick." He jumped to his feet, pointing his staff at me, too. "A ghost."

"I'm not a ghost, Chief. If I was, why in hell would I have come to this dump rather than picking somewhere more exciting to haunt?"

He lowered his staff. "Where *have* you been?"

"Away." His head would probably explode from jealousy if I told him I'd been to the Summer Court. "Any reason you're camping out here?"

"The necromancers have refused to let us into their headquarters for two days," said the Chief indignantly.

"I'm sorry about that," I said. "But there's a shit-ton of iron in there. It's not exactly a safe haven for your people. Can't you move back onto your own territory now the banshee's gone?"

"Our magic is no longer functioning," said the Chief. "I don't know what you did, Ivy, but the magic that sustained our territory—Winter or Summer alike—has disappeared."

"What?" Uh-oh. "Completely? It's gone?"

So it wasn't just me? Had *all* the faerie magic in this realm drained away? Destroying the cauldron surely hadn't done that much damage, had it?

"It seems so," the Chief said through gritted teeth. "It has been quite impossible for me to reclaim my leadership position without being able to offer any reassurances that our magic will return. The remaining mages refused to speak with us, so we came to the only other possible place."

"Er, you forgot the witches," I said. "You know, the ones who offered you shelter in their old leader's house. Remember?"

"The witches are a small force of power, limited within their covens."

"They have more magic than you have in your little finger." The witches were far more likely to offer the half-bloods help, and the coven had done exactly that to the ones who'd been driven off their territory. The Chief had been jailed at the time, but of all the places to come instead, why here? He and his people usually pretended the necromancers didn't exist, the same way they pretended death wasn't an inevitability. Being around gravestones, reminders that half-bloods weren't as immortal as their faerie ancestors, would send them into such an existential panic that it was no wonder they were so jumpy.

Admittedly, the intimidating facade of the necromancers' place resembled a stronghold more than the witches' run-down hall did, so I understood why they'd chosen it as their base. This place had withstood the invasion, in fact, but the iron in the walls would knock a half-blood out. Already some of them had ugly red welts on their faces and hands and splotchy marks from where they'd accidentally brushed against the mausoleum's iron-laced walls or floor.

"I won't accept judgement from you, human," said the Chief. "I will do everything I can to keep my people safe."

"I was just pointing out that a graveyard isn't exactly a place most people would consider safe." To say the least. "The witches offered you shelter. The mages would have done the same if they hadn't been attacked themselves."

"There you have it," he said. "Why should we trust any of you?"

"Because you don't have a choice." I scanned their group, my gaze landing on the kid who'd jumped me. He looked half-starved and terrified. "And because there are kids here, and it's a dick move to pretend nobody but you can offer them help. Take off the crown, Taive, and work with the human authorities."

"I *tried* to cooperate with the mages. They refused."

"As I said, they're in the middle of a crisis. Vance will listen to you once he's finished establishing a new council, but ignoring the witches' offer of help isn't fair to the others."

The Chief's face reddened. "You don't have any right to demand that we bow our heads to humans. It's the Courts who should answer to what they did to us. We would be in Faerie, working for our brethren, if Summer and Winter hadn't forced us to adapt to a world that is poison to our kind, or die."

"Nobody ever said life was fair, Chief," I said. "I've spoken to the Summer Court in person and your demands are pretty low down on the list. It might be unfair, but unless you plan to fight on Fionn's side in the war, you need to work with us. Get the kids off the streets first. It's not safe. Talk to the witches. Isabel and the coven will help you."

"You've spoken to...?" The Chief sagged on the spot. "You visited Summer? *You?*"

"Don't get too excited. They don't give a shit about any of us, as I always told you."

I understood his impulse to cling to any semblance of authority he had left, but that didn't mean it was fair to his fellow half-bloods to pretend the Courts would ever offer a helping hand. Yes, Summer and Winter *did* have a lot to answer for, but my own failure to gain Summer's cooperation drove home their disdain for mortals. Including the half-bloods.

"Come on, Taive," Killian said placatingly. Like the others, he had iron burns on his hands, his dark skin marked with red welts. "This place isn't healthy to stay in long-term and the necromancers won't care to help us. It should be safe for us to go back to the territory now *she's* gone, and so have her allies."

He meant the banshee. "Yeah, and believe me, they regretted choosing to betray you."

Not strictly true, but they'd certainly regretted letting Fionn slaughter them when I'd broken the cauldron and prevented them from being reborn as immortals.

"If you insist," the Chief said tightly. "Fine. I will talk to the witches."

"Be nice," I warned. "They don't have to take crap from you."

I made to leave, and the gate opened. Colby, the necromancer apprentice, ran in, brandishing a salt canister.

"Begone!" he yelled shrilly.

"I'm not undead, Colby." I sidestepped in case he did throw the salt in my face. "It's a long story, but I just got back from Faerie. You should also probably know that Fionn's likely going to come back and wage war on us again."

"I'm *not* surprised it's your fault," said the Chief. "What did you do this time?"

"I'll tell you later." I addressed Colby. "How many of you are left?"

"I don't know." Worry flickered in his eyes. "You came back from Faerie? Does that mean the Mage Lord—?"

"Yes, Vance is alive, and he's currently in the safe house setting up a new council," I said. "The mages are preparing for war. You ought to do the same."

"War." He gulped, his skin paling to milky white. "With whom? The faeries?"

"Among other things. Have any furies shown up out here?"

"What's a fury?"

Honestly. "Can I speak to Lord Evander? Or Frank?"

His face crumpled. "No. We can't reach any ghosts, not even our own people."

"That's not good." Oh, boy. Between the necromancers' struggles in reaching the dead and the half-faeries losing access to their magic, our defences against Fionn were looking decidedly shaky. And I was willing to bet he'd caused both by screwing around with the veil.

"Death has shut us out." He swallowed. "Can you help us?"

"I'm not a necromancer," I reminded him. "Just be prepared for things to go south at any moment. Ask Rick to call Isabel if you need anything. The witches are preparing for war, too."

I was probably being mean, but the necromancers were my lowest priority. The evidence that their ancestors had been too cowardly to protect anyone else in the last war was written on all those empty graves.

Leaving the apprentice, I returned to the Chief's hiding place. "Ready to speak to the witches? I'll walk there with you."

The group of half-bloods trailed after me out of the gate. I sent Vance a message explaining that I was going to take them to see Isabel myself, but before we'd reached the end of the road, they were already griping at my suggestion that they take the bus to save on time.

"There's too much iron," said the Chief. "It always makes me sneeze."

"You just spent days sleeping inside a giant iron box." I sighed. "Right, fine. Good luck dealing with any furies that decide to dive-bomb you on the way."

I took the bus to the half-bloods' old territory myself, intending to check how bad the damage was before I met the half-faeries at Isabel's place. Their magic had been in a bad state even before the banshee's attempted coup, and the impact was visible in the holes torn into the hedges and the lack of guards at the gate. Inside, the grass was yellow and dead, bearing crimson stains from the earlier conflict. The few plants present were dying, too, sad and drooping, and the distinct smell of neglect hung over everything. Not just regular decay, but decaying magic, the sort that attracted the worst kind of wild fae. No wonder the half-bloods hadn't come back. The presence of so much death should have made my sword react, but no response came. *This is wrong.*

Skin prickling, I continued to walk. I'd intended to drop in on the Hemlock Coven, but the last time I'd visited, I'd found myself repelled by the inbuilt defences they'd put around the forest and had had to travel on the spirit line to enter. This was not a safe place to leave my body unattended, but I figured it was worth seeing if they let me in on the ground this time.

As before, the forest had crept forward so that it extended over the giant trench the banshee had created when she'd bulldozed half the territory in an attempt to create a dividing line between Summer and Winter. I walked past the Chief's old clearing and found the entrance to the Hemlock witches' forest through which I'd failed to enter the last time.

I approached warily, prepared to be thrown aside when I tried to walk in.

This time, no resistance met me when I stepped over a large root. Weird. Had the witches lowered their defences because Fionn hadn't attacked yet, or was the magical drain affecting them, too? If so, that didn't bode well for the defences entrapping the monstrous beast that slept below their territory, nor the magic that prevented the god from breaking free and devouring the world.

Towering trees crowded me, ancient oaks and elms which belonged to a time before even the faeries had come here. The witches' forest had its own kind of magic, though Unseelie fae lurked here, too, and their snarls and growls filled the background as I walked. The wild fae wouldn't have had reason to flee the forest when the banshee showed up. Come to think of it, she'd only taken half-bloods with her, and Fionn had explicitly wanted the half-faeries to come and fight on his side. He'd left all the pure-blooded faeries in this realm behind, perhaps because the half-faeries were easier to fool, or because a larger number were half-Sidhe and therefore higher up on the faeries' social hierarchy. Dicks.

My steps halted when smoke coalesced on the path in front of me, forming the ghost of an older man. *Gerry.*

"Yeah, no," I said. "Nice try, but I already sent you on to the next world."

The illusion was proof the witches' magic was working properly, at least, but that I still had to pass some kind of test to reach them was irksome to say the least.

Gerry spoke without looking at me. "Avalin claimed a mortal woman… There were rumours of a child they had living in their quarters…"

Wait. This was a replay of the scene in the Vale, the last time I'd seen him. The Hemlock witches could read memories from those who entered their forest, which extended to my talisman, too. In my first visit, I'd viewed a scene prior to the invasion that nobody but Avalin and Velkas had been privy to.

"You want me to see this… why?" I asked of the forest in general. "*Is* Calder's mortal mother still alive?"

Gerry's ghost melted into the tangled mass of trees before me. The warped branches parted, forming an archway, and when I passed through, everything went dark.

"Hello?" I called. *Bloody witches. Couldn't give me a light switch, could they?* My talisman remained inert, and the last time we'd been in here, light spells hadn't been able to penetrate the darkness either. You'd think saving the witches' lives would give me a free pass to enter their forest without the theatrics, but apparently not.

"There is someone you wanted to see," whispered a raspy voice. Cordelia, the witch who led what was left of the Hemlock coven.

"Can you turn on the light?" I could clearly picture her wrinkled face staring from a tree trunk despite the absolute darkness, but not being able to see where I was going set my nerves on edge. "Why'd you let me in this time?"

"Because the veil is damaged," she said, "and it is not safe for you to travel on the spirit lines."

"I guess not." I scanned the darkness in a futile effort to see who I was talking to. "I assume Fionn's the reason the necromancers can't get into Death and the faeries can't use their magic?"

"You know that already, Ivy. You came here for another reason."

I stopped walking when my feet hit a tree root. "I do have some questions for you. If you can read memories from my talisman, can you show me where it came from, or where Avalin got it?"

"It's not that simple." The darkness lifted, revealing a tree with a wizened face carved into it like a stone sculpture. The bark cracked when Cordelia's lips moved. "The talisman's memories go back before even our time, and before the reach of our magic."

My hands dropped to my sides. "So you can't help me?"

"There is something else you seek, isn't there?"

I laughed emptily. "Sure. I'm looking for a way to beat an immortal death god without using the talisman I got rid of to prevent your forest from being destroyed—which, by the way, also got me kicked out of the Summer Court in disgrace."

"I rather think that is preferable to the alternative."

"I *know* that," I ground out, "but he's back at full power.

Fionn is. He has no weaknesses, and... and I guess you already know I destroyed the cauldron."

"Yes." Her tone was neutral enough that I couldn't tell if she approved or not. "An act that will ripple through the entirety of the faerie realm for infinite generations to come."

I tried to wrap my head around that and failed. Dizziness swept over me and I leaned against a tree, then I hastily stepped away in case the tree turned out to be alive. "Fuck. The cauldron actually was the source of the Sidhe's immortality? For real?"

"Yes."

"Wow." I sucked in air, my head spinning. "Fionn already abandoned his post, so nobody was getting reborn as they should have been anyway, but the Sidhe probably intended to find a replacement. Eventually." The Sidhe died infrequently enough that they might not have been in a hurry, especially given their last Huntsman had seemingly betrayed them.

"I cannot speak to the Sidhe's intentions," growled Cordelia, "but the cauldron's destruction will render their old ways obsolete."

I blew out a breath. "Then... then that means if I kill Fionn again, he's dead for real."

Iron had killed him before. I'd taken his life from within this very forest.

"I wouldn't assume an easy victory, Ivy... but yes."

I can kill him. The problem was, last time he'd immediately come back as a wraith, and my magic had been unable to destroy him. As a ghost, he was still formidable, but it was no wonder he'd thrown such a screaming temper tantrum when I'd shattered the cauldron. Once I forced him out of his body, he'd have a hell of a time finding another.

"If you ask me, the Sidhe need to work on making their magical artefacts less fragile," I remarked. "I mean, a single

Invocation spoken by a human broke thousands of years of immortality. Surely someone would have accounted for that."

"Of course not. You are as far from an ordinary human as it's possible to be, Ivy."

That was true enough. I glanced down at my talisman. "Yeah… I guess it's the gods at work again. I wondered if *they* might help, but I don't even know how to find them."

"You know the language."

"Invocations?" *Oh, right.* I'd been so focused on their magical capabilities that I'd forgotten the gods had once used the same language to communicate with one another. A language I knew… or at least, my talisman did.

"Correct," said the witch. "As to the whereabouts of the gods, I only know of one."

"Yeah, it's probably best to leave the Devourer where he is," I said. "Unless there's a chance of extracting the ring from where I threw it without destroying this realm. Can I can borrow it for long enough to permanently kill Fionn?"

"No," croaked the witch. "If you opened the rift again, your own world would fracture in the process."

I winced. "Yeah, thought so."

I lifted my talisman, my gaze skimming the glyphs visible despite its dimmed light. If even the forest couldn't track down its origin, did I have a hope of doing so myself?

Cordelia's pitted eyes followed mine. "If you're wondering why we cannot read all the memories from that talisman of yours, a part of that is because the Courts are inherently protected from having their secrets gleaned by the enemy."

"The Courts," I echoed. "Oh. The Vale… that's not part of the Courts, so I guess it doesn't count." That was why she'd been able to show me the memory of Avalin and Velkas discussing Fionn's plans to start the invasion. And if the talisman had been forged in the Courts, it made sense that the forest would be unable to show that process.

"Precisely."

"You showed me Avalin's memories," I said. "Some of them."

"As the previous owner, Lord Avalin's memories are still imprinted upon the blade, but it is difficult for us to isolate the ones you need. It's possible, however, that access to another's memories will help."

"Another?" I frowned at her. "What, another previous owner?"

"Not exactly."

The trees' branches parted, revealing a narrow crevice in which a woman sat hunched on the ground. She looked up at me, her eyes blank, dull. Human, but something was undeniably *off* about her.

"Her mind is damaged," said Cordelia. "Thus, we are unable to read her."

"Who *is* she?" No recognition dawned on the woman when our eyes met, but I hadn't a clue who she was either.

"Her name was Wilhemina Yarrow."

My mouth fell open. *Avalin's lover?* Wilhemina was painfully thin, her eyes blank and staring. Given the state of her, I understood why she hadn't raised Calder, why she'd abandoned him. Was there any life left in her at all?

"What did he do to you?" The words cracked something inside me. I'd been lucky. Avalin had never singled me out personally. The damage I'd suffered as his prisoner had been more passive, at least until our final duel, and I hadn't experienced half the horrors she must have, as his lover. It was hardly a fair relationship in any sense when she'd been kidnapped against her will and held captive in an alien world she couldn't escape.

No answer came. Angry tears burned my eyes. I'd failed

to save the other captives, but they were only the most recent of Avalin's victims. He'd been torturing humans for years before I'd fallen into his trap.

"I'm sorry, Wilhemina," I whispered, the tears slipping free. "It's okay. I can help you."

"She won't hear you," said Cordelia. "The Vale damaged her, made her dependent upon magic to survive. That's why she ran here when the faeries' power began to fade."

"What?" I scrubbed my eyes with the back of my hand. "Is all the faerie magic in this realm… gone?"

"No, but it's greatly weakened, and it won't be long before the situation is beyond saving."

"Then why…" I turned back to the blank-faced woman. "Can she help me?"

"There is a chance this woman has the memories you need, ones even the forest cannot reach. In order to gain access, however, magic other than ours is needed."

"What magic?" If the forest couldn't read her, who else could? Maybe the faeries had a way of extracting a memory, but their magic had gone. Or—wait. "Lady Harper?"

"Even her odds of success remain low," growled Cordelia. "This woman's mind is fractured. Killing her would be a mercy. She did not even know her own child and abandoned him without a thought."

Still doesn't make me feel sorry for Calder. He'd caused so much damage by freeing Fionn, and I didn't know if bringing back Wilhemina's memories would make her sorry situation any better or shatter her entirely. But if her memories contained clues as to how to use my talisman to destroy Fionn for good…

Wilhemina made a soft whimpering noise. She lifted her head as though she heard the witch's voice from the tree, but her eyes remained unfocused. I hated to leave her like this, but she was likely safer in the forest than outside.

"I'll come back," I told Cordelia. "With Lady Harper."

"Be careful with memories, Ivy," was her response. "If you aren't careful, the past can swallow you whole."

"I get that."

I left her and hurried out of the forest, retracing my steps down the winding paths as I thought over my plan. It looked like saving the world might just depend upon my ability to convince the bad-tempered former head mage, Lady Harper, to help me.

10

After I left the forest, my phone buzzed with a message from Vance confirming the mages were still mired in arguments and had yet to come to a resolution. Without him, my odds of persuading Lady Harper to help were low, and I didn't know where she was currently hanging out, besides. Another safe house? I cast my mind around and landed on the mages' storeroom. Despite the recent incursions, it was among the safest places in town, having once contained the life-drinker. I kind of wished I could leave it behind, as carrying two bulky swords around was a bloody nuisance, but Fionn's ability to walk through iron barriers as though they didn't exist meant leaving the blade unattended was out of the question.

The mages' storeroom also contained the Invocations. While Fionn had claimed not to need them, I didn't trust him not to try to steal them anyway, and having access to a list of the Sidhe's most powerful spells might come in handy even if Lady Harper wasn't present in the building.

I assumed the half-faeries were still trekking across town in search of the witches, but any desire to advocate on their behalf melted away in the face of more urgent matters. If nobody had checked in on the storeroom since Fionn had stolen the life-drinker, anything might have taken root inside, but most fae didn't share his ability to sidestep wards.

With my mind made up, I began to walk. No buses went to that part of the city, but I knew the route. Abandoned buildings became more prevalent the further I went from familiar territory, and within an hour I came upon the cemetery down the road from the mages' depository. The graveyard had once yielded some particularly nasty undead, but nothing stirred on the other side of the gates.

My skin prickled as I crossed the road to the otherwise unassuming building. A stark corridor waited inside, lined with old-fashioned unlit lanterns and doors covered in shimmering wards that made the whole building hum with residual energy. Vance had included me in the security spell that was usually restricted to the Mage Lords alone, so in theory, I ought to be able to enter the high-security room without him being present.

I reached for the door. My hands tingled but didn't burn, and the door opened on a room whose contents resembled a display of antiques in a museum with bizarre taste. The contents of most of the cabinets were unfamiliar to me, but at the back, a roll of parchment covered in symbols stood upright in a glass case. I approached, unlocked the cabinet, and gingerly removed the parchment. My fingers tingled and a metallic taste rose in the back of my throat. I averted my eyes, not wanting to look too closely in case the words tried to force me to say them aloud again. Usually, speaking an Invocation in this realm had some deeply unpleasant side effects. Like being ripped out of my body, for instance.

A distinct thud sounded outside. Stashing the document in my inside pocket, I drew my blade and ran out of the room, closing the door behind me. Outside the building, I collided with a small figure.

"Quentin!" I lowered my weapon.

Quentin peered up at me in surprise. "Ivy. What are you doing here?"

"Retrieving the Invocations before someone steals them."

His gaze went to my back, and the second sword strapped there. "You took the life-drinker?"

"Won it back fair and square," I said. "Vance is okay. I couldn't get back to Summer after Lord Burdock attacked me, and I ended up in the Vale."

"Yes, I know," he said. "You, however, should not be meddling with Invocations at a time like this."

"What else should I have done, leave them here?" I scowled at the brownie. "Fionn already got in here once. He gave the life-drinker to a half-blood kid who got a new body from the cauldron—who then went on a murderous rampage and captured Vance."

"Yes, he told me." Quentin's eyes simmered with anger. "Before he sent me here."

"I guess he's still tied up." I sighed. "Bloody mages. They don't have time to argue. Just like Summer doesn't have time to stick their fingers in their ears. I don't suppose you managed to change their minds after I was gone?" I added hopefully.

"I spoke to my other masters. They were concerned at the recent developments, but they carry little influence with the higher Sidhe."

"The invasion might come any second now." Impatience burned beneath my skin. "I know the Sidhe think we have all the time in the world, but we don't. I need to find Lady Harper. I thought she might be here."

A crash shook the building. I jerked forward, shielding my face against a shower of shattering glass and brick and falling roof tiles. Something—some*one*—had landed on the roof, a gigantic black bird with wings the size of sails.

The Morrigan.

"Hey!" I yelled. "There's nothing in there you want."

Fionn must have sent her. Why he hadn't come in person, I didn't know, but the Morrigan was a nasty piece of work on her own. Her ability—tearing souls out and devouring them —was too depraved even for Winter's unpleasant tastes. Her body was the size of a small car, covered in jet-black feathers, and her giant talons had crushed half the roof. It was lucky we hadn't been inside at the time.

I spun on her, brandishing my talisman. I was hardly equipped to fight her off when I hadn't even managed to wound her during our last fight, but I refused to let her get away with ripping out Vance's soul.

The Morrigan tore another chunk out of the roof with her taloned claw, revealing a metal band around her foot that hadn't been there the last time I'd seen her. The metal shimmered, and bright glyphs flickered across its surface. *Is that iron?* She didn't show any signs of being in pain, but for all I knew iron didn't hurt her the way it did the Sidhe. All the same, someone had put a binding on her, and I was willing to bet I knew who. Fionn, it seemed, had not wanted her to slither out of helping him.

I had zero sympathy. I willed magic to flood my veins, to offer me enough of a boost to jump up to the roof, but I barely made it halfway up the wall before the brief blue flash flickered and gave out. I landed at a crouch, my knees protesting at the impact. *Dammit.*

The Morrigan's gaze dropped to me. I averted my eyes to avoid the potent effect of her death-stare. A chorus of bird cries warned she wasn't alone. The air around her swirled with thick blackness, denser than fog. Crows, hundreds of them, if not thousands. Illusion or real, I couldn't tell.

"You can't fight her," Quentin growled.

"Not like I have a choice."

The Morrigan's huge black wings beat, and I threw myself flat to avoid being hit by a hurricane-force wind. As the crows surged downward in a torrent, I swung my sword at them, knocking a half-dozen feathery bodies aside. While the small birds were easy enough to hit, my weapon felt like a flimsy piece of wood without its usual blue glow, and my body was stuck on normal human speed.

The air rippled with a sudden current that sent the Morrigan flying off the roof with enough force to slam into the ground on the other side. The impact shook the building again, shattering glass, and Vance appeared at my side.

"Good timing," I breathed. "How'd you know I was here?"

"I had a hunch." His gaze passed over the Morrigan, anger shadowing his eyes. "She's mine to kill."

"Damn right," Drake ran up, wielding a flame in one hand, and gave a double-take when he saw the brownie. "Quentin, what are *you* doing here?"

"Quentin, if ever there was a good time to tell Summer we're being attacked by Winter's monsters, it's now," I told him.

The Morrigan rose upward, her wings billowing, and once again landed on the depository roof.

"Look away!" I yelled. "Don't look her in the eyes, whatever you do."

"I'll scorch her eyes out." Drake ran towards the building, throwing a handful of fire. The Morrigan scraped at the loose tiles with a clawed foot, and the three of us backed away from the shower of dust.

Vance disappeared. I heard him roar, and my heart plunged. He'd nearly had his soul ripped out once already, and I'd only been able to save him because the Grey Vale was so close to Death. I wasn't sure I could repeat the performance in this realm, without my magic working at all.

"Get out of there!" I screamed.

The Morrigan rose from the roof, in a beat of her vast wings, gripping Vance's body in her talon. He let out a pained snarl.

"Let go of him, you evil old bitch," I warned. "Or so help me, I'll tear *your* soul out with my bare hands."

"You took my souls from me," she croaked. "I'll take this one as recompense."

"No." I held up my sword, wishing my magic was at its usual functionality. "I don't care what Fionn told you to do. Let him go."

"It is not on the Huntsman's orders that I claim him," she said. "I will gain the souls I was promised, or I will reap them from this realm instead."

Vance disappeared and then materialised on her back, burying a knife in her wing. The Morrigan screeched, a noise that scraped my eardrums, and shook him off. Vance vanished mid-fall and landed on his feet beside us. I breathed out.

The Morrigan's wings beat, one slightly more crooked than before. Drake threw a handful of fire at her, but unlike the furies, the flames left no impact on her feathers. She uttered another painful screech and dove at us.

Readying myself for her to be within striking distance, I leapt, my sword snagging on her outstretched talon. The blade ripped into her claw and then stuck. As I tugged, trying to free it, her gaze connected with mine. The fear-effect hit immediately, my limbs freezing as fear flooded my body.

At my side, Drake had gone still, too—but Vance hadn't. A torrent of displaced air hit the Morrigan from behind, breaking her eye contact with us. I swung my blade at her claw, but her other talon hit me first, knocking me off my feet. Pain tore up my leg; blood soaked my jeans. Eyes watering, I looked up to see Vance and the Morrigan grappling with one another, shifter against shifter. No—shifter against death goddess. His claws locked with hers, neither able to gain ground. My leg burned with pain when I tried to stand. I sank down, scrambling in my pocket for a healing spell, and my fingers brushed the parchment with the Invocations. My last shot.

I tugged the parchment loose and scanned the symbols, their meanings sliding into my mind, like a distant object coming into focus. Despite the lack of magic in this realm, I could still read them. One stood out like a beacon: *Leave.* A banishment spell.

The Morrigan hit out, and Vance flew back, sprawling on the ground. Heart lurching, I lifted my head and screamed the word. *Leave.*

My sword ignited in a pulse of blue light. I tasted copper in the back of my throat as the word I'd spoken shuddered through my bones and shook the ground beneath my feet. My fingers trembled to their tips, and I fought to maintain my grip on my body as the same tremor shook my spirit as well as my physical form.

The Morrigan threw her head back, emitted another bone-shaking screech, and vanished, leaving nothing behind but a flurry of black feathers.

My body swayed as a grey haze intruded on my vision, and for an instant, a strange cold emptiness pulsed through me, as though I'd touched on the bone-deep pain of some great and terrible loss.

Blackness as dark as her wings rose to swallow me.

———

"Ivy," said Isabel. "Ivy. Rise and shine."

"Ow," I groaned, my eyes flickering open. I lay on a sofa in a living room I didn't recognise. Isabel stood over me, wearing an expression somewhere between exasperation and relief. "Where am I?"

"Francine's old house," she replied. "It's become kind of a central hub, since the mages keep inviting themselves in here anyway."

Vance had entered the room, his angry expression softening into relief when he saw I was awake. "Ivy, how do you feel?"

"Like I have the hangover from hell." I rubbed my forehead. "I banished the Morrigan, right?"

"Yes, and it knocked you out cold for two days," Isabel said accusingly.

"I didn't miss the end of the world, did I?"

"Not quite." Drake entered the room behind Vance. "What did you *do*?"

"Used an Invocation to send the Morrigan back into Faerie before she killed us all," I clarified. "I wasn't sure it'd work, given that there isn't much faerie magic left in this realm—which is Fionn's fault, too, by the way. I was going to tell you everything after I got back from the storeroom."

"No, you were going to keep running around the city until you ran into another near-fatal trap." Isabel propped a hand on her hip. "Really, Ivy."

"Vance should have put a chain around *your* foot," Drake added, and then yelped when a current of air hit him in the back of the head. "Just kidding."

"Don't even," I said. "I didn't expect Fionn to send his second-in-command this soon. I don't know what she was even looking for at the storeroom. Not the life-drinker—wait, where is it?"

"Your talismans are over there, don't worry." Isabel pointed to a table across the room. "The Invocations, too."

"Good." I sagged back on the sofa, exhaustion threatening to claim me again. Since my wounded leg was no longer bleeding, someone must have used a healing spell on me, but pretty much everything else hurt. "I spoke to the Chief, too. Did he make it here?"

"Yes, after a fashion." Isabel's lips pursed. "We don't have any spare rooms left and the Chief refused to sleep on the floor like a commoner, so Shana and Chloe let him and some of the others stay in their house. I think they're having second thoughts."

I bit back a laugh. "The Chief has been sleeping rough in a graveyard for days. You'd think he'd show some gratitude."

"Some of the other half-faeries did," she said. "His partner… Killian, right? He's actually been helping Shana and Chloe prepare some spells for the coven. Possibly to avoid being kicked out of their house because of the Chief's attitude problems."

"I'm glad some of them appreciate the help." I smiled up at Vance, who moved to the sofa's side and handed me a mug of the energy restorative he sometimes used when his powers were overtaxed. "Didn't know you could brew this so fast."

"Quentin did," he said. "He's also making dinner."

"Quentin's here?"

"He goes wherever I do," he said simply.

"You two made it up?" I'd have to ask for the details later. "And the other mages? Are they at the safe house?"

"Yes, but it's easier for me to move back and forth between there and here than for them to travel through the city. There are still furies on the loose."

"And the manor's not secured yet?"

"Not yet, though Lady Harper is there," he said. "I believe she and Wanda are working on resetting the wards with the help of some witches."

"They are?" That reminded me. "I actually need Lady

Harper to help with something. It's kind of important, so I might need you to employ your powers of persuasion on her."

Vance blinked, startled. "What could you possibly need her help with?"

"I may have taken a detour into the forest when I dropped in on half-blood territory."

I told them all about my visit to the Hemlock witches while Quentin showed up with dinner and all but bullied us into eating. Not that I usually needed the encouragement, but the brownie's presence struck me as bizarre in its sheer normality after his temporary estrangement from the mages. If Vance had forgiven him, I'd reserve judgement on the brownie's past actions, and he was a good enough cook for me to tolerate him hanging around while I explained Cordelia's unexpected request to find the grumpy former Head Witch.

"You met Calder's mother?" Vance's eyes widened in surprise. "She's alive?"

"He broke her mind." I lowered my gaze. "She ran into the forest when she came back to the mortal realm because it was the closest place to Faerie. I'm not sure she even remembers she had a child."

"You think Lady Harper can reach her missing memories?" he asked. "That sounds difficult, but I wouldn't be surprised if she did have that capability. There isn't a mind mage I know of who's on the same level as her. But... it might not be pleasant to be the person on the receiving end."

"I don't *want* to subject someone who's already in so much pain to that, believe me." Guilt dug its claws into me. "But if Avalin ever confided in her, ever gave her information that might help us defeat Fionn, it might be the difference between life and death. For all of us."

Vance inclined his head. "Then it's worth trying. I'll ask Lady Harper."

"Anyway, tell me what else I missed while I was out cold," I said. "Did you sort out your new council?"

"Temporarily," Vance said. "The other regions' mages cancelled their visits when they found out about the attack on the former council, but they keep calling my office asking to speak to me. Someone has been spreading muddled versions of the story, most of which involve me being dead."

"Was that Lady Granville, by any chance?" I gave an eye-roll. "I'm sure she was devastated you survived and she didn't get to swoop back in and claim power here."

"She wants to come back for Lady Penrose's funeral, but I can see her using that as a means to get a foothold in with the new council."

"Leave her out in the cold. This is war."

"I told her there won't be a proper funeral for the deceased council members until after our current state of emergency is laid to rest." Vance's bleak tone made his meaning clear: he expected there to be more deaths, many more, before the end.

I sought a change of subject. "I wonder why the Morrigan went to the storeroom? I assume Fionn sent her to steal something."

"It's one of the last obvious sources of powerful magic in the city, aside from the forest," Vance said. "Given that chain on her foot, she was likely following Fionn's orders."

"Honestly, it's unfair that one side gets all the immortals and the other doesn't," I muttered. "Who made the rules? I want to have words with them."

His mouth quirked. "I'm glad you're feeling like yourself again, Ivy."

"Never better." I stood up and the world swayed a little. "Okay, I might need another nap before I duel Fionn."

"Do that—and both of you, too," Isabel told Vance and Drake. "You two haven't slept since before the fight with the Morrigan. I know."

"There's no time—" Drake began to protest.

"There's no time for the two highest ranked Mage Lords to get knocked out of the fight due to exhaustion," she retaliated. "Quentin's been telling you the same."

"She's right," I put in. "We've driven the Morrigan off. We have some leeway. Which is good, because it'll probably take a week to convince Lady Harper to come and visit the Hemlocks' forest."

"I'll talk to her," Vance said. "She'll understand the importance of our mission."

"I bloody hope she does." I crossed the room to pick up the Invocation sheet again, my gaze skimming the list of spells. One nudged at my eyeballs, and I bit my tongue to avoid speaking aloud, focusing instead on the banishment spell I'd used on the Morrigan. *Leave.* I'd never spoken the word before, but before I'd passed out, I'd had this odd sense of familiarity, as though I'd experienced it before.

Wait. Was that the same spell the Sidhe used when they banished one of their own? When I'd experienced a vision through Avalin's eyes in the forest, I'd felt the echo of his pain at being ripped away from Faerie, and a similar sensation had hit me when I'd done the same to the Morrigan.

"Damn, that's strong." Had I kicked her out of this realm permanently? *God, I hope so.*

The front door slammed open. Isabel jumped, and so did I. "Who's there?"

"Sorry." Vance rose from his seat. "I didn't expect her to arrive this soon."

"What is that?" demanded a familiar voice. "Who left that lying around the hall? I could have broken my neck."

"Grandma, stop!" said another, younger voice. Wanda.

I put down the Invocations and ran from the room. Wanda, Vance's assistant, stood beside her considerably more fearsome-looking grandmother. Lady Harper leaned on a walking stick, glaring bloody murder at the plant pot she appeared to have tripped over on the way in. At a guess, one of the half-faeries had been responsible for that.

"You're alive," I said to Wanda. "You've no idea how happy I am to see you."

"Ivy." She hugged me. "I'm glad you're okay, too. I heard you were unconscious?"

"For a bit." I looked behind her at the sturdy old woman, who glowered back at me. "Erm. I kind of need your grandmother's help. Specifically, we need her memory-reading ability."

11

"I can't believe you're dragging me into the forest," said Lady Harper. "Can you really find nobody else to help?"

"No." Anyone else might have taken that as a compliment, but the old mage wore a long-suffering expression as if we'd dragged her to watch a school pantomime instead of to help save a world from certain destruction. And save a woman from the aftereffects of Avalin's depravity.

Lady Harper was one of few mages who held any ties to the Hemlock witches, as they'd once served on the Council of Twelve together. In addition to her prior experience as a Mage Lord, she'd temporarily rejoined the mage council after the invasion to help rebuild the city, and her own ability, which involved being able to extract memories and influence thoughts, made her one of the most powerful mages in the city. Even though she was pushing eighty-five and walked with a cane, most of the wild fae we encountered on the path ran away from her.

"How are you even doing that?" I asked. "Poking them with your mind?"

"Essentially," she said in an irritable tone. "This had better be important."

"I already told you it is." To say Vance's old mentor wasn't fond of me was an understatement. She hadn't liked me *before* I'd witnessed Fionn's rebirth and his attempts to instigate a repeat of the events that had claimed the lives of most of her family as well as half the planet. Even my bringing Vance back from Faerie had done zero to change her attitude towards me, probably because she blamed me for getting him captured in the first place.

While I might have stuck to my word to wait until I'd rested a little more before coming to the forest, Lady Harper had made that impossible. She'd roamed around Francine's house criticising every aspect of the décor before I'd opted to get this excursion over with before Isabel set a glitter spell on her out of sheer frustration. Persuading the old mage to come had taken surprisingly little effort on Vance's part. Despite her relentless complaints, Lady Harper must know we wouldn't have asked for her help unless we had no choice.

"There's a human woman in here whose memories might be able to end the war against Fionn before it starts," Vance told her. "We need your help to extract those memories from where they were lost when a Sidhe damaged her mind."

That was stretching the truth a little. I doubted Avalin would have confided all his secrets to a human, but who knew, maybe he'd messed with her head for a reason. Or maybe he was just a fucking depraved individual who deserved the fate I'd bestowed on him.

Lady Harper gave me an appraising look. "You want me to break into the mind of someone who has already suffered greatly?"

Guilt tugged at my chest. "Lord Avalin is the one who broke her mind. It's his secrets I need to access."

"Who?"

"What rock have you been living under for the last year?" I forgot, momentarily, who I was talking to. "Avalin. Depraved Sidhe lord who captured humans for fun. The guy who owned my talisman before I killed him. You *saw* him when you rummaged around in my head."

Lady Harper's cutting stare sliced into me. "And yet you want me to do the same to someone else, someone whose mind has already been severely wounded."

"I never said I liked the idea." I halted, recognising the clearing in which I'd encountered Cordelia during my last visit. "Hey, that was fast. The forest didn't play tricks on us this time."

"Obviously," said Lady Harper sniffily. "They have too much respect for me to resort to cheap trickery."

Figures. They'd happily screw with *my* head, but even the Hemlock witches respected Lady Harper.

Wilhemina Yarrow didn't appear to have moved since my last visit. She crouched beneath a tree with her knees drawn up around her ears and gave no reaction when I lowered myself to look into her blank eyes. Why had Avalin spared her life? I'd seen him torture people in a thousand ways before putting them out of their misery, but for some reason, he'd left her alive. Had he wanted her to take care of Calder, their son? Or had he been careless, and hadn't meant to damage her at all? As was becoming clear, the Sidhe were as fallible and prone to making errors as humans were, and with enough power to turn a simple mistake into a catastrophe.

Lady Harper approached Wilhemina, leaning on her stick as she peered down at her. "Yes... her mind is fractured. I've never seen anything like it before."

"I guess that's what happens when a Sidhe scrambles your mind." I swallowed against a lump in my throat. "Can... can you reach her memories, though? Without hurting her too badly?"

A moment passed. Wilhemina let out a shallow whimper and began to rock back and forth, her blank eyes locked on Lady Harper.

Around us, the forest warped and shuddered like ripples on the surface of a lake, then everything went dark.

The sound of a baby crying brought me back to alertness. I blinked, and the darkness peeled away, revealing a room with deep crimson carpets, stone walls, elaborate furniture. An arrow-slit window on my right offered a view across the forest. Not the Hemlock Coven's forest, but an expanse of silver-leafed trees.

Whoa. Was this Wilhemina's memory? As before, I couldn't move or speak, entrapped within the person whose eyes I watched through. In my arms was a bundle of clothes, containing a baby.

Calder.

My insides recoiled, instinctively, but from this angle, he resembled any other sleeping human child. I might have expected Avalin's offspring to be born with some kind of visible sign of the monster he'd grow up to be, but he didn't even have any obvious signs of faerie blood, like pointed ears. Just a squashed-looking face, relaxing into sleep as Wilhemina rocked him in her arms.

I was her. Lady Harper's magic had worked... but which memory had I been brought into?

"You're back," said the woman whose eyes I watched through, her tone trembling with relief or perhaps fear. "I missed you. Look at him! Look at your son."

"He's mortal." The voice came from my right, and Avalin strode into view. Visceral horror hit me as it always did when I saw him, his tall form clothed in the same armour, and his sword—the talisman—in his hand. The glyphs lit up blue as he drew closer to the baby, wearing an expression more like a child disappointed with a birthday present than a loving father. "He has none of my strength or power."

"He will be powerful, Lord Avalin," said the woman quietly. "He'll be a worthy heir for you."

"I don't *need* an heir," said Avalin. "I'm immortal."

The woman—me—flinched. "Then he will be your ally, and your warrior."

"He looks human," said Avalin. "Humans are weak and pathetic. He doesn't have any magic."

"He will," she insisted. "Like you did."

"Yes." He spun the sword in his hand, revealing the glyphs gleaming on the hilt. "I did. Tell me why I no longer have the magic to which I was born. Tell me." His voice gained a sharp edge.

"Because the Court stole it from you," she whispered. "But now you are more powerful than you ever were."

"Precisely," he mused. "He *might* have some trace of the Unseelie within his veins, but nothing compared to what I now possess. To claim this talisman, I took the darkest path down the Vale, a path that the gods once walked, and the gods themselves answered my call. I am beyond any other Sidhe, and I have spent more than enough time in this miserable place."

"I don't understand," she whispered. "You told me you wanted to stay."

"I did, and I lied." A manic glow shone in his eyes. "The Courts took away my inability to tell untruths. A favour, perhaps, in the end… and one I will wield against them.'

"It's *him*, isn't it?" said Wilhemina. "He told you to leave me, didn't he?"

"You humans truly believe the world revolves around

your limited existence." His lip curled. "Why ever did I decide to taint my blood with a mortal's?"

"You…" Her voice faltered. "You love him."

"Do I?" The light in his eyes intensified. "I think not. A fragile child will have no part in this war, and nor will you."

"You promised." The plea in her voice made me want to scream at her to get out while she could. To run for her life.

Avalin laughed, high and chilling. "And I promised revenge upon the Courts. I will have that and more, when I march on Winter with the army he gifted me."

"He won't keep his word." Her voice trembled. "If you can lie, so can he, and I've seen—seen how he looks at you. He's going to betray you. He won't want to share power. When he becomes Huntsman—"

"You *dare* to argue with me?" His voice echoed off the walls. "I have no need of a pathetic child *or* a snivelling mortal who doesn't know when to keep her mouth shut. I will rise and take Winter back, and you will stay silent or suffer dearly."

Wilhemina whimpered, clutching her child to her chest. "I only worry… I worry for you. For us. That's all."

Avalin advanced on her, his blue eyes alight with the magic pouring from his talisman. "Then you need worry no longer."

The whole room shook, and a cry sounded as the baby woke from sleep.

"I will have no more of you," roared Avalin. "You will never speak to me again. You will never set foot in my castle as long as you're alive. And you will *forget*."

The world fractured. Screams—the woman's and the child's—combined in a terrified clamour as the word rang through my head. I'd spoken the same word myself, but hearing it from Avalin's mouth was infinitely more primal and terrifying.

Forget.

I snapped back into my own mind, lying flat on the forest floor. More screaming filtered in, and I sat up, hitting my head on a tree branch. Ow. Branches surrounded me, caging me in a space hardly big enough to stand in. There was no sign of the others.

I took in a breath, examining my own memories quickly to make sure the Invocation hadn't affected me somehow. It shouldn't be possible, but Avalin had shot that poor woman in the face with an Invocation, and reliving the moment felt like the gods themselves had scrambled my brains.

Before that, though? Hearing of Fionn's betrayal was no surprise, but Avalin's words had unearthed a new batch of questions. *I took the darkest path down the Vale... and the gods themselves answered my call.* Did that mean he'd literally met the god whose power was contained in his—my—talisman? Surely not. He'd had no magic when he was exiled. He wouldn't have survived the encounter. What, then, had he meant?

As my grip on reality reasserted itself, it dawned that I could still hear screaming. I tried to crawl through the branches, but they wouldn't budge. "Hey. Hemlock witches? Care to give me a helping hand?"

"Are you ready to fight?" Cordelia's voice asked.

"Depends if you let me out." I craned my neck but was unable to see through the interlocked branches. "Where are the others? What's going on out there?"

"You were attacked. Our forest was breached. We expelled the intruder, but too late."

"Wilhemina?"

"Dead."

My heart lurched. "Look, just let me out. Please."

The branches pulled back. Only then did I appreciate that the witches' magic had stepped up to protect me from harm while I was trapped in the vision. The forest was awash in carnage, a large section ripped away as though giant claws had pulled the trees out by their roots and left the ruined bodies of fae in their wake.

I clambered out, leaping over fallen branches and broken tree trunks, following the sound of screaming. No—screeching. *Furies.*

I skirted a fallen trunk and spied Lady Harper and Vance standing side by side as three furies circled them from above. I ran to Vance's side and flung an iron dagger through a fury's skull. The beast fell out of the air, and the knife disappeared and reappeared in my hand.

"Thanks," I said to Vance.

He was covered in fury blood, but he didn't look injured. His own blade sliced at his opponent in midair, severing its spine.

The third exploded. Blood, feathers and guts rained down on our heads. I gagged and spat, blinking crimson out of my eyes. "Thanks for that, Lady Harper."

"You're welcome," she growled. "I'm sorry to say that woman was killed in the fighting."

"Wilhemina." Had she ever recalled any sense of her own identity in the end? Lady Harper's powerful magic coupled with the witches' forest had brought some of her memories to the surface, but now it was too late for her to ever regain her sense of self.

Tears pricked my eyes. The faeries used up humans so casually, discarding them like old clothing. I spat again at the furies' remains, wiping gore from my face.

"Are you going to tell us why you decided to take a nap?" Lady Harper enquired.

"A vision," I said. "I saw into Wilhemina's past, like I wanted."

"And?" She looked at me expectantly.

"What did you see?" asked Vance.

"Avalin being a dick." I wiped more fury guts from my neck. "And confirming that he and Fionn made a deal that he'd help Fionn steal the Huntsman's title in exchange for a share in his power. We all know how that turned out."

"I thought you came here to learn crucial information about that sword of yours," said Lady Harper.

"I did." I ran a hand over my blade's hilt. "He claimed to have walked on the same path the gods did to claim its power. Not sure what he meant. The whole Vale used to be their domain, and I doubt he *met* the god."

"Well, that's no use," said Lady Harper. "In the meantime, the enemy noticed our presence here. You endangered the Hemlock Coven for naught."

"Don't you start," I returned. "I never got the chance to ask what *you* did when you were all on the Council of Twelve together."

She hadn't been around when Quentin had revealed that he and Vance's grandparents had helped form a secret agreement between all the disparate groups of supernaturals and the Sidhe, but Lady Harper displayed no surprise that I knew.

"It was my job to carry messages between the mages and the Hemlock Coven," she said. "I played my part in helping to prevent the forest being infiltrated when the Huntsman attacked."

"And you didn't think to mention it to anyone?" I asked. "Whatever confidentiality agreements you were under must have been invalidated when most of the council was killed, and when Fionn came back, you must have known he'd try the same again."

"None of us can get into the faerie realm, you foolish girl," said Lady Harper. "Reforming the council is not possible."

"I can," I snapped back at her. "And that's no excuse. You might have at least told Vance."

"What would that have achieved?" She scoffed. "The Council of Twelve can never exist as it did before. Moreover, the last council were only able to achieve victory over the Huntsman by making use of the ring he stole—which, again, is no longer an option."

"I know." While I'd already suspected the ring had been his undoing, she'd confirmed that we'd have to find a new way to repeat the previous council's victory. "Well, this time he doesn't have the cauldron either. He can't make an army of immortal Sidhe to serve at his side."

"You're a fool to believe that makes him less dangerous," she growled. "You saw what a single Sidhe did to that woman's mind."

"That was an Invocation," I explained. "The language of the gods. Not Fionn, but the actual ancient gods of Faerie. My power came from there." I tapped the hilt of my sword. "Unfortunately, Fionn didn't give me too many clues about where I can find its original owner."

"*Find* the gods?" said Lady Harper. "Have you not learned your lesson from what you witnessed in the forest?"

"Nope," I said. "That wasn't the god I was thinking of, anyway. There's one I *can* speak to, because I know exactly where he is."

A shadow passed over Vance's face. "That seems... unwise."

"I know." I was all out of any better ideas, though. "If the Sidhe won't help, the only person who might know how to defeat someone masquerading as a god is the real deal. I'm the one who imprisoned him, so I should be able to find him again."

"The danger from the god himself aside, we also run the

risk of encountering Fionn while we're there," Vance said. "Are you sure you're ready?"

"Not in the slightest, but we don't have much choice," I said. "We've got to go back to the Grey Vale and find the dragon shifter god."

12

The following morning, we set off for the Grey Vale. Mercifully, Lady Harper hadn't stuck around. I didn't know which safe house she was staying at, but Isabel didn't need to deal with her complaints on top of the half-faeries making a nuisance of themselves. According to her, the Chief and Chloe had had a storming row that had only ended when the Chief's attempt to leave the house had nearly resulted in him being decapitated by a fury. I was disappointed it hadn't finished the job, personally.

Vance and I opted to enter the faerie realm via the spot where I'd originally bound the shifter god after my fight with the Lady of the Tree. We'd left extensive instructions behind with the mages so they'd be ready to spread across the city to protect the vulnerable in the event that Fionn did launch an attack while we were gone. All possible safe houses were open, including those run by the witches. Any necromancers who could fight were prepared to deal with a potential influx of undead and ghosts. And the half-bloods were ready, too, despite their lack of any access to their power. I even saw a fair few humans walking around carrying iron weapons or setting up wards outside their homes.

Wise of them, because the supernaturals couldn't defend the whole realm alone. We outnumbered them collectively, but the shifters, one of the largest groups, had ignored our invitations to fight at our side. Which meant entering Faerie via their territory was a risky move, but they'd rarely ventured near the Ley Line since some of their fellow shifters had been killed in a battle orchestrated by the Lady of the Tree. The house that had once belonged to Vance's uncle Wyatt lay empty; he'd been forced to move after the dragon shifter had awakened down the road from his home, and Vance's extended family were currently at a safe house, as far as I knew.

The Ley Line was easy to track by the jagged hole in the ground that cut through the field, surrounded by chunks of broken iron nobody had been able or willing to move. A beast with the strength to rip through iron like tearing through paper was someone I wanted on my side, but I wouldn't hold out too much hope. When the dragon shifter had been set free, I'd been unwilling to risk the others' safety by letting an ancient god roam freely around the city and had opted to put him back to sleep in the Vale. It had seemed like the right decision at the time, but now I had to undo that spell, I was braced for a confrontation.

Vance swept me into his arms and kissed me. I savoured the moment of his strong arms wrapped around me and committed it to memory before I pulled both of us into Death.

Greyness surrounded us, and the next second, we landed on the path of the Vale, a thick layer of fallen leaves under our feet.

"Okay," I said quietly. "My ability works as normal. Let's see…"

I drew my blade, which instantly lit up in blue light. Relief warred with suspicion, and then dread when a visceral jolt of fury rang through the blade as my magic ignited in response to the burning anger I associated with one individual.

Fionn was here.

Vance, seeing my alarm, unsheathed his own sword. "Where?"

I scanned the trees, seeing nobody but the pair of us. "Not sure. He's been here, recently, but I can't see him."

I needed to move fast. Transferring Helena to my other hand, I reached across my back and pulled out the life-drinker. Green light flared across the blade, and its humming resonated through me, through the air. Threads extended, reaching out. Searching for their master, or for someone's life to drain.

"You know where to go," I murmured to the sword. "Take me to your owner. Preferably not via Fionn."

The threads shifted westward. Telling me to turn left? I took that path and Vance fell into step with me, his mouth pulled into a frown.

"What is it?" I asked him.

"Nothing." He shook his head. "The power in the sword belongs to the god, correct?"

"Yeah," I said. "Why?"

"If the shifters are from the same bloodline, none of them inherited any of that power," he elaborated. "Shifters don't have magic."

Oh, right. Like all shifters, Vance was indirectly descended from the gods—not that the other shifters were willing to acknowledge that link. "Huh. Good point. Does your mage blood cancel it out?"

"Perhaps, but I'd have thought I would have heard if my father or uncle had the ability to drain the life out of someone. And we would certainly be aware if any of the other shifters shared that talent."

"Maybe the power gets diluted with each generation," I said. "That's how it works with the Sidhe. They lose their immortality the instant they interbreed with humans."

Vance looked at the sword, then back at me. "The gods are immortal, too. Shifters certainly aren't."

"No, and I reckon there's more faerie blood in the mortal realm than anyone thought." I stopped, spying a familiar construction ahead of us. "We're here."

The fortress I'd created when I'd bound the god resembled stone but infinitely stronger. The threads of green light from the life-drinker crept along the ground and slid up the walls, and a door rippled into view.

"Damn. Didn't expect to find it so soon." I retrieved the parchment with the Invocations from my pocket, though with the glyphs gleaming on the life-drinker's hilt, I might not need it. "If the dragon attacks us, get out."

"No," said Vance.

I looked at him. "Is that it? No? That's your argument?"

"I think it suffices."

"Cooperate with me, Vance. I'm not letting you die here out of stubbornness."

"I rather hope you plan to make use of those powerful words in your hand before I'm forced to make that choice."

"Yeah, well. The gods *invented* this language."

Vance's mouth tightened. "I'll wait outside."

"If you see Fionn, let me know. Don't try to fight him alone." I pushed on the door, then pulled, but it didn't open. I pushed again. "Bloody thing."

What did I need to do? *Hmm.* I'd used the combined power of both swords to create this prison, so maybe I needed them both to get back inside.

Doubly glad I'd retrieved the life-drinker, I returned the

Invocations to my pocket and drew Helena again. With one sword in each hand, I let their magic flow into me, green and blue energy swirling in a turquoise vortex.

As soon as the swirling threads touched the door, it swung open. The dragon shifter lay curled up exactly where I'd left it, impossibly huge, filling the space within the dungeon from corner to corner. Black scales covered its body, huge wings were bunched behind its back, and its head rested on clawed hands.

Holy crap. My heart drummed in my ears. I wasn't entirely sure *how* to wake up the creature. I'd used an Invocation to put it to sleep, but I didn't know how to reverse the spell. The Lady of the Tree had simply used the two talismans, so I held out the life-drinker alongside Helena. Green magic swirled outward, eagerly reaching out to its former master, while blue light melded into a turquoise haze again.

Both talismans flashed, glyphs igniting on the hilts, and the dragon's eyelid flickered. I took a step back, my breath catching. *Too late to turn back now.*

The dragon's eye opened—grey, sharp—and locked onto me.

13

"Hi," I said to the dragon shifter. "So... I'm sorry I locked you up."

The dragon's teeth snapped, and I leapt back before they closed around my feet. *Okay. This is a bad idea, Ivy.*

The dragon roared, and the whole dungeon trembled. My body shook, my eardrums vibrating until I heard and felt nothing else but the primal noise that erupted from the dragon's throat. Its teeth snapped at me again, catching the edge of the life-drinker, and I unfroze.

"You want this?" I said through chattering teeth. "You want the sword?"

No surprise when someone had ripped out some of the beast's power to place in the talisman. I doubted the dragon had given it up willingly, however it had come about.

Life-drinker. If the sword could drain the life out of someone, I could only guess what this beast was capable of, but maybe giving the sword back as a gesture of goodwill would make the dragon shifter less inclined to bite me in two.

I laid the sword down carefully. The dragon watched my

every movement with those shrewd eyes, then leaned forward, and its teeth closed around the sword. A flash of green light enveloped the room. I squeezed my eyes shut against the glare, hoping I hadn't made a fatal error.

When I opened them, a man lay face-down on the dungeon floor. Before I could utter a word, he rose upright faster than I'd ever seen a human move, and his arresting grey eyes hit me first with a piercing glare that sent a quiver through my very being. His body was cloaked in black armour edged with silver, while his face was a blur that suggested either he was using some kind of glamour, or the gods shared the same trait as the Sidhe that made it hard for humans to look directly at them. My eyes skimmed over strong features, longish dark hair, and clear grey eyes similar to those that had looked into mine countless times.

This man wasn't Seelie or Unseelie, but something else altogether.

More to the point, the god was a *shapeshifter.* It seemed obvious now, given his similarities with both the shifters and the faeries with which he shared his heritage, and he'd just happened to be in dragon form when he'd been put into that enchanted sleep, hundreds or thousands of years ago.

Ah, shit. If he'd been stuck in that tomb for centuries or more, he wouldn't have interacted with a single person since then. He definitely wouldn't speak modern English. Not that *I* could speak at the moment.

Peering into the room behind me, Vance broke the silence first. "We're sorry to disturb you."

"Yeah." I swallowed against my dry throat. "I'm… I'm sorry I locked you in here, too."

No reply. At my feet, the life-drinker sword's bright glow had dimmed, but my own blade was as vibrant as ever, as were the swirling glyphs on its length. *Invocations.* Symbols from the time of the gods, like the magic inside my talisman itself. Invocations were like an ancient faerie language, so logically he was more likely to be able to understand me if I spoke in that tongue, but if I wasn't careful, my words would cause unwanted real-world side effects.

The man spoke in a deep rumbling voice. I shook my head. No translator. *Come on, magic, if you can wake a god, you can at least help me speak to him.*

"I'm Ivy," I said to him. "No idea how to translate that into god-speak."

I'd never had that issue with the Sidhe, but as their appearance shifted depending upon who looked upon them, so too did their speech. As a result, I always heard them speak in English because it was the only language I understood myself, but why did the same not apply to this guy? Didn't he predate the Sidhe by centuries beyond counting?

I held up the parchment with shaking hands. "Can you read this?"

He spoke a single word. The paper rippled in my hands, vibrating hard enough that I almost dropped it, and then my ears popped.

"I would not speak those words lightly, human," he said in a rumbling voice that echoed from the walls of the dungeon. "They will break your fragile mind."

"I've heard that one before." I steeled myself. "I need your help. Erm. Life-drinker… whatever your name is."

"Eraenar," Vance supplied.

The dragon shifter's grey eyes gleamed. "Yes. The name is Eraenar, human, and I do not take kindly to being imprisoned underground."

"We're not really underground." I backtracked. "I don't know who originally imprisoned you, but it wasn't me."

"You maintained my prison and brought me here. I remember."

Uh-oh. "My realm was under threat. I didn't know if you planned to attack my fellow humans."

"A danger I know very well, human, but every kingdom falls."

My heart sank. "I know I just woke you and I'm sorry I trapped you here, but I seriously need your help. There's a dangerous outcast named the Huntsman running around, and if I don't stop him, he'll destroy both the human and the faerie realms. If I hadn't come here, he'd have reached you first and probably forced you to fight on his side."

"He would not have succeeded."

"Wouldn't he?" Risky words to say to a god, but I'd got the better of him myself long before Fionn had woken. "He stole the Huntsman's magic. He calls himself a god."

"Fool," growled the dragon shifter. "There are no gods but us, and the Sidhe took our essence and banished us from their realm."

He remembers. "Did you ever meet the Huntsman before?"

Likely not. I didn't know when the real Huntsman had begun ferrying the Sidhe's souls to the cauldron to be reborn, nor if this deity had ever been to the Grey Vale or if he'd been imprisoned in the mortal realm even before then.

When he didn't answer, I added, "Do you remember when the Sidhe took your power to forge their talisman?"

"Yes." His gaze followed mine to the sword. Its green vibrancy had dulled, and a distinct crack split the length of the blade. *Whoa.* Either he'd bitten it harder than I'd thought or the effect of waking the god had caused the talisman to break of its own accord. "And its power is now back where it belongs."

He took the power into himself. The talisman held no green glow, not even the glyphs on the hilt, and I was willing to bet that if I gave it a swing, no magic would answer my call.

Which meant the odds of me putting the god into an

enchanted sleep again if he turned violent were pretty much zero.

"Good." I tried for a smile but didn't quite get there. "Summer doesn't deserve it."

"Summer destroyed their own people in order to forge this blade."

My mouth parted. "They did?"

"Yes," the shifter-god said. "The dryad who belonged to the tree they cut down to forge that blade… it was she who woke me."

"What?" I stared at him. "The dryad… the Lady of the Tree? They cut down her tree to make your talisman?"

If so, no wonder she'd been ready to reclaim the talisman as hers. And if those dryads I'd encountered in Summer had been right, the Sidhe had exiled her to the mortal realm to prevent her from enacting revenge upon them.

"Yes," he growled. "The Sidhe stole my power and bound me into an eternal sleep. And *you* killed the one who woke me."

"She wanted to destroy my realm," I protested. "She didn't give a crap about you, either. Also—you're the shifters' ancestor, aren't you? She murdered a bunch of them in her quest for power."

"Shifters," he repeated. "Yes. I suppose I am."

The dragon's gaze moved to Vance. The resemblance wasn't *too* obvious—aside from the eyes—but recognition flared in the shifter's gaze. "Who are you?"

"Mage Lord Colton."

Shock and anger crossed the dragon's face. "That's what became of my progeny? They intermingled with *humans*?"

Oh boy. Evidently, this guy didn't like humans any more than the Sidhe did. Hardly fair, given that it hadn't been humans who'd bound him, as far as I knew. And now I'd lost one of my talismans, I'd better hope to gain the cooperation of the one who'd carried it.

"Times change." Vance met the dragon shifter's gaze and didn't look away. "And it happens we may have need of your people again."

"My people," repeated the shifter. "What did I just say? We were exiled, imprisoned, and I know not what became of the others."

"But I have this." I held out my other talisman. "It contains the power of another god. Is it possible to find them?"

"They're all lost," growled the man. "If anything remains of the others, they are incapable of helping you. What do you want from me?"

"Like I said, there's another god trying to destroy all the realms," I said. "He's immortal, immune to all magic, and if I don't stop him, we all die."

"My kin are gone," said Eraenar. "Whoever you face, he is no god."

"No, but he pretty much made himself one," I said. "He attacked the mortal world a couple of decades ago and nearly destroyed us. Now he's trying the same again. I can't beat him in a fair fight. He's immune to my magic, which I took from... I don't suppose you've heard of Lord Avalin? He's the one I took this talisman from."

His expression was blank. "I have been imprisoned a long time, mortal. Whatever other talismans the Sidhe foolishly forged are outside of my knowledge, and you will not convince me to fight alongside of the mortals who polluted my bloodline and the Sidhe who stole our power and banished us from our home. If one of their own betrayed them and stole that power back, they will fall, as they rightfully deserve."

"Maybe they do, but innocent people are going to get caught up in this."

"Would you sacrifice the lives of your own children on a battlefield they never asked for?" asked Vance. "Your descendants wanted no part in this war. They are no enemies of yours."

"They are nothing to me." Coldness emanated from his voice. "This realm in which you imprisoned me stands as proof that the Sidhe do not deserve anything short of their own destruction. They turned our own magic against us and severed us from our home, creating this prison in its place— a realm entirely void of magic and home only to the dead."

"I know," I said. "It wasn't right, but believe me, the Sidhe hate humans as much as they hate you. They don't care if we die. I gave you your talisman back, didn't I?"

"That you stole, human."

"I'm not the thief." My voice rose in desperation. "And I didn't mean to steal this one either. I had no idea where its power originally came from. Listen—if you won't help, can you at least give me some direction? Its owner must have originally been banished here, too. Can I find them?"

"You ask the impossible," he said.

Despair crept in. "Fionn—the Huntsman—he *is* going to come for you. And he has the Morrigan on his side, too. She can rip out people's souls, so the pair of them practically have control over life and death."

"I sincerely doubt it," said the shifter. "If that's what passes for immortality in this day and age, the Sidhe will die out sooner rather than later."

"What do you mean?" I asked. "The cauldron, right? The source of their immortality? Yeah, I destroyed it. If that's not proof that I'm not on their side, I don't know what is."

A moment passed in which the dragon shifter studied me, his piercing eyes raking over me from head to toe. "You lie, human."

"Nope." I gestured to the glyphs shimmering on my

blade's hilt. "I used the word *break*. You know I can speak these words. I used them on you."

"Yes," he said. "You did. You really mean to say that you broke the absurd immortality cycle the Courts have worshipped for eons?"

"I guess I am, yeah." My heartbeat quickened, but I pressed on. "That means Fionn will die permanently if I can get the upper hand, but he's immune to my magic. I don't know why. That's why I thought I should ask—ask the god it belongs to."

My mouth went dry as his intense stare pierced me again as though to see through to the magic swirling within my soul. "That would not be wise. As I told you, our language is not used lightly even by the Sidhe. They know that we can sense when someone speaks of us, and that uttering the name of a god will draw its attention, whatever form it exists in."

Did that mean I could speak to the god just by voicing its name? "Can you tell me which—?"

"*No.*" The command rang out as sharply as an Invocation, and the words died in my throat. "I will not teach you how to speak the language the Sidhe stole from us, mortal."

"I—I'm sorry." Could I figure it out myself? Maybe, but from the murderous intent in the dragon shifter's expression, I wasn't convinced I'd survive an encounter with *this* god, let alone another. "This was—a mistake. I shouldn't have bound you. I was scared. I didn't know we could communicate." I tripped over my words and felt Vance's steadying hand on my shoulder from behind, but he didn't speak, knowing that he had to tread with extreme caution.

"You will betray us, too." The dragon shifter's voice resounded with anger, yet beneath lay a hint of something that I might have called vulnerability if I hadn't known better. "There are always fools who think they have the right to usurp our power. The Sidhe drained all magic from this part of their world deliberately. They wanted us to expire."

"Shit. I didn't know that, either." Did that mean he was weaker here than in Faerie? This realm was friendlier to death magic, to Winter, than Summer, but he was from neither. Not originally. The talisman containing his magic had been tied to the Summer Court, but that had been the Sidhe's doing, and the deity himself belonged to no Court. The Sidhe's arrogance knew no bounds, and I didn't blame the dragon shifter for hating them, but that didn't mean I'd let innocent people suffer as a consequence.

A faint whistling noise sounded from somewhere outside the dungeon.

I tensed. "There's someone outside."

The dragon shifter moved in a gliding motion that carried him past us and through the open door. Vance and I exchanged grim looks and followed.

As we left the dungeon, Eraenar collapsed in the door-way, blood spraying from a wound in his chest. I raised my sword, shock and panic setting in a second too late. *What did that?*

"Ivy!" Vance shouted as the air thickened with grey and fog swept in.

I shoved the Invocations one-handedly into my pocket and conjured a magical shield around Vance and me. Not a moment too soon. Ghosts flickered into view, hundreds of them popping into existence around the giant stone construction. I recognised some of them as from among the half-bloods who'd been left behind when the cauldron shattered.

I held my sword up in warning, its glow already vibrant with their anger and hatred as I scanned the trees beyond the swarming spirits. Who had hit the dragon shifter? Ghosts couldn't harm the living, and I'd never have thought a regular weapon could leave a mark on a god.

"Who else is out there?" I called.

The ghosts parted to either side and the Morrigan landed beside the dungeon, her claws splaying on the ground and stirring up flurries of leaves.

I should have known. I'd banished her, and now she was back for revenge. Around, the ghosts gathered, eyes angry and accusing.

"Hey, don't look at me like that. I'm not the one who snagged your souls."

I took aim, calling my magic into a blast that I sent at the Morrigan, but the attack bounced clean off her feathery hide. Vance disappeared and reappeared behind her and swung his blade, but a mass of ghosts pushed him back before his sword connected. *Dammit.* Vance's ability didn't work to its full extent in this realm and he was forced to get in close to strike the Morrigan, which ran the risk of her severing him from his body once again.

Not on my watch. I tapped into the ghosts' pain and drew it into me, into the vibrant glow circling my blade as their anger and despair fuelled my talisman's strength. Yet raw magic alone hadn't left an impact on the Morrigan. My magic was fuelled by death energy and so was hers, and I guessed it made sense that my talisman alone wouldn't work against someone who was the embodiment of death herself.

"This one's soul was meant to be mine." She raised a talon towards Vance, revealing the glimmering chain that marked Fionn's binding. "Now I will take him."

"No, you fucking won't." I launched myself at her. My blade drove into the joint of her wing, slicing upward. She screamed, not quite on a banshee's level, but enough to make my ears burn. I dug deeper, spraying crimson tinted with blue.

Vance ducked underneath her talon and drove his claws into her other wing, pulling her downward. Together we held her half-pinned down but neither of us could deal a killing blow from this angle, and the dragon shifter remained inert on the forest floor.

The Morrigan shook her wings, dislodging us both. Her wings trailed crimson as they beat, and I readied myself to jump again.

A sharp, violent surge of energy shook the world. Even the ghosts fled, swept away in a torrent. I braced myself in vain as my spirit flew loose from my body and into the air, above the dragon shifter's bleeding body, and above Vance, who held onto a tree for balance as the current of death energy roared through the world.

The current stilled, and I fell downward, dropping back into my body as violently as I'd been ripped loose. My knees hit the ground, drawing blood. I lifted my head, fighting against the threads of death magic wrapping around me, trying to pull me out of my body again.

"That wasn't part of our agreement," said Fionn's voice, addressing the Morrigan.

14

I *knew it. I knew he was here.*

Coldness spread through me, my hands numbing as ice flowed across the ground and up every tree. The temperature dropped at least ten degrees as Fionn appeared, sitting astride his dark-pelted horse. Evidently, this time he was playing Huntsman, not shapeshifter, but I'd never seen him use magic like that before. He'd frozen this entire area of the Grey Vale. Did he have a powerful Winter Sidhe on his side, or had he stolen yet another talisman?

I spoke through chattering teeth. "You can't just make a normal entrance, can you?"

Vance stepped forward, his claws out and his blade in one hand. "What's your game?"

"This is no game," said Fionn. "While I grant that I find it deeply amusing to watch humans' endless capacity to run yourselves into fatal errors, I cannot afford to let you roam around the Vale any longer. You've done too much damage already."

"If you mean killing your pet Sidhe, you shouldn't have handed the life-drinker to a twelve-year-old with a god complex. And you sure as fuck shouldn't have had him kidnap the Mage Lords."

"Your mage seems fine to me," he said dismissively. "You seem to care little for his safety yourself, as you brought him here with you despite knowing the Morrigan desires his soul."

"Is there any reason you attacked him first?" I glanced at the dragon shifter, wondering if I should be alarmed at the amount of blood spreading across the pale snow. I didn't know if he could heal like the Sidhe could, but for all I knew, a healing spell would have no effect on him either. "He might have helped you."

"Is that what you thought? That I desired the help of an expired god who was tricked into imprisonment by a human?" He laughed softly. "No… I have grander aspirations."

"I bet." What was grander than a god? With Fionn, it was probably unwise to ask that question. He'd lost his chance to form an immortal army, but he still had a bunch of exiles at his command, including several reborn Sidhe, and god-knew-how-many ghosts at his beck and call. And his Horsemen of the Apocalypse.

"This is very enlightening," growled Vance. "But if you mean to attack our realm again, you won't find it undefended."

"What makes you think I would waste any more time on you?" Fionn's head tilted on one side. "Your realm *will* fall, but whether you defend it not, the outcome will be the same. All realms are intertwined, after all, and what happens to one affects the others."

"Fascinating. Please tell me all about your evil plans." I was under no illusions that either of us would be able to harm Fionn as he was now, but our only ally on the same power level as Fionn was bleeding on the ground, and my sole option was stalling until we found a way to heal him. Eraenar lay inert, unresponsive, and I couldn't tell if he was even breathing.

"The faerie realms are more resilient than yours is. More so than their inhabitants." A smile curled his mouth. "Even gods can die."

"Including you." Out of the corner of my eye, Vance began to move closer to the dragon shifter, and I sought to keep Fionn's attention on my face instead. "Not that you're a real god. You just pretended to be one after you fled the Courts."

"I never fled them." His smile vanished. "I am the only person who has ever turned my back on the Courts without suffering the pain of exile."

"Only by tricking others into helping you," I said. "You enlisted Avalin to help you steal the Huntsman's magic and didn't even share any with him. No wonder his talisman is so pissed off at you."

"Ah. You spoke to…" He looked at me questioningly, and I remained quiet. He didn't need to know where I'd learned that information. "No matter. Crossing between realms was the least of what I required the Huntsman's magic for."

"I'm sure the Sidhe appreciated you running off with the power that made them immortal."

"Now, that's a less severe crime than that committed by *you*, Ivy." His mouth twisted. "If not for my own aims, I'd dearly love to see what the Winter Queen would do to you for destroying her means of continuing her rule."

"The cauldron?" I forced a smile despite the dread coiling inside my chest. "Bet you didn't plan for that. I really fucked up your plans, didn't I?"

"Less than you might think." His expression darkened. "You have audacity, Ivy, but we all know how this will end. The gods thought they would rule forever. The Sidhe proved them wrong. The Sidhe themselves thought they would rule forever, and—"

Fionn's horse tipped backwards when a knife buried itself in his shoulder. Vance appeared, his hand on my shoulder, pulling me towards the dragon shifter, who was stirring.

"*No.*" Fionn's voice was a clap of thunder as potent as the surge of energy that had announced his arrival. The frozen forest was lost in sudden darkness as absolute as the Hemlock Coven's lair, and both Vance and the dragon shifter vanished from my sight.

"Hey!" I called into the dark. "Where are we?"

"This way," said a singsong voice. A ball of light appeared in midair above Fionn, who sat perched on his horse a few metres away.

I glared. "Where are we this time?"

"I thought it would be easier to talk in a place we're less likely to be disturbed. Don't you agree?"

"Easier for you not to get hit by stray knives, you mean," I said. "Where the hell is Vance?"

"Don't worry about him, Ivy. Worry about yourself. The shadows are hungry for blood."

Cold softness brushed the back of my neck. I gritted my teeth, fighting the instinct to panic, knowing Fionn was employing some of Faerie's cheapest tricks to wring a reaction from me. I pointedly ignored the feather-light shadows caressing my arms and legs as I walked leisurely towards him, hands clenched around my sword hilt.

"Lousy effort, Fionn." The shadows receded and the ground beneath turned to frosted grass. Leafless trees were visible through the light hovering behind him, and a chill breeze swept in, biting at every inch of my exposed skin. "Where the hell did you take Vance?"

"Wouldn't you like to know." His teeth flashed in a wide smile that I wanted to punch clean off his face. Technically I *could* cause him physical damage, but he'd just heal himself. Losing the cauldron hadn't taken away his invincibility, and my magic had no effect on him whatsoever.

The light widened, exposing a path leading uphill to a vast structure. Not the castle Vance had been imprisoned in last time, but built along similar lines.

"You haven't an original thought in your head, have you?" I gave an eye-roll. "Let me guess, your castle contains a giant ballroom where a human band is cursed to play until they die, while you waltz around beheading people for looking at you the wrong way."

"Avalin did that?" Fionn laughed. "He did have a certain taste, or lack thereof."

"We can agree there, but that doesn't mean I'll play along. If you want to fight, I'll do it here and now. If you don't plan to attack my realm, there's no point in dragging this out, is there?"

"You're right," he said, startling me. "Targeting the mortal realm should never have been my priority. I've learned from my mistakes, Ivy. Where do you think we are?"

"Some new hellscape you've created, no doubt."

"We aren't in the Vale any longer, Ivy," he said. "In time, all the magic of Summer and Winter will flood the realm they left to die and allow the Vale to be born anew, but for now, I have claimed the Death Kingdom as mine."

Death Kingdom? The Morrigan… this was *her* domain, and as she was bound to him, he must have claimed leadership over the land as well, despite this realm being part of Winter instead of the Vale. In fact, did his actions here also account for the damage to the veil in the mortal realm, and the necromancers' inability to reach Death?

"As I said," he whispered, "my ambitions go beyond a single realm."

Holy shit. He'd certainly hijacked some of Winter's magic

for his own, if what he'd done to the Vale was any indication, but for all I knew he was draining the Winter Court dry as we spoke and taking that power into himself. While the talisman I carried was fuelled by the pain of the dead, whose very essence haunted this realm, that power had no effect whatsoever on my enemy. How was I supposed to best him, especially when my allies had been left behind in the Vale?

"It takes time to build an empire," Fionn added. "Come with me."

He rode ahead until we reached the top of a hill that afforded us a clear view of the vast palace he'd claimed as his. Fionn's new domain gleamed under a silvery moon, its bright sheen suggesting it was made out of either glass or ice. Probably the latter, given the temperature.

"Wow." I shook my head at him. "You know, you might be a power-hungry warmongering dick, Fionn, but I always thought you weren't like the Sidhe. You might have hated the Courts, but you're just as wasteful and extravagant as they are, and just as empty. It's pitiful."

A growl sounded behind me. I tilted my head, seeing a huge leonine shape emerge from the bushes. Hot breath warned me to jump aside as a stream of fire came from its jaws, turning snow to water. *Chimera.*

I spun around and cut its throat. Blue-tinged blood splattered the remaining snow, and the half-lion half-lizard beast sank to the ground. I moved away from the blood seeping out from underneath its heavy body, shaking droplets off my blade.

"Nice try." I rotated back to Fionn, who watched, thin-lipped, from the back of his steed. "I'm sure Winter will be thrilled that you're bringing fire-breathing wild beasts into their territory."

"Not as thrilled as Winter's foot-soldiers," Fionn said. "Use that resourceful mortal mind of yours, Ivy."

"What?" Wait a second. "You didn't."

A yowl came from the trees, followed by the sound of skittering footsteps. Lots of them. Oh, *shit*.

"It was you who spilled blood on the redcaps' territory, Ivy. You might mock me for following the example of the Sidhe, but trickery works for a reason, does it not?"

"Redcaps." I sighed. "Anyone would think you cared more about making a spectacle than achieving anything meaningful."

"Wrong."

Again, his word hit like a thunderclap, and again the world distorted. Instead of darkness, a large hall rose around us, pillars springing up in place of trees. A ribbon of moonlight shone from a ceiling high enough to vanish out of sight, illuminating the open space between the pillars. Dark figures crowded around the edges like a crowd awaiting a show.

"What is this, an arena?" Now he was poaching ideas from Calder of all people?

Fionn didn't answer. He sat astride his horse beneath a column of light that reflected off his pale features and highlighted his grin as he surveyed the dead chimera. Despite the change in scenery, the body hadn't budged an inch, and the sound of dozens of pairs of tiny footsteps grew louder as redcaps swarmed into the room.

I stepped back, calling magic to my hand and taking aim at Fionn. A stream of blue light surged from my palm and fizzled out as he spoke words that slid through my mind, my body, my very essence. A suffocating pressure cloaked me, and the magical shield I'd unconsciously conjured vanished outright.

The redcaps swarmed before I could figure out which Invocation he'd used. I swung my blade, burying it in a redcap's skull, and tried to reform my magical shield. Not so much as a wisp stirred, and even my blade's light had dulled.

Grasping hands tore at my clothes, sharp nails scoring lines across my skin. I cut at the redcaps, but even speed and agility were reduced to ordinary human levels.

He cut off my magic?

I sent a redcap's head flying in Fionn's direction and glimpsed him smiling at me from his horse, holding the parchment that listed the Invocations. Not that he'd needed it, but he hadn't been able to resist taking away another of my rapidly dwindling assets.

I tugged my sword out of a redcap's chest and slashed at its grasping hands. Even without magic, my sword was sharper than any mortal blade, but there were too many of them to hit at once. The tide of redcaps was relentless, and my heart plunged when I saw Vance fighting, too, surrounded by screeching, laughing creatures wearing caps drenched in crimson.

"Get out!" I screamed, to no avail. Neither of us had a hope of breaking free of the crush, and towering horses bearing masked figures in armour blocked every possible route of escape. The horsemen of the Wild Hunt. So that's where the fuckers were hanging out. Had they even noticed or cared that they were taking orders from an impostor?

Vance snarled, tearing into the redcaps, but he was bleeding from long scratches on his face and I assumed he either couldn't use his ability in here or he'd been too concerned about me to transport himself out.

Kicking a redcap aside, I dug one-handed in my pocket and my hand closed around the small jar hidden alongside my spare dagger. I ripped it free and tossed it into the crowd. Glass shattered, and redcap screams tore at my eardrums as they trod on the iron filings I'd scattered under their feet.

Simple works best, eh, Fionn?

I'd slowed them, but Vance remained beyond my reach and the tide of redcaps seemed never-ending. How had

Fionn gathered so many in one place? He must have perpetrated a massacre, possibly in this very room. Redcaps were battlefield faeries, and the arena under our feet was stained in blood. Stinging cuts marked my face and while my healing power might be functioning to some degree, Vance had none of that advantage. He'd sustained several stab wounds already, and panic gripped me when I saw the bloodied state of his face.

"You have to get out!" I shouted to him. "I'll distract Fionn somehow."

"Haven't we been through this?" Blood streamed down his cheek, but his eyes gleamed with a fierce light as he continued to slash and hack at the redcaps. "I wouldn't be anywhere but at your side."

I cut down a redcap before its grasping fingers gouged my eyes out. Two fell simultaneously under Vance's blades, but two more took their place. Our enemies might be weak, but they were relentless, and Fionn showed no signs of intervening. This was pure entertainment to him, nothing more.

"Quit fucking around!" I skidded sideways when a wrenching crack sounded, and the arena floor split in two. Redcaps fell, screeching, into the gap, and Vance and I staggered back, watching one another across the rapidly growing crack in the ground, drawing in any redcap

unlucky enough to get too close to the edge. Their fighting didn't cease and they even turned on each other, stabbing with short knives and gouging with pointy fingers.

Fionn rode his horse through the melee, offering me a smile and a wag of his finger. Spitting curses, I fought on, sheathing my blade in redcap blood, moving closer to the crack spreading across the floor. I could still make the jump.

As my feet skirted the edge, Fionn's voice spoke in my ear. "Don't bother."

He extended a hand, grabbing me by the scruff of my

neck. I kicked, my boots striking redcaps' skulls, my blade unable to reach its target. "You're both already dead, Ivy, but you get to choose who dies first. You—or him."

"Absolutely not." Damn him. If I died, Vance would, too. He couldn't get out of here without me.

"Him, then."

The tide of redcaps pushed at Vance, driving him away from the crack in the floor and away from me. Three more horsemen parted the crowd, each armed with a long spear.

"No!" I screamed. "Not him."

I kicked hard, broke free of Fionn and leaped for the gap in the floor as though the air might catch me and make me fly.

As I soared, Vance dodged the first spear. The second caught him in the arm and knocked him to the ground.

The third hit him in the heart.

My scream flew upward as I tumbled into oblivion, into a place without hope or light.

15

I didn't expect to wake up. I didn't *want* to wake up. But I did. The abyss had spat me out onto an unbearably soft bed in an elaborately decorated room that mocked me with its fitted mahogany furniture and gold-leaf patterned wallpaper. No window, of course. No way out.

I still wore my bloodstained clothes, but one quick check confirmed the contents of my pockets had been emptied. The Invocations were lost. All my weapons, gone. My phone, too. Someone had even removed the spare dagger I kept in my bra. The visceral jolt of disgust that hit me at the realisation opened the floodgates. I was a prisoner, at a Sidhe's mercy again, and Vance was—dead.

There was no faking it. I'd been close enough to him, for the brief moment before we'd been torn apart, to know it was really him.

Fionn had killed the man I loved, right in front of me.

Rage propelled me across the room. My fist struck the door hard enough to draw blood. A tingling sensation followed, indicating my healing power at least was functional. But that didn't matter, because Fionn had shut off my magic, he'd taken my talisman and Invocations, and he'd ripped out my heart.

Rationality briefly reared its head. Recalling how I'd escaped his castle in the Vale, I willed my spirit to leave my body and pass into Death. *This has to work. I have to get out.*

Nothing happened. An invisible force pinned me to my body, and no matter how hard I tried to reach the spirit world, I remained solid, awake, and trapped. Fionn had accounted for everything, but it was beyond me to guess if this was a side effect of him binding my power, a spell he'd put on my room to prevent my escape, or just a general effect of him screwing around with death and claiming the Death Kingdom.

Where were the dead now? Where was Vance?

A keening noise rose in my throat. I hammered at the wall until my healing ability couldn't keep up with the skin being torn from my knuckles. I screamed my throat raw, my fists pounding the stone, as though the physical pain would ease away the agony tearing my chest apart like a scalpel. If my magic had been functioning, I might have brought the entire palace crashing around our ears with the force of my rage and despair.

But in the end, the only thing broken was me.

Vance. I never should have brought him here.

Oh, who was I kidding? He'd never have consented to be left behind. In addition to his insistence on standing at my side, we'd both thought Fionn intended to attack the city at any moment. But our realm had never been his priority. His revenge upon the Courts took precedence, and if his earlier gloating had been any indication, our realm would be caught up in any aftereffects that ensued, and without Fionn having to lower himself to setting foot there in person.

And I'd waste away my remaining time here, unless something resembling a miracle showed up. The living couldn't help. The dead were out of reach. If Vance was on the other side of the veil, I'd never know.

My nails pierced my palms as anger and grief battled for dominance. My hands tore at the door, blood streaking the wood, but I hadn't made so much as a dent. The sensible part of me whispered that using up all my energy on futile escape attempts would only exhaust me with no real benefit, but Fionn had already tied my hands, and he'd killed Vance to shatter my hope. Knowing that didn't make the bleeding stop, didn't seal the hole in my heart.

For a wild moment, I wished I had the Invocations, not to use on Fionn but to use on myself, to wipe my memories of this pain. Wilhemina might have suffered horribly, but who was to say if recalling the memories of her torture wouldn't have been a thousand times worse than being without any at all? In this moment, being able to forget would be a blessing.

No. No, it wouldn't. If nothing else, Vance wouldn't want you to.

I sank to my knees and cried until the minutes blended into one, until oblivion crashed down on me again.

I woke with my head throbbing and my mouth dry. Despite the pain tearing at my heart, my survival instincts stirred. I rose upright on shaky legs and found that my room contained an adjacent bathroom even equipped with a proper shower. That was new. As Avalin's prisoner, I'd had to bathe in the river and hope nothing came and ate me, but if Fionn hoped to win me over, he was sorely mistaken. I glared at the fancy gold-plated fittings and scooped water from the tap into my mouth. The mirror above the sink showed my eyes were puffy and red, my face smudged with tears. I didn't care. Nor did I care for the fine clothes left out on the floor beside the shower. He wanted me to clean myself up, dress well for my execution. I would not comply. I wouldn't allow

Fionn to steal my identity on top of everything else he'd taken from me.

For all his claims that he understood me on a deeper level than anyone else, Fionn could never truly grasp that this wasn't the first time Faerie had ripped away the people I loved and trapped me in hell. He couldn't comprehend the struggle, the years fighting with no hope of victory, waging a futile battle against the odds. For all his claims of the wrongs the Courts had committed against him, I wasn't convinced he'd even gone through the pain of being exiled the way the other Sidhe had. He'd certainly never know what it was like to be stolen away from everything you loved, to be thrown into a pit of darkness—and to still find a light to follow to the surface.

Maybe that was why I didn't want to die. Not even with Vance gone, and with nothing in my future but my own end.

I wiped the tears from my face, gathered the shattered pieces of my resolve, and I waited for Fionn to show up. The moment he did, I'd be out of here or dead. I'd rather cut off my own hand than pretend to play nice with the bastard who'd killed Vance.

He'd wanted to break me, yet he hadn't taken my life. Not yet. He must have some fresh horrors saved up for me before he dealt the final blow.

Seconds passed. Minutes, blending together. I waited. And the instant the door finally began to open, I launched across the room at Fionn, tearing at his chest, punching at every part of him I could reach.

My hands had no effect on his armour and each hit further ripped apart my knuckles, but I kept striking him, again and again, until his palm rested against my shoulder and gave a gentle push. I swayed back on my heels, looking into his calm gaze as it travelled from my bloody hands to the crimson smears on the door and wall. "There's no need to take your rage out on the furniture, Ivy. I made this room especially for you."

"Rage," I repeated, my voice husky from screaming. "You haven't seen anything yet, Fionn. Tell me what the hell you want or I'll run into your sword and take away all the fun you planned to have with me."

"You think this is fun?" asked Fionn.

"Oh, I don't know, maybe you enjoyed feeling me up when you were taking away my weapons."

"You flatter yourself, human. I didn't lay a finger on you."

"What the hell's that supposed to mean? That I should thank you for not violating me while I was unconscious?"

"You hold little interest for me, human," he said. "Humans are so fragile, so breakable. I confess it would be greatly amusing to make you utterly dependent on me, as often happens whenever a Sidhe chooses a human lover, but the novelty would soon wear off."

"How honourable," I spat. "You disgust me."

"I know you spoke to Avalin's former lover, too." His mouth tilted in a smile. "Did she tell you anything useful?"

"Why do you care?"

"I'd like to ensure there aren't any unpleasant surprises ahead, but I suspect not. Avalin was predictable to a fault, and his brief dalliance with that fragile mortal was of little consequence. Although I do have his progeny to thank for my revival." His teeth flashed in a grin. "It's strange how these things turn out, isn't it, Ivy? You and I both owe Lord Avalin, in a way. After all, if he hadn't taken you captive, you wouldn't have survived the destruction of your realm."

"Bollocks." My hands curled into fists. "Go on. If you really want to kill me, get on with it."

"I'm surprised you have any fight left in you," he mused. "I forget you've suffered loss before."

"Whereas you've never cared for anyone enough for their loss to matter."

"I beg to differ," he said. "Some would call you fortunate to die so soon, given that your time was always going to be limited."

"Didn't I tell you to get on with it?" I glared at him. "Seriously. I'm starting to think you don't *want* to kill me. You're so deeply insecure that you need someone you can kick down occasionally as entertainment. The Sidhe are exactly the same. They need to feel superior, and if you sit alone on a throne made of your enemies' corpses, what else is left for you to do?"

"Isn't that what we all desire?" he said. "To stand alone, apart, to watch others kneel at our feet? You carried the Invocations, Ivy. You might have remade the world."

"I wouldn't have, because I'm *not like you*." I spoke through gritted teeth. "How many times do I have to tell you? Is that why you can't let me go? Because you're used to having everyone either flee or fawn all over you? Am I getting under your skin because I don't give a shit about you?"

The angry line of his mouth told me I wasn't far off the mark. He might pretend not to be a Sidhe, but in the end, they were all fixated on being liked. Or worshipped, which to a Sidhe, was essentially the same. Refusing to comply was the sole victory I had left to claim.

"Out of words?" I goaded. "You were never a slave of the Courts. You were one of the, and like the other Sidhe, your ego will be your undoing. You think you're invincible, and you're willing to drain even *Death* dry to ensure it. But you're not. Sooner or later you'll slip up like Avalin did, and even if I'm not there to see it, someone will be. Someone will be desperate enough to snatch your power out from underneath your nose and cut your throat. Because I'm not unique, Fionn. I just got lucky. And I hope another human does, too."

He slapped me. The blow carried me off my feet and onto my back. The soft carpet cushioned my fall, and despite the throbbing pain in my face, I bared my teeth up at him in a grin. Fionn looked down at me, his emotions swept behind a mask that didn't fool me in the least. I'd cracked his shield without lifting my sword.

"You're proving how pathetic you really are." I stood up, one hand to my aching jaw, and met his eyes defiantly. "If you were really secure in your power, you wouldn't need to strike me."

"It is you who should know your place, Ivy. Get on your knees."

The words rang through my body and my knees bent against my will, sinking into the carpet. *That fucking vow again.* He turned, addressing someone behind him. "Bring her."

A small figure slipped into the room, but my neck refused to straighten enough for me to see them. The newcomer slipped behind me, and a pair of cuffs clamped over my wrists. Out of the corner of my eye, I glimpsed my captor, a young girl with dark hair and pointed ears. A second set of cuffs appeared, chaining my left hand to her right one. *Roseanne.* Fionn must have captured the Morrigan's daughter along with her palace.

"Come quickly," Fionn said. "Both of you."

I rose upright, still chained to Roseanne, and walked into the corridor. A chill wind cut into me underneath my leather jacket, and not a sound disturbed the silence. I wondered if Fionn had left anyone alive in here at all.

"Roseanne," I whispered. "He found you?"

She shot me a wide-eyed look and didn't speak. Either out of fear, or because he'd put her under a vow, too, to ensure her utmost obedience.

"It's okay," I whispered. "I'm here. I'm with you."

Her eyes widened in surprise. Likely nobody had ever said that to her before. She'd killed innocents, but the crimes she'd committed hadn't been her own. They'd been Fionn's.

Someone had to bring him down. I hoped it would be Roseanne, if not me. And if nothing else, if I died today, I might see Vance again before we passed through Death's gates. Together.

16

I held onto that thought as Roseanne and I walked down the corridor. The palace walls were dark stone, coldness seeping through crevices. Standard Unseelie, but I had to wonder where Fionn had banished the Morrigan to. Was she imprisoned somewhere in her own palace?

The outline of a winged creature the size of my hand hovered over my head like a giant moth, tugging at my hair. I tried to swat it, causing Roseanne to turn around and shake her head frantically at me. I dropped my hand and fell into step with her again, but Fionn didn't spare us so much as a glance. He knew neither of us was going anywhere.

We reached a staircase and climbed down one level, then a second. The third ended in a pitch-black room. Roseanne whimpered, and I felt her trembling next to me as the darkness enfolded us.

"It's okay," I whispered. "Fionn's just trying to freak us out."

"Come along," Fionn called, his voice lost in the gloom. "Your fate awaits you, Ivy Lane. Hers, too."

"Don't you have a light switch?" I could no longer see the stairs, but I moved that way, Roseanne clanking against me.

My shoulder fetched up against a cold wall. No trace of the stairs—or Fionn.

"You still here?" I called out. "I assume you have some kind of night vision. It won't be fun if you can't see us die, will it?"

Fionn didn't say a word, nor did he reveal himself. With one arm against the wall, I edged around the room, Roseanne uttering the occasional whimper at my side.

"Roseanne," I whispered. "Can you speak?"

"No," she moaned. "I can't."

"You just did." I peeled my arm away from the cold stone wall and stood on tiptoe, tilting my head back in the hopes of catching a sliver of light above. No windows broke through the darkness, and the ceiling might have been a mile off for all I knew. "Did he put you under a vow?"

"Yes." She gulped. "He told me not to speak to you. Said the vow would hold until my death. That means we're gonna die in here."

"No, we aren't." I wriggled my wrist in the handcuffs, trying in vain to reach my magic. Still nothing. "Fionn wanted to make a spectacle of my death. He won't leave us to die in the dark."

Or would he? As was abundantly clear, Fionn didn't *have* a clear plan. Not just because I kept thwarting him, but because he was as capricious and unpredictable as any Sidhe, and I wasn't meant to be his priority. I was nothing more than a stubborn, annoying human who kept on needling him long past my planned expiry date.

Roseanne let out a sob. "Yes, he will. He told me he kept me alive because you—you cared about me."

"Damn." If he'd kept her alive for the purposes of

tormenting me alone, odds were that he'd brought me here to watch *her* die first. Or worse… force me to kill her.

Roseanne sobbed again. "He came here, stole my mother's palace, and… and he laughed when he found me. Said he hoped I'd lived."

"How did he enslave her?" I asked. "The Morrigan? I thought they were on equal footing. He promised her those souls, and she—"

A slap connected with my neck.

"It's *your fault*," she cried. "He blamed you for destroying the cauldron. You took away my chance at being immortal and you made him angry enough to turn on my mother. We're gonna die because of you."

"Which of us believed his lies when I *told* you not to?" I fired back at her, my temper snapping. "Everything I said to you was true. You had a choice, and you picked the faeries who abandoned you over the father who would have given anything to spare you from that fate."

"You bitch!" She hit me again, sharp claws raking the side of my chin.

"*Ow.*" Her hands must have shifted to her animal form. Damn, that hurt.

A laugh resounded above. Light streamed in, once again revealing Fionn's grinning face as he peered down at us from a balcony that I was positive hadn't been there either. "Fighting already?"

"Want to come and fight us yourself?" I called up at him.

Roseanne screamed as a jagged crack split the floor in two directly below my feet. As I fell through the gap, the cuffs holding us together pulled her after me, and there wasn't enough light to see what awaited at the bottom of the pit. A grisly death, I was willing to bet.

"Shift!" I shouted up at Roseanne.

The world swung around me as her free hand shifted into a claw and dug into the ledge that had once been a floor. She flailed, gasping, not strong enough to pull us both to safety. Nor could her beating wings support my weight on top of hers.

"I can't!" she sobbed. "I can't hold on."

"Then let go and use your claws to undo the cuffs so you can fly back up." My wrist burned, the cuffs pressing into my skin as I dangled below her. "Free yourself."

"You'll fall," she said. "You'll die."

"Probably that's how it's meant to go." Only one of us could survive. "Or he'll change his mind and rescue me at the last minute so he can kill me in a more satisfying way. Go on. Save yourself."

She sobbed, then screamed when the ledge tilted and more of the floor vanished. Fionn's laughter resonated above. The meaning was clear. He *wanted* her to let me fall to my death.

"Go on!" I pressed. "I'll be fine." A blatant lie, but I refused to literally drag her down with me.

Roseanne's clawed hand slipped free from the edge. As we began to fall, she reached down, her claws stabbing at the cuff linking us until I felt the tightness around my wrists loosen.

The cuffs broke free—she'd unlocked the one binding my hands, too—and as I shook them loose, I began to fall faster. Roseanne descended, this time reaching out with both hands to grasp mine. Her wings beat behind her back, unable to rise higher, unable to support my weight.

"Don't," I gasped. "Roseanne, it isn't worth it."

Roseanne's gaze dropped and she let out a scream. I twisted my neck to see the pit into which we were falling had turned to solid floor and was covered in what appeared to be a solid mat of spear-sharp spikes. No, those weren't spikes, but thorns, as sharp as any wielded by the Princess of Thorns.

"Still stealing other people's ideas, Fionn?" I snarled between my teeth, conscious that we continued to fall in height as Roseanne's fragile wings struggled to keep us both in the air. "Sorry, Roseanne. You'll have to let me go. Don't blame yourself for this one. It's all on him."

"No." She whimpered. "I hoped he'd spare me if I agreed to… to serve him."

"Not your fault." If my healing ability worked, I *might* survive the thorns, but odds were higher that I'd bleed out slowly instead, while Roseanne was forced to watch.

A faint flash of light caught my eye as something fluttered past, a slip of what looked like gold foil. No, a piece of shredded paper. More fell around me, displaying remnants of what had once been glyphs.

The Invocations. Fionn had torn the parchment to pieces, shredded the words so that nobody could read them and nobody could use them against him again. A final 'screw you' as I fell to my doom.

The spikes loomed higher. Roseanne uttered another howl.

"Let go of me," I told her. "Please. Fly away. Far away. It's okay."

"I can't."

"Seriously, now is not the time to play the hero—"

"I *can't!* Look up."

I lifted my head. The floor—or ceiling—had sealed above our heads, and the underside gleamed with sharp thorns, too.

Oh, fuck.

In vain I scanned the falling Invocations, willing the glyphs to reform and show me a way out, but the scattered pieces continued to tumble towards the oncoming thorns. We had maybe thirty seconds before we were crushed into a human sandwich between floor and ceiling and no miracle on the horizon.

I wondered if Fionn would be satisfied with my death. Wondered how to spend my last words.

Someone else spoke. Or rather, they *roared*.

The floor exploded.

Thorns and stone burst upward in a reverberation that caused Roseanne to let go of me with a shriek of alarm. I had no time to take in the rapidly forming hole where the floor had been before I fell into it, my legs scraping against thorns as the world narrowed to a tunnel.

I slammed down on hard stone, and then yelped when Roseanne landed on top of me. "Ow."

"Ivy." Roseanne scrambled off me. "Are you hurt?"

"Yes… no, not really." I rose upright. My body ached, but nothing was broken, and the sharp thorns protruding above were a reminder of the dire fate we'd escaped. "Where are we, do you know?"

"Tunnels, probably. They bring the bodies out underground… what *was* that?"

"I don't know." I'd heard… an Invocation? Someone had blasted a hole in the floor, and it sure as hell hadn't been me. That sound, though, had not belonged to a human.

I squinted, peered ahead, and stifled a yell when a giant grey eye stared back at me from amid an equally huge face, reptilian and covered in black scales.

Roseanne did scream. She flailed, wings beating, and tried to fly away. I grabbed her talon first and pulled her down, my heart thundering in my chest. "It's okay. He's a friend."

I think. I wasn't entirely sure why the dragon shifter had saved my life, but he wouldn't have gone to that level of trouble if he intended to kill me after all. I didn't know if the same applied to Roseanne, though.

The eye blinked and then the head turned away. I

followed the sound of heavy footsteps through a tunnel that grew progressively darker as we drew away from the opening through which we'd entered. Now the adrenaline from my brush with death had worn off, my hands and feet rapidly numbed, and my body ached all over. Roseanne sobbed quietly at my side, and when I tried to take her hand, or claw, she pulled away from me. "No."

"It's all right. We'll get out."

Roseanne sobbed. "I can't. I'm bound to him still."

"So?" I listened out. The dragon's steps had faded, suggesting we were close to an exit.

Soon the tunnel began to slope upward. Light filtered in from somewhere above, and Roseanne took flight, lurching above my head. I hurried after her and tripped headlong over a body. Redcap. Ugh. I kicked it aside and saw a smaller winged shape flitting around my head. A piskie. Hadn't I seen one earlier? Wait. Was this same one I'd freed from the tower back in the Grey Vale? I couldn't imagine there were a lot of piskies in the Death Kingdom, let alone working for Fionn, and I'd lost track of the little creature after I'd left the Vale.

"Did you bring the dragon shifter to me?" I asked the piskie. "Where is he?"

The piskie chirped and flew ahead, out of the tunnel, which opened into a mass of dead bodies piled on the snowy ground. Redcaps, goblins, half-bloods, even the odd ogre. I gagged on the smell of decaying flesh. "Lovely, Fionn."

No way out except through the corpses, so I waded through and held my breath, my eyes watering. Most of the dead were redcaps, their teeth bared in sneers.

"You bastards." I kicked at them, a fresh wave of anger rising within me. "You fucking killed—"

I couldn't say his name. Couldn't face the possibility that now I was free, that I'd survived, I'd have to live without him.

And that his body might be here, among the dead.

"Alive, mage alive!" yelled the piskie.

"Go away! All of you, go *away*." I kicked a dead redcap viciously, embedding my foot in a tangle of intestines. The piskie continued to circle my head as I swore, pulling my foot free from the redcap's guts. "Do you want to join the dead, you annoying little shit?"

"Alive!" the piskie screeched. "Mage is alive."

What? "Don't you fuck with me. He's *dead*."

"Alive!" said the piskie, undeterred. "Alive!"

Gritting my teeth, I kicked the redcap aside and tried to ignore the piskie's meaningless screeching. It *was* meaningless. In Faerie, nothing was constant, and everything was changeable, whatever my senses told me.

Except for death. Death alone was absolute.

Yet hope dangled in front of me, tantalising even with the presence of so many dead. I waded through corpses, below the piskie's zigzagging flight path, hoping that we were too far from the palace for anyone to hear its screeching.

"Be quiet," said a male voice. "You foolish creature."

"Ivy alive!" yelled the piskie. "Mage master alive!"

I kicked the bodies of fallen redcaps alive and climbed over a dead troll without even registering the sensation of my boots sinking into its rotting flesh. Not when I'd heard a voice I'd never dared hope I'd hear again.

Vance stood amid the sea of corpses, covered in blood and very much alive.

As he studied me, I stared back. Looked for every one of Faerie's tells, every hint at a glamour or illusion. None came. The snow was real, the dead bodies were real, and Vance was —alive.

The piskie flew around his head, yelling indistinctly. My limbs unfroze, and I ran to him, grasped his bloody hands in mine. "Vance. You're alive. How?"

His hands were icy cold. Then again, so were mine. His body had gone completely still, and he stared down at me, his face pale underneath the blood. "Ivy. I saw… I saw him kill you."

"I saw him kill *you*." My words came out as sobs. I wrapped my arms around him, buried my head in his shoulder. "Vance, I swear it's me. I'm alive. I'm here, Vance."

"Ivy." He hugged me back, held me close to him, and let me sob into his arms until my tears were spent.

"Vance, I thought you died." I wiped my eyes and my hands came away smudged with red. So much red. "I got redcap guts all over you. Sorry."

"You're sorry?" He still didn't let go of me. Behind the blood and grime on his face, I swore his eyes were damp, too. "The dragon shifter—"

"Fuck. It was him." I looked around, but I'd lost sight of him. "He got me out. He spoke an Invocation and broke the floor."

"I thought so." He breathed out. "He… healed me. I woke up out here and he was standing over me. He'd shifted."

"He healed you." I swallowed, fresh tears leaking from my eyes. He'd been stabbed to death in front of me. It'd take a long while for me to forget that sight, if ever. "You died."

Vance stroked my hair. "I didn't feel much pain before I blacked out. I woke up somewhere over there near the tunnel. I'm not sure if Fionn had any intention to bring back my spirit after my death."

"I couldn't even reach Death." I shuddered at the memory of being trapped in that luxurious room. "I tried to leave my body and couldn't. Granted, he also blocked my magic, which probably includes my ability to shift into Death, but something's screwed up in here. Badly."

"Yes." Vance stepped back from me when the piskie flew

lower, skirting above my head. "This piskie showed up when I was outside and led the dragon shifter to find you."

"That piskie was in the Vale, locked in the same tower as you," I explained. "Must've followed us."

"I'm glad it was here to help." Vance followed the piskie's erratic flight movement with his eyes. "Eraenar, too."

"Yeah." The dragon shifter had the power to drain the life out of someone, so it made sense that his ability could also heal others, but the real miracle was that he'd helped us at all. "Please don't do that to me again. I should ask Isabel to make me a spell that'll cover you in bubble wrap the next time we end up in a faerie castle. I'm sure she can make something that specific, given enough time."

He laughed quietly and brushed a strand of hair from my bloodstained face. "Ivy Lane. What am I going to do with you?"

"This?" I leaned in and kissed him. His hand wound into my hair, and I lost myself in him as though this was our last minute alive.

"We should go," he murmured against my lips. "I doubt any of this was part of Fionn's plan."

"Definitely not the piskie part." That was enough to convince me this wasn't a dream, because in my experience, reality was way more screwed up than anything in my head.

"No." Vance scanned the sky. "I don't know where the dragon shifter went."

"Nor me." The only person I saw was the piskie, who'd flown a short distance away as though trying not to intrude on our private moment. "I don't know if he left. I imagine it took a lot out of him to speak an Invocation to let me out. Fionn tore up mine, you know. And—" Oh, *shit*. He'd also taken my weapons.

Vance saw the question in my eyes. "Your talisman? If we

get close enough to the palace, I might be able to use my abilities to fetch it."

"Are you sure that'll work?"

"I've moved your sword dozens of times."

"True, but we don't know where it is." I beckoned to the piskie. "Where is my sword? Have you seen it?"

The piskie buzzed around my head. "Sword in east tower! This way!"

All my instincts told me to run like hell, but I refused to leave my talisman behind, and the place was so absurdly massive that Fionn might be anywhere inside its walls. There didn't seem to be any rhyme or reason to the design. It looked like someone had mashed together several pictures of what they thought a castle should look like and thrown buckets of snow all over it. Towers twisted at impossible angles, and the corpses spilling underneath formed a moat of old blood against the ice-white walls.

I tried not to look too hard at the bloody river as we followed the piskie along the bank. Vance skirted the edge, and at one point he crouched down, reaching over the edge of the moat. I wondered what he was doing, and then saw he'd taken two curved daggers from the redcaps that lay amid their slaughtered kin. "It's not ideal, but they'll work if we run into trouble."

"Thanks." I took one of the daggers from him, hoping that nothing worse than redcaps lay ahead of us. With no magic, most fae could trounce me with ease, and there wasn't so much as a shard of iron present in this realm. I'd thrown my jar of iron filings away when I'd been surrounded by redcaps.

The piskie flew above my head, jabbering and pointing at a tower looming on our left.

"That's the place." I halted, seeing two huge brutish ogres positioned in front of the door. "Vance, can you reach my sword from here? My daggers and my phone are probably in there, too."

"I'll try." We edged closer. I gripped his hand for balance as we skirted around a particularly slippery snowbank, and the ogres perked up, lifting their clubs. They'd seen us.

One ogre roared and charged, its huge feet tearing up the snow. A short dagger wasn't the best weapon to fight an eight-foot-tall beast with, but I ducked underneath its huge green arm and stabbed. The ogre bellowed with rage as blood spurted—I'd hit an artery, as I'd planned—and Vance moved in behind it and plunged his own knife into its leg. The creature sank, unbalanced, and I went for the throat.

Ogre blood splattered the snow, and as it crumpled, the second guard took a swing at me, too fast for me to duck. I flew several feet into a snowbank, the wind knocked out of me. Vance snarled in rage and drove his knife into the ogre's back. As I sat upright, a current of air lifted the hair from my scalp, and my sword appeared in my hands in the same instant.

A surge of energy had me on my feet, revelling in the familiar feel of the hilt in my hand and the whistle of air as my blade swung. The ogre's head flew wide, hitting the snow. Magic buzzed through me like an electric current. Wounds healed. My senses heightened, like a light turning on in a dark room.

I felt like I could conquer the world.

"Ivy." Vance walked over to me, holding my phone in his hand. "Are you okay?"

"Oh, yeah." I flashed him a grin and took the phone from him. "I figured Fionn wouldn't have much use for that."

He handed me my daggers next and I slid them back into their sheaths. Energy buzzed in my veins, but tiredness lurked beneath the surface and the adrenaline would wear off soon.

I'll come back, Fionn, and I'll kill you.

"Where's that dragon shifter?" Vance scanned the area. "I thought he was waiting for us somewhere out here."

"Yeah, we can hardly leave him behind after he saved both our lives." There were only so many places a giant dragon could hide, so I began to retrace my steps uphill.

I overtook Vance when I spotted the shifter's body lying in a snowdrift. He was back in his human form and appeared to be unconscious, his eyes closed and his hair plastered to his face with melting snow.

"Damn." I *hoped* he was unconscious and not dead. "I don't think he has any more miracles in store for us."

"Can you get us out?" Vance asked.

"I managed to reach the Vale from Summer. Stands to reason that Winter is the same, and we're probably closer to it here in the Death Kingdom than anywhere else."

I sure hoped so, anyway. I crouched beside the unconscious shifter and took his hand in mine, reaching for Vance with my other hand. The piskie landed on my shoulder, evidently determined not to get left behind this time.

Take me to the Vale, I thought, tapping into my magic, gladder than ever that I'd lifted the spell Fionn had used to bind my power. Blue light swirled around me, turning to grey.

The Death Kingdom faded, the cold temperature returning to something more neutral. The Vale was back to normal, its silver-lit paths deceptively quiet. I breathed out, then coughed on the smell of redcap guts. Without the cold freezing my breath, the stench was even more prevalent. As soon as I got home, I'd have to douse my clothes in a dozen cleansing spells or just throw them away.

"Never thought I'd be glad to see this place." I glanced down at the dragon shifter, who hadn't stirred during the crossing. He must have expended a great deal of power saving Vance's life and getting me out of that castle. I owed him more than I could ever repay in my human lifetime. "We can't leave him in here."

"No," said Vance. "We can't. This is going to be somewhat difficult to explain to the mage council."

"I don't know, maybe the threat of being swatted into oblivion by a god will make everyone listen to us for once."

And on that note, we shifted out of the Vale and back into the mortal realm.

17

"Rise and shine, sleepyhead," said Drake's voice. "Now's not the time for a nap."

"Oh, god." I tilted my head, finding that I lay on a bed and not a sofa, though once again I didn't recognise the room. The plain cream-coloured walls and crooked wooden furniture might have belonged to anyone. "Where am I?"

"In a spare room at the witches' place," he said. "You passed out on shifter territory. Really good job none of them were there."

"Oops. Is Vance okay?"

"He's fine. But he won't say what really went down over there in Fionn's castle or how you found that shifter dude."

"It's… slightly complicated." I flopped back onto the pillow. "Damn. I lost my magic, got it back, and now I've lost it again."

"Ivy." Vance entered the room and sat down on the bed, leaning over to lift a strand of hair from my forehead. "Are you feeling all right?"

"Sure." Better than fine, knowing he was alive. He wore

fresh clothes and was thoroughly bloodstain-free. "We spend way too much time on one another's deathbeds these days."

Vance's mouth tightened, but he attempted a smile. "It's a terrible habit."

He leaned in and kissed me. I twined my hands into his hair, kissing him back like there wasn't enough air, as though my touch might erase those terrible hours when I'd thought he was gone forever.

"And that's my cue to leave," Drake said. "Call if you need me for anything."

"I need a shower." I rubbed the back of my head, expecting to find blood. Instead, my hair was clean. I no longer felt like I'd taken a swim in a river of corpses, which was always a bonus.

"The witches objected to getting redcap guts on the carpet, so I used a cleansing spell or three," explained Vance.

"Ah. God. I'm starving. How many days did we lose this time?"

"Five." He passed me a cup of the energy restorative he used when his ability was overtaxed. "Isabel left you cookies, too."

"I don't deserve her. I keep disappearing and ditching her."

"She was somewhat calmer about our absence than the mages were."

"That's because they're almost as dramatic as the half-faeries." Isabel appeared in the doorway and offered a smile. "I thought I heard your voice."

"Yeah." I sat up, throwing my jacket aside. "You didn't have to give me a room here, you know. I thought most of the rooms went to half-faeries."

"They left," she replied. "Mostly. Shana and Chloe are still having to deal with the Chief hanging around making a nuisance of himself. He said that he doesn't feel safe going back to his territory without any magic."

"And the dragon shifter?" I asked. "Is he still out cold?"

"Yes, he's in the room next door," Vance said. "Quentin's watching him. I'll see if anything's changed."

He left, while Isabel studied me. "I can't believe you brought him here. Are you *sure* he's on our side?"

"He saved my life. And Vance's." I didn't need to say more. To Isabel, I was an open book, and she knew I meant that in a literal sense and on the most profound level possible.

"All right." She released a breath. "I can't pretend it's not weird having a literal *god* sleeping in the house, but that talisman of yours is partway there and it's been with you for months."

"Exactly." I looked for my sword out of habit and released a breath when I saw it propped against the bedside table. "I'm gonna shower. I realise I've been doused in cleansing spells, but it'll be a while before I forget I spent ages crawling through a sea of corpses."

"Charming." Isabel shook her head. "And yet, precisely what I expected of you."

I grinned and then grimaced when I took a drink of the foul-tasting liquid Vance had given me. At least the energy boost made me feel slightly less like a zombie and I managed to shower without falling over. I felt even better when I returned to the bedroom and found Vance had set down two trays of homemade lasagna on the desk. I had to admit that Quentin's cooking alone was reason enough to forgive him for almost any transgressions.

Vance gestured to the chair next to his. "I know it's not much of a date, but I'd like you to come and join me for dinner."

"No, it's perfect." I sat down and dug into my meal. "Who else is here?"

"Drake. I don't think he's having a good time staying at the mages' shelter now Lady Harper is there. Other than that, half the Laurel Coven is here, plus our dragon shifter friend."

A shriek came from outside.

"And the piskies," he added. "Erwin doesn't get along with the one we brought back with us. Isabel keeps having to break up fights."

"We can take the other piskie with us to the manor,' I said. "When it's secure enough for us to go back."

"I believe all the wards are in place now," Vance said. "But it's up to you. When the war's over, and Fionn's gone…"

"And things are back to normal?"

He smiled at me. "Normal?"

"No such thing, I know."

Vance updated me on the current situation while we ate. There'd been sporadic attacks from furies over the past few days but no major incidents. Vance had told the council that we'd encountered Fionn and the Morrigan and both were still at large, but not that we'd come so close to annihilation. Everyone knew we'd brought an unconscious shifter back with us, too, but Vance had opted not to share the details. He'd left the decision up to me.

I got to my feet. "I guess I should check on our guest."

I went through the corridor into the neighbouring bedroom. The dragon shifter had been carefully laid on the bed and presumably doused in a cleansing spell, because he wasn't covered in blood any longer. While sleeping, he looked more humanlike than godlike and I could actually focus on his face this time around. He and Vance had the same strong-boned features, but I only picked up on the resemblance because I knew they were very distantly related, and Vance was so familiar to me.

"Wonder why the shifters don't have magic like he does?"

I murmured to Vance. "I guess shapeshifting is a kind of magic in itself, though."

"Yes," Vance said, "and the gods were stripped of most of their power a long time ago."

"There is that." The implications made my head swim. I looked down at the unconscious shifter again. "It's probably for the best that I never got the name of the other deity out of him, but… well, I'm starting to wonder if I should pay a visit to the Winter Court. I can't imagine they want Fionn squatting in the Morrigan's castle."

"No, I expect not," Vance said. "I would hope that they'd feel a sense of responsibility, too, given that he was originally from their Court before he betrayed them."

"Not sure the Sidhe know the meaning of the word." Their irresponsibility had kicked off this war to begin with. "But yeah, I think they'd want to know their Huntsman was an impostor. I'm surprised they haven't assigned someone to take his place. I can only assume nobody important has died in recent years, or else they'd have chosen a replacement sooner."

"That doesn't seem like the kind of job offered to just anyone," Vance observed. "Even the Sidhe have standards."

"I guess not." I thought. "Well, Fionn still had the Huntsman's magic when they bound him. That might've caused complications."

"In what way?"

"Well, the Huntsman's magic is… not the same as the other Sidhe." To say the least. "He can't be affected by Invocations, for one, because his duty makes him immune. The Sidhe didn't want their enemies gaining control over someone who literally chooses whether they're reborn or doomed to eternal suffering."

Vance inclined his head. "That makes sense. Invocations

are stronger than almost all other magic, and they wouldn't have wanted any loopholes."

"Nope." I groaned. "Wait. Shit. Fionn stole the parchment with the Invocations from me and ripped it to pieces. I forgot."

Vance's eyes widened. "You don't remember any of them?"

"I can still read the symbols." I ducked my head. "Sorry. I guess they were your family's property."

"It's not your fault," he said. "If Fionn's magic makes him immune to commands, that would mean the other Sidhe can't use Invocations to fight him, either."

"Exactly." Ingenious, in a way, that he'd made himself all but bulletproof. "When Fionn betrayed them, all the Sidhe would have needed to do when they found out he was a thief and a traitor was to use one of those Invocations to rip away his magic, but he evaded them."

"Unlike the other exiles."

"Yeah." I took in a breath. "You know, when I sent the Morrigan out of this realm, I'm sure I used the same Invocation the Sidhe use when they exile one of their own. Not sure if it's as effective coming from me, but it'd be nice to think she's permanently locked out of our world. I never saw her in the palace, so I'm not sure if he has her imprisoned or if she's roaming around Faerie."

"I doubt he wants her out of his sight." A muscle ticked in Vance's jaw. "Did Fionn say anything else to you while you were imprisoned? Any hints at how we might get the upper hand on him?"

"He got pissed off with me for calling him a spoiled brat throwing a tantrum," I said. "Otherwise, he said our realm would fall as a side effect of him fucking up the Courts. I wondered if his shenanigans in the Death Kingdom are the reason none of the necromancers can reach the afterlife. I bet he's responsible for the faerie magic draining out of this realm, too."

"Yes." His mouth thinned. "Enslaving the Morrigan is bound to have had other effects throughout the faerie realm as well as in ours."

Guilt gnawed at me. "He took Roseanne, too. I left her behind again. She took off before I could get her home." What of the Morrigan, though? Why had he put her in chains? The last time they'd worked together, they'd had an agreement: he'd give her half his army of half-faerie ghosts in exchange for her assistance, but I was still unclear on how she fit into the next part of his plan.

"She's free, though?"

"He bound her with a vow." My chest tightened. "The Morrigan, too, I assume. No idea why."

"She's a goddess of death," Vance said. "Fionn wants to avoid dying by any means possible, and without the cauldron, he's lost that insurance."

"Oh." A possibility nudged at me. "If she can tear out souls, maybe she can reattach them, too. Without the cauldron, Fionn is more vulnerable than before, and he wants to cover his bases. As a bonus, her being chained to him means she can't rip his soul out if he annoys her."

"That means if we kill her first, we can prevent him from resurrecting from death, if only temporarily."

"Yeah... that's true." Like with the ring, Fionn had been determined to account for every possible weakness that might be used against him. And that, above all, proved he could be beaten. "You know what? I think we can get him. He's as weak to iron as ever, and the Morrigan isn't immune to Invocations like he is. Might be as easy as extracting fire imps from a burning house, but I reckon we have a shot."

"We'd have to kill him in Faerie," Vance reminded me. "I don't doubt you're capable of repeating your last victory over him, but we have yet to find a way to stop him coming back as a wraith."

"Dammit, Vance." He was right, though. If I killed him, even with iron, Fionn would remain a wraith until he found a way to secure a new body, with the Morrigan's help or otherwise. 'Easy as extracting fire imps from a burning house' had been upgraded to 'easy as putting out a fire with a chimera's tongue'. Which is to say, almost impossible.

Not if our army was all human.

"That's not to say we can't do it," he added. "But we'll need the Sidhe's help."

"Yeah… I just don't know how to convince Winter where I failed with Summer," I admitted. "The Unseelie Queen is probably as inaccessible as the Erlking of the Seelie Court."

"Not if we have a strong case to bring to them," Vance said. "Representatives for our cause."

Oh. "We need to reform the Council of Twelve."

"Yes," said Vance. "A unity of all the supernaturals across all our realms. It won't do to meet in secret like before, either. Everyone needs to know this time."

"You're right. We wouldn't be in half as much trouble if the last council had decided to share the truth outside of their ranks before they all got killed." Though there were some glaring obstacles in the way. "Not sure we can get *all* the supernaturals to join, though. Outside of the mages and the witches, I'm not sure the necromancers will have any volunteers, given that they don't even have a leader. Oh, and the shifters probably won't listen to us."

"I intend to speak to them tomorrow."

"And the half-faeries?" I didn't know how they would react to finding out that Fionn had invaded Winter's territory, either. The Chief himself might be loyal to Summer, but some of his allies were Unseelie, though none of them would be of much use in battle without their magic.

"We'll let them sort out their own leadership issues first," he said. "Like the necromancers. However, I believe that contacting the Sidhe is the highest priority. Quentin has been in communication with his other family in the Summer Court, and they'll be aware of what's happening in Winter by now."

I made a sceptical noise. While Fionn's threat wasn't as ignorable now he'd trespassed into their own realm, Summer and Winter were estranged enough that one wouldn't jump to defend the other. "It's Winter who are the most at risk, but I'm not sure they'd willingly ally with humans, even to save their own realm."

The Unseelie Queen wouldn't take an attack on her territory lightly, but it didn't sound like she or her people were fans of the Morrigan, and her response might depend on whether the rest of her Court disliked Fionn more than they did the goddess of death.

"It's worth trying," he said. "Quentin said that his family in Summer has agreed to send emissaries to meet with us tomorrow morning."

"You made it up with him?" I asked. "Was that when I was unconscious after fighting the Morrigan?"

He inclined his head. "It seems petty to waste time on grievances amongst ourselves at a time like this."

"I don't think it's petty for you to be mad at him for lying to you your whole life."

"He didn't lie. He couldn't. I just didn't ask the right questions." He shook his head. "I followed my grandfather's example when I allowed him to stay in the manor and work for me. I never felt entirely at ease with the decision. It felt like exploitation, and I never understood why he refused payment."

"Faeries don't have any concept of money," I said. "You were probably way nicer to him than the Sidhe are. I bet they're nasty to their servants."

"You'd be surprised," he said. "Brownies have powerful magic of their own. They don't often get taken advantage of. However, this dual arrangement is unusual."

"No kidding," I said. "He didn't tell you about his other family. That's a big enough red flag on its own, isn't it?"

"He assumed they were lost to him after the invasion," said Vance. "He told me that until recently, he hadn't been to visit them since before the faeries came."

"I guess to the Sidhe, that was five minutes ago." I rolled my eyes. "I guess I can see where it would have come in handy for the council to employ someone who had a foot in both worlds, but… I don't know."

Whatever I thought of the brownie's divided loyalties, forgiveness was for Vance to offer, not me.

"Quentin has made up for lost time in telling me everything he knew of how the Council of Twelve was set up," he added. "Enough that I think we can do so again, provided we get enough people."

"Isn't that just the problem," I said. "Sure, we might be able to get someone from Summer, but every Winter faerie I've met has been a total menace. The Unseelie Queen must know Fionn is encroaching on her territory, but the Sidhe have this annoying tendency to make everything into a complicated song and dance and dither around as though we have all the time in the world. Which we don't."

"Precisely," Vance said, "which is why we need to speak to her sooner rather than later."

"How? I can't get there from here, and I don't have an invitation to their Court even if I could."

"You know how to get there," said Quentin from behind

us, making me jump. "Do you remember the clearing where we first entered the faerie realm?"

"Yes, I do." I looked askance at him. "I also remember telling you I don't like people sneaking up on me."

"My apologies," he said evenly. "I thought it prudent to tell you that both Courts are joined to the mortal realm along the same path. If we enter the Summer Court the same way we did the last time, you merely need to follow the path in the opposite direction to reach Winter's domain."

"Are you sure?" I asked. "You've never been, have you?"

"No, and I am not permitted to enter Winter," he said. "You'll have to go in alone, and there is a strong chance you will run into danger."

"Child's play," I said. "Compared to Fionn's castle, anyway."

I was only half serious, knowing what total shits Winter faeries could be. The brownie ducked his head and slipped out of the room as stealthily as he'd entered. Maybe I'd been unfair when I'd snapped at him. I couldn't bring myself to mistrust him, not when he'd evidently been going out of his way to make it up to Vance. Like it or not, he was my only route into Faerie. My one chance to speak to the Courts.

"There are days when I wish we only had to deal with would-be rivals trying to oust me from my position on the mage council." Vance smiled and shook his head.

"And then you met me."

His steady gaze connected with mine. "I wouldn't change a thing."

"Neither would I," I said. "Never. But Vance... I'm going to Faerie alone tomorrow. I don't want to put you at risk. If he's there..."

"Absolutely not," Vance said. "We've been through this before."

"You *died*. I watched you—I watched him have you slaughtered." Tears burned my eyes and I blinked them away.

"I'm coming with you."

"I love you, Vance, but seriously. Eraenar won't be there to save you next time. There won't be any second chances."

"This is my fight, too," he said. "Fionn is the reason my family is dead."

My throat closed up. I had no argument there.

"He's the one who sought out our safe houses and destroyed the wards," he said softly. "I'm sure of it, and I'm sure he knew there were undefended children in the shelters who hadn't even come into their powers. He might not have killed Sarah himself, but he orchestrated her murder, and I have every right to stand against him alongside the mages."

"Of course you do, Vance." A tear ran down my cheek. "But I couldn't bear to lose you again. Never."

He gently touched a thumb to the teardrop, his other hand cupping the back of my head. "I've told you before, Ivy. I'm not going anywhere."

I dabbed my eyes with my knuckles. "It's so fucking ridiculous. We're on the brink of a war, and I'm starting to think killing Fionn is going to be easier than getting everyone to cooperate."

"True, perhaps," he said, "but a common enemy is a uniting factor, and it's possible that the war will spur everyone to make decisions on a much faster timeline than usual. Anyway, that's on the agenda for tomorrow."

"And what's on the agenda tonight?"

"You." He kissed me lightly and released the back of my head. "We're going for a walk."

"We are?"

"Not a long one." In a blink, Vance transported us both to the bedroom in the manor. The curtains were drawn over the balcony, though moonlight streamed in through the gap onto the plush carpet, and candles burned softly on the desk.

"I came back here while you were resting," he explained. "The manor's been cleaned out and the wards put back into place, but it's up to you if you'd like to come back afterwards."

"Yes… you didn't need to bring me here to tell me that, though." His tone suggested he was working up to something, but while the bed had been re-made since we'd last been here, I had a hard time believing he'd be this coy if he'd brought us somewhere quiet to have an extended make-out session without everyone in the witches' house overhearing us.

"No." There was a short pause. "Ivy?"

"Yes?"

"This isn't how I planned to do this. I know it's a little soon, but we might be fighting a war tomorrow. I had every intention of waiting for the opportune moment, but waiting doesn't always work in our favour."

No way. Heat seared my cheeks, and my heart began to beat faster.

Cool air blew into the room, making the curtains flutter and raising the hair on my head. A box appeared in his hands, and the next second he was down on one knee. My mouth dropped open.

"Vance? You're serious?"

He smiled. "Are you going to let me say the words?"

"Yes. I am." *I think.* Of all the surprises he could have come up with.

"Ivy Lane, would you marry me?"

My throat was dry. He'd really said it.

"Are you sure you're serious?"

"Very much so." His smile was sincere, maybe a little nervous. The ring he held out was a simple band inset with a white diamond. My heart drummed against my ribcage. I'd faced Sidhe, faced living gods, but I'd never faced this before. Never believed I'd meet someone who truly saw me, chose me above all others, and offered me his heart.

"I expected more of a performance."

He took my hand. "I suspected it'd make little difference to you either way. I'd like to spend the rest of my life with you, Ivy, if you'll have me."

And just like that: the decision was easy. Whoever I'd been before—before Faerie, and after—I wasn't that person now. I'd stared death in the face, felt the despair of losing the one I loved, and I'd never look back.

"Of course I will. Yes, Vance, I'll marry you."

"Good." A smile lit up his grey eyes. "We can make the arrangements afterwards."

"Gives me another incentive to survive." I ran a finger over the ring, which disappeared as a cool breeze stirred the air and skimmed against my skin. "I think you did have an ulterior motive bringing me here. It's quiet."

He drew his arms around me and nuzzled my neck. "That may have been a factor. I think some of the others might have guessed, and I didn't want Drake to hang around listening at the door."

"Ha. He probably would. Is he going to be the best man?"

Vance frowned. "I didn't even think about that."

I poked him in the arm. "You just asked me to marry you. Stands to reason we get to have a wedding, right?"

"Yes." He groaned. "Last time Drake was invited to a wedding, he ended up running away with two of the bridesmaids."

I cracked up laughing. "Well, someone else will have to supervise. I'm not letting you out of my sight."

"Agreed." He wrapped his arms around me, his warm gaze

capturing mine. "I don't want anything else more than I want this."

"Nor me. Isabel's going to freak out. I'll have to wait until after the battle to tell her. She'll start designing dresses and bouquets. Of course, I might just show up in jeans and my bloodstained jacket. Just to screw with Lady Harper, obviously. Wait, have you told *her*?"

"I haven't. This was… a rather hurried decision."

"No kidding." I leaned my forehead against his, hearing the sound of his rapid heartbeat. *I knew he was nervous.* Strangely, that made the idea of a wedding less daunting. I wasn't marrying the Mage Lord, but Vance, the man I loved. I breathed in the scent of him, felt his closeness, wished I could bottle this moment and take it with me when we entered the upcoming war. But whatever tomorrow brought, we still had tonight.

Vance kissed me again, softly at first. I went along with it, happy to enjoy every second of being just us, and pretending the outside world didn't exist. His arms circled me, pulling me against his hard body. The kiss turned more fevered, more intense. His gaze simmered, eyes dark with need. For me. A thrill went through my bones, and my hands became more brazen in their wandering. There were too many layers of clothes between us. I grumbled something along those lines, and he whispered in my ear, "I can take care of that."

A faint breeze tickled the back of my neck as he expertly removed every article of clothing from both of us without his lips leaving mine. Now that was some skill. But he still didn't move beyond kissing, just manipulating the air to brush against my back, my shoulders and arms, then the insides of my thighs. I didn't want to rush the moment, but the teasing was too much to handle. I might not have *quite* the same array of tricks up my sleeve as he did, but I knew exactly how to get him to respond the way I wanted him to.

I trailed a hand down the tight muscles of his chest, eliciting a shudder as I reached his erection. He dropped the teasing and transported us both onto the bed, where his fingers delved into me with expert movements that had shivers racking my spine. I moaned and dug my hands into the muscles of his shoulders, pulling him onto me.

My breath came out in gasps as pleasure surged through me in hot waves. Tenderness became urgency, and my body clenched around him as desire rose and dragged me under. He gasped my name, raining kisses on my neck as we both collapsed onto the bed.

My heart's drumming beat calmed, my body relaxing against his. Vance's hands rhythmically massaged my shoulders and back, as though he couldn't stop touching me for a single moment. I stretched out, enjoying the sensation, enjoying the calm.

As my mind drifted, something came back to me.

"Vance?"

"Hmm?"

"Quentin said..." I began. "Back in Summer, he said because we're together, I count as part of your family. For the purposes of whatever vow binds him to the Coltons. Did... did you know that?"

He propped up on an elbow. "Yes, he told me. I think he knew I planned to ask you. If I didn't know better, I'd say he's starting to like you."

"Ha. Next I'll be on Lady Harper's Christmas card list."

"She does like you." He smiled. "Just save the world and you'll be in her good graces forever."

"No pressure, huh." I rolled onto my back, my gaze catching on the small box on the bedside table. I gently picked up the ring between my fingers. "I don't want to lose this in the battle."

"It's fine. I can keep it somewhere safe. Think of it as..."

"A promise? A vow?"

"If you'd prefer not to…"

"I'm good with the regular kind of promises." I smiled up at him, and a breeze skimmed over me as the ring disappeared from my hands again.

Vance leaned over and kissed me. "Good, because I can promise I'll be waiting for you when the battle is over."

"Me, too."

18

The following morning, we rose early for a long day of negotiations that might or might not end in a war, if our presence in Faerie caught Fionn's attention. Or else he'd already planned to strike against us after learning of our escape from the Morrigan's palace. Either way, we had to be ready to fight.

"I am," said Isabel, when I said so aloud. "The witches are with you, one hundred percent."

"I'm glad someone is," I said. "Because the others are being a bloody nuisance."

Vance had been unable to get through to the shifters, while the other mages were back to their usual bickering and the half-faeries had been driving the witches out of their minds with absurd demands. The one upside was that Summer had agreed to send an envoy at nine o'clock, but it was beyond me to guess if the Sidhe knew how time worked over here or if they intended to show up in a week instead. Quentin insisted they'd come, but so far, we just had the witches as definite yeses for the new council, and even then, we only had Isabel as a confirmed volunteer. Shana, her

Second, was less than enthused. In fairness, some of that might be because the Chief had turned the inside of her and Chloe's living room into a greenhouse.

"I want him out," Chloe hissed at Isabel when she entered the living room with her wife. "Can't he go back to his own territory?"

"Not while there's no magic," I said apologetically. "He won't take the risk of someone stabbing him in the back."

"If he carries on the way he is, he'll wish he'd chosen the easy way out." She cracked her knuckles, scowling.

"Don't skewer him yet. We might need him." The other half-faeries had left, for the most part, but we didn't have anyone from among their number who was an obvious pick for the new Council of Twelve. The same went for the necromancers. While they'd cooperated with the mages and had even offered some people shelter in their headquarters, their leadership issues were as prevalent as ever.

The witches, by contrast, had already set about transforming the downstairs room of Francine's house into a base for war preparations. At Isabel's instruction, they arranged spell circles on the floor to make a fresh batch of explosive spells and defensive wards ready for anyone who might need them.

"Did you say Summer was sending people here?" Isabel asked me in an undertone, supervising the preparations from the doorway so she wouldn't have to tread around a dozen spell circles to answer the front door.

"Supposedly they're meeting us at the mages' safe house, but you know what they're like. They could appear in five minutes or turn up when it's already over." I checked the clock mounted on the wall. We had maybe half an hour left until the designated meeting time. "Vance is over there now. The other regional Mage Lords are making noises about showing up after all, as if we don't already have enough bull-shit on our hands."

"Why would they come?" Isabel asked. "To help in the fight?"

"I wish," I said. "No, to argue and undermine Vance and probably stand in the way of our attempts to set up the new council. I realise that it might be a bit premature to start an official thing now, without consulting the other regions, but we've got a war on our doorstep."

"I know."

Isabel was dressed for it, too. Recently she'd changed out of her usual flowery dresses into more subdued, dark-coloured outfits, and she wore bands on both arms with defensive witch runes marked on them. That was in addition to the glyphs that appeared on her skin whenever her life was in danger, marks designed to protect the coven leader. The witches might not be at the centre of the battle, but she'd still be a potential target for trouble.

A few minutes before our planned meeting, Vance and Drake appeared in the hallway.

"The Sidhe aren't here yet, but Quentin's adamant that they'll be punctual," said Vance. "Did you ask your coven about our plans for the new council?"

Isabel nodded. "They don't object to me stepping forward, but none of them have volunteered to join me yet. You need twelve people in total?"

"Doesn't have to be," I said. "Two members of each super-natural group should stop any potential arguments about favouritism, though."

"Agreed," said Vance. "Quentin has volunteered to get things started, since he's a previous member. I imagine the Hemlock witches would like to be involved, at least on an advisory basis. Lady Harper, too."

That did make sense, though I hoped the latter would turn us down. "We'd need someone from Winter as well, to match Quentin. And a noble each of the Seelie and Unseelie Courts. Oh, and the half-bloods. They won't want to be left out. And…"

"You," said Vance.

"Me?" I blinked. "I'm human."

"With faerie magic," said Drake. "Winter, right? There's no saying whether the Unseelie will volunteer one of their people."

"Probably not, but I don't count as Winter, given that my power comes from… oh, fine," I relented, as the three of them gave me pointed looks. "You win. So, there are eight of us so far. We'd need at least one more witch, a couple of necromancers… and shifters."

Vance's jaw tensed. "They still haven't answered my calls."

"Aren't they worried?" asked Isabel. "I mean, some of them live right next to the Ley Line."

"You know what they're like. Stubborn to a fault." I shook my head. "They'll probably be the last to volunteer. Knowing them, they'll show up when the meeting's already in progress and demand to know why we left them out."

"That's a possibility," Vance said. "I do think the current issues with the veil are also affecting the shifters, so there's a chance they'll be more amenable after the battle is over."

After it's over. We kept talking like there was a future, as though it didn't wait on the other side of a vast gulf that might contain anything from a horde of rabid piranhas to a giant dragon shifter.

"Well, I hope you can stop the war before it starts," Isabel said. "Shouldn't you be going?"

"Yep. Let's see if the Summer Sidhe keep their word."

I hugged Isabel and then joined Vance and Drake. We landed at the mages' safe house a heartbeat later, where Quentin waited in the front garden. *He'd better be right.*

Dead on nine o'clock, a flash of green light announced the arrival of several horsemen, all dressed in the green-and-gold finery of the Summer Court. Evidently, they *could* keep to human time, if they wanted to. Upon seeing them, Quentin dropped into a bow that seemed mostly directed at a fair-haired Sidhe whose horse stood next to Lord Raivan's. *Is that his other master?*

"Nice to see you again, Lord Raivan." At least he wasn't accompanied by his backstabbing friend Lord Burdock this time, but I didn't know any of the other Sidhe who'd come with him. The Sidhe who Quentin had bowed to looked similar enough to Lord Raivan to make me wonder if the two were related, though it was hard to tell with the Sidhe.

"Ivy Lane," he said. "Quentin tells me you have a proposal for the Summer Court."

"Correct," I said. "You might have noticed Fionn has taken Winter's entire Death Kingdom hostage, and he won't stop until he's conquered the whole of Faerie. That includes your Court, if you didn't pick up on the implication."

"I see you have reunited with your mage companion," said Lord Raivan. "Surely you have no further need of us."

"Hello? Didn't you hear the part about a war knocking on Summer's door any second now?"

"We are not permitted to enter Winter's territory without a prior arrangement with the Unseelie Queen."

"You must be able to sense that almost all the magic has drained out of this realm," I said impatiently. "That's Fionn's doing, and I wouldn't put it past him to try doing the same to you. He's also enslaved the Morrigan. You know, the death goddess who can rip out souls, including yours."

Lord Raivan's mouth tightened. "What would you have us do?"

"Fight with us," I said. "There's no magic left in this realm, so it's easier for us to fight him on his own turf." *Also, he's fucked around with Death, so killing him here would make it impossible for me to destroy his spirit as well as his body.*

"I will not trespass on the territory of the Winter Court," he said tightly. "They would punish us greatly."

"Winter will be on your side," I said. "I haven't had a chance to talk to them yet, but I will. They don't want their territory invaded by a usurping wannabe death god."

"Winter are not our allies," said Lord Raivan. "Neither are the humans. The last time we intervened in a war on your behalf, we paid the price in blood."

"Some of you stopped Fionn from destroying all our realms, thanks to an alliance with the humans. Now you have the chance to do it again. And you can't kid yourself that he won't come after you next. He wants the Courts obliterated."

Lord Raivan cast a look at the other Sidhe. From their expressions of blank indifference, I didn't know if they'd listened to a word I'd said. "This is unprecedented. We cannot act without the Erlking's permission, and conveying the urgency to him would require all the Sidhe lords of influence to come to an agreement."

A chorus of yowls interrupted my reply. Erwin and the other piskie came flying out of the house, brawling in midair like fighting street cats. They pulled at once another's ears with tiny hands, punched one another with enthusiasm, and generally made an ungodly racket.

"Oh, for god's sake." I'd thought we'd left them back at the witches' place, but apparently not. "Erwin, stop that. Can't you see we have visitors?"

"Traitor!" Erwin yelled, punching the other piskie in the mouth. "Traitor piskie human."

"Shut *up*." I grabbed the other piskie by the scruff of his neck while Vance caught Erwin's wing between his fingertips. "Have you not noticed the Sidhe are here?"

Erwin sank into a bow in midair, his wings fluttering. "Apologies, Lord Sidhe. This traitor piskie is—"

"Sorry, I have no idea what he's going on about." I fought to stop the other piskie from squirming out of my hands. "Keep still."

"Are you aware that the one you're holding is human?" Lord Raivan enquired.

"What?" My gaze dropped to the piskie. "Seriously?"

"Yes. He's bespelled, but he was not always in his current state."

Damn. Was that why he'd been Fionn's prisoner? "Erm… can you undo it?"

"In this realm, no, I cannot."

"Then in Faerie. It's important. This piskie—he was spying on Fionn. He might know how to beat him." Unlikely, admittedly, but the piskie had helped the dragon shifter find me while I'd been in Fionn's castle, and I was curious to know how he'd ended up being held prisoner alongside the mages.

"Humans aren't allowed to enter the faerie realm."

"Oh, for god's sake." I sighed. "How about the Grey Vale? I'm guessing you've never been."

His blank expression confirmed my guess. "Is that not where your enemy is based?"

"Not now he's stolen the Death Kingdom as his own," I replied. "I can take you to the Vale myself, but we'd need to be on a spirit line. Or in Faerie itself. Whichever you want."

From Lord Raivan's expression, I might as well have asked him if he fancied attending a summit at the necromancers' guild. "Absolutely not. The Vale is for exiles only."

"Actually, it was made for the gods," I said. "There's more magic there than here. It'll take five minutes."

"Swear on it."

"What, like a vow?"

"If you intend to harm me, or if you lie, you will forfeit your life."

"No problem," I said easily. "I accept those conditions. Now come *on*."

Lord Raivan walked to my side, wearing a scowl. This was a ridiculous diversion, but I was kind of curious to know who the piskie really was. And who knew, maybe a trip into the Vale would give the Sidhe an idea of what they were really up against.

I released the piskie. "You want to be human again, don't you?"

"Yes, human, yes!" He landed on my shoulder and dug his clawed feet into my jacket.

"We'll go with you." Vance approached, with Quentin at his heels.

"Lord Torin has offered permission for the Mage Lord to come to the Summer Court," the brownie said to Lord Raivan, when he began to voice an objection. "He comes with us."

"Fine." Lord Raivan gestured, and a flash of green light enveloped the garden. As it faded, the ordinary street was replaced by the clearing through which we'd entered the Summer Court. Lord Raivan gave me an expectant look. "You can find this Vale from here?"

"Yes." This was going to be awkward. With the piskie hanging onto my shoulder, I took Vance's hand in mine and reached for Lord Raivan with the other. "Better hang on tight."

Lord Raivan's jaw tensed when I grabbed his wrist, as though the very notion of being touched by a human offended him beyond measure. Ignoring his reaction, I felt my way out of the clearing, reaching towards the grey nothingness of the Vale.

The instant our feet touched down on the silver-lit path,

the piskie launched into flight, shrieking. I waved a hand, already regretting this whole endeavour. "Be *quiet*, or else I'll leave you behind." The piskie fell silent, whimpering, and I turned to our silent companion. "Are you okay over there, Lord Raivan?"

"What *is* this place?" He stared around, horror distorting his features. "It feels—dead."

"Didn't anyone teach you?" You'd think his centuries-long existence would have brought him to this hellhole at some point. "Your fellow Sidhe created this place as a prison. Now, come on. Work your magic and we can get out of here."

Lord Raivan raised his hands. There was a clap of thunder, a flash of green light, and Larsen lay crumpled on the path in front of us.

"Larsen?" My old boss was alive? His clothes were torn and bloodied and his straw-like hair was in disarray, but it was definitely him. "Who turned you into a piskie?"

Fionn? No, it was more likely to have been the big-mouthed Sidhe who'd captured the mages and locked them in that tower.

Larsen lifted his head and emitted a couple of high-pitched noises before he found his voice. "Ivy Lane, what have you done?"

"Turned you human again. You're welcome."

"Where am I?"

"Grey Vale. You know that. You've been here for weeks."

Larsen gaped. Then his eyes rolled back in his head and he keeled over, unconscious.

"So much for him being a useful spy." Sticking around in the Vale wasn't wise, so I looked to Lord Raivan. He was staring down the silver-lit path as though contemplating a coffin with his name on it. "Hey. We're leaving."

The Sidhe lord jerked his head in acknowledgement. With reluctance, I took his wrist again and reached for

Larsen with the other hand. *Ugh. Better wash my hands when we're home.*

Vance rested a hand on my shoulder, and together we crossed the veil. We landed on the edge of the pit where we'd once found the dragon shifter.

Problem: it wasn't deserted this time. A dozen shifters milled around, and they zeroed in on our mismatched group at once. At least they were in human form, but based on their expressions of absolute outrage, that would not be the case for long.

"Ah." I held up my hands to show I was unarmed. "Sorry. Didn't mean to cross over here."

A blond man stepped in front of the others, his muscular form coiled tight as though ready to shift at any second. "You're on our territory."

I know that. I hadn't consciously thought about where to cross realms, but my magic must have brought me to the area closest to the mages' safe house—and the shifters had decided to come to the Ley Line at precisely the wrong moment.

"Why have you brought one of *them* here?" A heavyset female shifter looked at Lord Raivan in disgust.

Predictably, the Sidhe raised his staff and addressed the shifters in haughty tones. "I am a knight of the Seelie Court, and I will not be spoken to in that way by mortal degenerates."

"He doesn't mean that," I said, as a collective growl went through the shifters. "Seriously—*stop it.*"

The blond shifter leaped at Lord Raivan, his hands shifting into furred paws. Vance raised a hand, and the shifter was thrown backwards mid-dive.

"Think carefully," Vance said, stepping between the shifters and our group. "Do you want to start a war with the Faerie Courts?"

"They're invading our territory," spat the shifter. "This *is* war."

"It's my nephew," said a familiar voice from the middle of the group of shifters. "He never had any respect for us. He is my brother's child, through and through—causing disruption wherever he goes."

The shifters parted to make way for Wyatt Colton, Vance's uncle. His wife and daughter didn't seem to be here, thankfully, but I'd bet my sword he was behind this impromptu gathering.

"It was my idea," I said, with a sideways look at Vance. He and his uncle had been at odds since an argument that Wyatt had had with Vance's father prior to the invasion, the details of which even Vance didn't know. While Wyatt's grudge was also tied to the mages' treatment of shifters in the time before the invasion, I'd never understand how he could blame Vance for events that had taken place before he was even born, let alone Mage Lord.

"Your idea," said Wyatt. "Of course. It seems fitting that my nephew would ally himself with someone with a worse reputation than he has."

"Thanks for the compliment." I turned to the blond shifter. "By the way, Wyatt hid underground in the invasion while Vance's father fought to protect this realm. He was also the person responsible for that." I pointed over my shoulder at the hole in the ground where the dragon shifter had once been imprisoned.

Wyatt went purple when all the shifters' eyes turned to him. "I—I was manipulated by one of her faeries."

"I *killed* the faerie responsible," I said. "And you'll get worse if you ignore what's coming. Either go into hiding or come and fight. There's no other option. Don't say I didn't give you fair warning."

"You turned away my emissaries," Vance added. "My

mages have sent warning no fewer than five times, but each time, you refused to listen or to allow them to explain."

"The last time your mages came to our territory, people were killed," said Wyatt.

"By the *faeries*," I said. "And trust me, if you think the Lady of the Tree was bad, you should see Fionn. I don't want you to die, believe it or not, but we're short on time and I'm not kidding when I say you'll probably be the first to get trampled if he comes through the Ley Line. I'll be taking my own army over into the faeries' realm first, but if they attack while I'm gone, there's nothing I can do to stop them. What I *can* do is ensure you won't have to fight them alone. We're forming an alliance across all supernaturals and we want to invite you to join."

"Your former Mage Lords tried to tie us to treaties that took away our rights," said the blond shifter. "We don't forget our history."

"There won't be a formal agreement," said Vance. "Just an understanding. We're offering to help you defend your territory, alongside the witches, necromancers, mages and half-faeries."

"The faeries are the enemy," snarled another shifter. "Aren't they who you say is invading this realm?"

"The half-bloods aren't. Okay, Fionn might have some of them in his army," I amended. "Not the ones already in the city. They won't hurt you. They can't even use magic in this realm, anyway."

"I will not spend another second here." Lord Raivan vanished in a flash of green light that kicked off a chorus of exclamations and roars of indignant rage.

"You dare bring your magic to our territory?" bellowed the blond shifter.

"He got bored with your yelling," I shouted back. "Fine. Vance, let's just leave them."

"Wait." Vance addressed Wyatt. "Are Rita and Anabel at the safe house?"

"Yes," his uncle ground out. "Even though you had the audacity to send my family to the home of the dead."

"The necromancer guild is one of the safest places in the city," Vance said.

He'd sent them to stay with the necromancers? *I guess it is the closest safe house that doesn't belong to the mages.*

"So are you going to fight this time?" I asked Wyatt. "Or hide underground like before?"

"You wouldn't understand, girl. You were a kid."

"I nearly died in the invasion because I was kidnapped and taken to Faerie," I said. "You hid underground while Vance's parents died, and you'd have to make some seriously messed-up logical leaps to blame him, considering he was ten years old when the invasion happened."

"Let them die? They willingly looked the other way while the shifters were massacred."

"That isn't true," said Vance. "You know perfectly well that there was nothing the mages could have done to prevent the effects of the Ley Line opening upon your people, no more than they were able to stop the Sidhe from killing so many of their own."

"And yet they were hailed as heroes anyway."

"Look," said Vance through gritted teeth. "I don't know what you said to my father before the invasion, or what he said to you, but the world would be in a considerably worse state if the mages hadn't fought back against the Sidhe. Now we intend to do so again, and we would like to invite you to join us. The Sidhe are coming either way, but there's strength in numbers. Think on it."

Before his uncle could reply, Vance transported us away. Our small group—Larsen included—landed in the hallway of the witches' headquarters. Isabel, who was still in the doorway, jumped at our sudden appearance. "Oh—Ivy. I thought you were at the mages' place."

"Change of plans." I indicated Larsen's unconscious body. "Turns out *he* was the other piskie. Lord Raivan had to turn him back into a human."

Behind her, Erwin flew around the main room and yelled about bad faeries. He must have flown all the way here from the mages' headquarters after we'd gone into the Vale.

Isabel winced at the noise. "Fionn turned him into a piskie? Why?"

"Why do the Sidhe do anything? Because they can." I prodded him with my foot. He stirred a little but didn't get up. "How much time have we lost?"

"A couple of hours," Isabel said. "I've been talking to the coven. And the mages, but I think they had some other visitors show up."

"Not the other regional mages." Annoyance flickered across Vance's face. "Now is not the time."

"Bad human!" Erwin yelled from behind Isabel.

Larsen groaned from the floor. "Where *am* I?"

"Home." I nudged him with my foot. "You passed out after you were turned into a human again."

Erwin flew out of the room and tried to dive-bomb him. Isabel reached out and caught the piskie mid-flight, shushing him. "Relax, Erwin. We'll get him out of here soon enough."

"What?" Larsen climbed to his knees. "You... Ivy Lane?"

"That's me." How much of his own senses had he retained while trapped as a piskie? From the way he'd talked at the time, it had sounded like his brain had shrunk to match his new body, and he hadn't had a lot in that department to begin with. "Please tell me you overheard something useful while you were stuck in Fionn's tower. How'd you end up there anyway?"

"I don't remember," he said. "One second I was at... the

guild." His moment's hesitation suggested he'd been about to say 'casino' instead. He sure hadn't been fighting the furies amongst the other mercenaries, anyway. "Then some faerie grabbed me."

"Seriously?" I said. "I guess Fionn thought you might be a useful hostage."

Which was laughable, but another piece of evidence that Fionn didn't really know me at all.

Isabel held Erwin at arm's length and gave him a push. "Go on, wait outside. He'll be gone when you come back."

Larsen shuddered. "I was tied up in this tower, and… and I don't remember much after that. Except when you showed up and escaped with the mage. I tried to follow you out, but I got lost, and the next thing I knew I was… there. In that palace."

"Did you see anything inside the palace?" I asked. "Do you remember it?"

He lowered his gaze. "I was in this… this giant hall, and there was this massive crow."

"The Morrigan," I surmised. "Did you see him, too? Fionn? He wasn't the same faerie who took you. That was one of his allies. He might have been riding a horse."

Another shudder racked his body. "Yes. There were a few of them, horsemen wearing masks. They pinned down the giant crow and put this chain on her foot, while one of the horsemen—he killed people. Faeries."

"Sacrifices?" I guessed. "He probably needed to take lives from Summer and Winter to bind her to him."

Which meant the binding was permanent, in all likelihood.

"Sacrifices," he repeated. "I never asked to get dragged into this bullshit. What did I ever do to deserve it?"

I bit back a laugh. "I mean, there was the whole thing

when you had your people turn off my wards and let fire imps into our back garden. Isabel remembers, too, right?"

Isabel scowled. "Yes. I lost a whole batch of valuable herbs that were meant for the coven."

His face flushed. "That wasn't me."

"You didn't try to stop them," I retaliated. "And you've been trying to poach our clients ever since Isabel and I set up shop independently. Don't bother denying it."

His flush deepened. "You badmouthed me behind my back."

"I didn't say anything that wasn't true," I pointed out. "Do you recall anything else from the palace? Did Fionn actually say anything to the Morrigan? To the crow?"

He stared at me for a moment. "He said—words. I didn't understand them."

"Invocations?" I guessed.

"I dunno, but he also said she was bound to him, that she'd… she'd preserve his soul if he died. I don't want to think about this shit, Ivy."

"None of us do." I'd confirmed my guess that the Morrigan was Fionn's insurance. And the key to his ongoing immortality. "Luckily, you don't have to. If you run fast enough."

Isabel opened the door. "Be thankful. You might get turned into worse than a piskie the next time the faeries think you have something they want."

He gulped and fled the house, pelting down the garden path faster than I'd ever seen him move. Isabel closed the door on him with a satisfied nod. "Well, that was enlightening," she said. "I wonder if his personality will improve after spending a while as an eight-inch twiglet with wings?"

"I have my doubts." Vance said. He'd let Isabel and me berate Larsen without getting involved, though he'd clearly had some choice words of his own. "If the mages from outside of the local region have shown up at the safe h ouse, I need to head there right away."

"Because what we really need right now is our least favourite bureaucrat stomping around." I rolled my eyes. "Her *and* Lady Harper in the same room. You know what, maybe I should have stayed in the Vale."

"I'll make it clear that I'm still making the decisions," Vance said. "You don't have to come."

"Oh, I'm there." Whatever Lady Granville wanted, I refused to let her divert everyone's attention from the real emergency.

Vance transported us to the doorstep of the mages' safe house, where we found Drake lurking outside.

"What are you doing?" I asked.

"Waiting for you," he retaliated. "Or... okay, I'm hiding. Lady Granville's in there, and she's already got half the regional mages answering to her beck and call."

"Did you mention our plans for the council?" Vance asked.

Drake shifted on his feet. "Erm... no. You know she'd prefer to hear it coming from you."

Vance sighed. "Then let's go in."

As we did so, a commotion erupted and the council members rose to their feet. The room was much more crowded than earlier, and I recognised a number of familiar faces among the newcomers. Including Lady Granville, a forty-something mage wearing a funerary black outfit instead of her usual mouldy yellow or green ensemble, her customary scowl even darker than usual. She and Lady Penrose had been friends and co-conspirators in their attempts to oust Vance from his position as head mage, but even in the depths of grief, she'd managed to find time to ruin my day.

Vance silenced everyone with a stare. "My apologies for

the delay. I was meeting with representatives from the Summer Court."

"I thought we were at war with the faeries," said Lady Granville.

"Not those faeries," I said impatiently. "The exiles. Haven't you had time to get up to speed yet?"

Drake laughed, then fell silent when Vance gave him a warning look.

Taking a seat, he addressed the council. "We're currently at war with the exiles of the Vale, and we're currently gathering allies and preparing for the upcoming fight. I assume that since you're here, you came to join in."

Ha. Lady Granville's tight-lipped expression told me she'd expected an easier victory. The other mages stirred, but none of them raised their voice to argue.

I sat on Vance's left and Drake took the other side, smirking at Lady Granville. "That's right. We'd really appreciate the help."

"Actually," she said, "we're here because we heard you were having difficulties establishing a council after the shocking deaths of your fellow members and the Mage Lord's capture."

Or to take his place. "Vance is fine, which you ought to know, since you've spoken to him several times since his return. Anyway, like Drake said, we're forming alliances. If you're not here to fight, you can help us do that. The coven has agreed to lend their support."

"As have the necromancers," said Vance. "I have extended the same offer to the shifters—"

"What?" said one of the mages. "We can't work with them."

Vance flashed him a dangerous look. "We can and will, if necessary. We're outnumbered by far and the shifters offer us many advantages."

"I fail to see how allying with the shifters helps our cause," said Lady Granville. "They're as likely to turn on us as not."

"I disagree." Vance addressed the mages at large. "Petty differences are far less important than our own survival."

"There aren't enough of us anyway," said the first mage who'd spoken. "Not to take on all of Faerie."

"So we make up the numbers by recruiting other supernaturals," said Drake. "You'd better believe I'm with Vance on this one. We need the shifters. They lost as many as we did in the first invasion, if not more. They're baying for blood, and we're going to give it to them."

"Also, it isn't all of Faerie," I added. "Just one egomaniac who thinks he owns the universe. The other supernaturals have skills to offer in the fight, including the shifters."

However stubborn they might be, they'd fight with us where it mattered, which was more than I could say for Lady Granville and her ilk. It figured that the people she'd brought with her were the sort who'd unthinkingly abandon their own districts to interfere in another for the sake of their own ambitions, but every moment she forced us to waste was another potential gain for Fionn and his allies. At least Vance's people outnumbered hers, but looking at everyone gathered around the table brought the sudden chilling realisation that the mages of the invasion might have gathered in this room once. Vance's parents—hell, the parents of most people in this room—had been killed, and the entire generation of mages who'd been at the peak of their power during the last invasion had been decimated. Only a scant few had survived, most of whom were present at this very meeting. If Fionn won the upcoming battle, none would remain to salvage what was left a second time.

No. We won't let history repeat itself. We won't let him win.

"I won't be a part of this," said Lady Granville haughtily. "What's this ridiculous proposal for a cross-species council?"

Oh, great. She'd found about that, too?

"Vance's idea," said Drake. "Vance and I will represent the mages. You don't have to get involved."

"Ivy," Quentin's quiet whisper came from below the table, somewhere near my leg. "The Summer emissaries have gone, but you're unlikely to get another chance to visit Winter."

I caught Vance's eye, torn, and he nodded.

I rose upright and faced the table. "I have another appointment to keep. For all our sakes, I hope you come to a decision before I'm back."

Quentin waited in the doorway; glad of the chance to escape, I followed him through the hall and out of the house. "You can take me there now?"

"Of course," said Quentin.

"Wait." Vance emerged through the front door. Behind him, I heard raised voices, chiefly belonging to Drake and Lady Granville. "I don't want you to go alone."

"You're needed here," Quentin told him. "Moreover, the Winter Court is more likely to elect to speak to Ivy alone."

Vance looked at me, at my hand where I'd be wearing the ring when this was over. For now, it was our secret. I smiled at him. "It'll be okay."

"All right," he said quietly. "Please—come back as quickly as possible. You know where to find me."

I kissed him quickly. "Love you, Vance. I'll come back."

I turned to Quentin and took in a steadying breath. He inclined his head, and there was a bright flash of green light.

The house disappeared, replaced by the same bright clearing we'd visited during our last trip here. The blue sky and birdsong were the same as ever, but Quentin turned away from the forest and gestured towards a path that ran in the opposite direction, winding out of sight.

This sky darkened noticeably when I stepped onto the

path. Trees crowded on either side, no longer draped in leaves but stripped bare, and a chill lingered in the air.

"Keep walking that way," said Quentin. "I'm unable to enter Winter myself, but you will know when you cross the border."

"All right."

Unease slid down my back, but I'd made up my mind. As I walked, a cool breeze rattled the branches of the thick oak and ash trees. A thick canopy blotted out the sun, and with every step, the temperature plummeted. Snow soon coated the branches I passed, and my teeth chattered. *You will know when you cross the border. No kidding.*

It was time to introduce myself to the Winter Sidhe.

19

The Unseelie Court was, to put it mildly, bloody freezing. Ice coated the trees and crunched beneath my feet. I huddled inside my jacket and walked faster to warm up, aided by the boost to my magic that had accompanied my arrival into Faerie. Winter had none of the brilliant colours and vibrancy of Summer, nor the overpowering flowery perfume or lilting music. I passed by a series of trees the colour of bone, their sharp branches forming eerie sculptures like faces distorted into screams of agony.

"Nice decor," I muttered, rubbing my hands together to keep them from numbing, and wondered where everyone was. The Court seemed awfully quiet, but maybe that was typical of a place so desolate. There were no delicate beings here like piskies and brownies, who would never survive the cold. Winter was harsh and uncompromising, inhabited by brutish ogres and trolls, vicious redcaps, flesh-eaters and sluagh. Grateful that my magic was back to full functionality, I kept my sword out as I picked my way along the winding path.

The coppery tang of fresh blood reached my nostrils. I

tensed, looking around for the source, and spotted a group of redcaps feasting on some poor unfortunate creature. They howled when I sent a blast of magic at them and scattered into the bushes. Otherwise, I didn't see anyone around. There must be some kind of security close to Summer's border, but they might be hidden with glamour. Quentin had told me Winter was militant about protecting their domain, much more so than Summer. It was one of the reasons I held out hope that they wouldn't take Fionn's invasion lying down.

Ten long, freezing minutes later, I came to a division in the paths near an ice-covered house amid the trees. Its solid stone walls looked downright plain by the Sidhe's usual standards. What was it, a guardhouse?

A tall, sharp-featured man stepped out from behind a tree. Like the Sidhe I'd met in Summer, he carried the same aura that made it impossible for the human eye to focus on their features for too long. My flickering vision showed me his skin was paler than the snow, his hair black as pitch, and his eyes equally dark, the latter an unusual feature in Sidhe. His finery was less ostentatious than the Summer Sidhe I'd seen, consisting of silvery-grey armour without adornment, and he carried a sword strapped to his waist. Its sheath gleamed with silvery glyphs, confirming the weapon to be a talisman.

"Why," he said softly, "is a human wandering in our forest?"

"I'm here to speak to a member of the Winter Court." The Unseelie must know what was happening in the Death Kingdom. If they had any level of self-preservation whatsoever, they'd listen to me.

He glided closer, one hand on his blade. On instinct, my hand jumped to my own sword's hilt. Its glyphs shone as bright as his own, reflecting in his odd pitch-dark eyes.

"That talisman is one of ours."

"I claimed it as my own." Magic rose in a blue mist around the blade as I pulled it from the sheath. "From Lord Avalin."

A shadow passed over his face. "We do not speak of the exile."

"He's dead," I told him. "I killed him and won this talisman from him. I'm Ivy Lane."

"I am Lord Lyle. You're human. How did you kill a Sidhe?"

"Short version is, he underestimated me. So did Fionn, and he's the reason I'm here. You must know who *he* is. The Huntsman. Whatever he used to call himself."

"Mortals should not speak of such matters." His teeth gleamed impossibly white, sharper than any person's had the right to be. A chill raced down my back, and I didn't lower my sword.

"It's a long story, and one I'd prefer to share only with your queen," I told him. "Let's just say Fionn is a legitimate threat to the Courts, and I'd like us to form an alliance to fight against him before he destroys both Faerie and the mortal realm. He's already moving onto your territory. You know he is."

"The Unseelie Queen forbids alliances with mortals," said the Sidhe. His dark gaze never wavered, and his pointed teeth hinted at an animal side lurking beneath his almost-human exterior. Maybe he was a shapeshifter, like some of the other Winter Sidhe. "It is a waste of your time for you to speak with her, and likely to end only in your demise."

"It's in her interests to listen to me," I said. "Fionn has enslaved the Morrigan and has claimed the Death Kingdom, and he's just getting started."

He gave me a dismissive look. "The Death realms are a

lesser territory. The Unseelie will not fight for domains outside of our Court."

"The Death realms are part of Winter, right?"

"They exist under the jurisdiction of the Morrigan," said Lord Lyle. "Not the Unseelie Queen."

"Don't you care that Fionn is also stealing your magic?"

He didn't react at all to my raised voice. "Magic does not belong to one single individual."

"But if he steals all your magic, you'll die, won't you?" I pressed. "Also, he broke about a thousand of your rules into pieces when he killed the former Huntsman, took control of his army, raised a rebellion in the place you send exiles and attacked the mortal realm, killing at least one of your own in the process. Don't tell me you're completely ignorant of all that."

"The Huntsman was punished for his crime and was imprisoned outside of this realm." The Sidhe's impassive face made my anger rise, made me want to scream words that would banish the maddening calmness from his expression. But if *your people are going to die and your realm is going to be conquered* didn't cut it, what would?

"Don't you want to punish him for what he did?" I tried. "He stole at least one of your talismans, like he did to Summer. The Seelie Court have agreed to help us. Why can't you do the same?"

"The Seelie Court and the Unseelie Queen have never been friends, let alone allies."

"There's a traitor invading your territory. Isn't that a good reason to forget your old arguments? He'll come here whether you join us or not. I reckon there's strength in numbers."

The air froze, and I gasped as my throat burned and my lungs tightened. Ice spread inside my chest and spots winked before my eyes as my body lifted from the ground, my legs dangling beneath me. Blue crept into the corners of my vision, and death beckoned, thick with grey smoke and the waiting dead.

No, I thought, fighting the pull of Death. Faces flashed before my eyes—whether real or hallucination, I didn't know—and a blue glow arose from my hands and my blade. Its vibrant light cut through the grey, breaking the spell, and I dropped to the frozen ground. Landing at a crouch, I gasped, trying to catch my breath long enough to curse him. "What—what the hell was that?"

The Sidhe wore the same indifferent expression as before. "It seems the magic does indeed serve you."

"You could have checked without strangling me." I massaged my throat and then my chest; a tingling sensation told me my magic was working overtime to heal the damage. "Fionn is coming for you. If you don't act now, there might not be anything left of your realm to fight for."

"Even if I had the authority to lead a war, which I do not, the Unseelie Queen will never consent to listen to you."

"She'll seal you in ice," said a female voice. "Such is the fate of any human foolish enough to cross her."

A female Sidhe appeared, her dark hair clouding her pale face and her eyes like glittering blue gemstones. She wore armour in black and silver with the edges sculpted to resemble sharp thorns, a balance of beauty and danger which fitted an Unseelie noble. Had she been lurking in the shadows and listening to our conversation the whole time?

"And you are...?"

"Lady Rive," she said. "This territory is mine."

Oh boy. "My name's Ivy," I told her. "I'm here to speak to someone willing to listen to my warnings about the impostor calling himself the Huntsman. He's infiltrated your territory and enslaved the Morrigan."

"A bold cause, for a human to stride into our midst and make demands."

"It's not a demand," I said. "I don't know if you heard what I said to Lord Lyle, but the person who was imprisoned twenty-one years ago and is now on the rampage wasn't originally the Huntsman at all. He stole the Huntsman's title and his magic and is now trying to take over your Court. Some of us intend to fight back, and we'd like to invite you to do the same."

The Sidhe woman's eyes glittered. "Humans are strangely fixated on the past. We do not worry about what *was*, only what *is*. There is one Huntsman, always."

"Even if he's an impostor?"

"It is in the nature of my Court to fight for what we want. If someone set his sights on the Huntsman's mantle and won the battle fairly, then we shall accept the result."

"What, you're okay with him being a traitor?" I said in disbelief. "Even if you accept that it's in the nature of things for your people to murder one another for power, I'm pretty sure he used one of Summer's talismans to kill the Huntsman in the first place. Not to mention he stole a bunch of *your* talismans."

Her icy blue eyes flashed. "The matter is for the Unseelie Queen to judge, not us."

"You do realise that without a Huntsman, you aren't really immortal?" I wasn't sure how much the other Sidhe knew of the cauldron, but I'd have thought at least one of them had died in the past two decades, or however long had passed in this realm since the invasion.

"We do not die easily, human. The matter of the Huntsman's betrayal is between myself and my Court, and I will not discuss those matters with a human."

Dammit. Twenty human years was probably nothing to the Sidhe, and if nobody important had died here in the interim, they wouldn't have been in a hurry to find a replacement for the Huntsman. With the cauldron gone, the Huntsman's job was obsolete now, but I'd prefer to be as far away as possible when *that* bombshell fell on their heads.

"Your realm's tied to ours whether you like it or not," I retaliated. "Fionn's actions have drained the magic out of the mortal realm, and there's no reason he can't do the same to yours, too."

"Wrong," said Lady Rive. "Your realm is impermanent. Ours is everlasting."

"No, it isn't." The words slipped out. "Your gods used to rule, but you exiled them. The faerie Courts weren't always the ruling class. If you're not careful—"

Ice spread up my legs, locking me to the ground, but I held my chin up. "You're only attacking me because you know I'm right."

"You're nothing more than a child. We have lived for eons."

"And never changed an inch, by your own admission." I met her stare defiantly. "I bet I've spent longer in the Grey Vale than anyone in this Court. I'm aware of my mortality. I've been reminded of it every day since Fionn tried to destroy my world—and if he'd succeeded, you'd have been destroyed, too. We're tied together. The realms are inseparable."

I held my breath as her eyes raked over me, gleaming like blue gemstones. Then the ice receded from my legs. "You make a reasonable argument, human, but the man calling himself Fionn is not one of our people. He was exiled some immeasurable years ago after he was caught stealing from the Unseelie Queen, and he was sent beyond our territory's boundaries."

"You didn't take away his magic." I frowned. "That's what you do to exiles, isn't it?"

"Yes, we do." Her gaze slid to Lord Lyle. "A practise that started because of several incidents in which exiles attacked the Court from the outside and stole our talismans."

"Including Fionn." I'd been right when I'd guessed he'd never been through the soul-sucking pain other exiles were subjected to, and which he'd entirely deserved. "I know all this. I know he stole from you and from Summer, too, but his worst crime was stealing the Huntsman's magic and gaining access to the cauldron. You can't *want* something that valuable in the enemy's hands." I was dancing on the edge of the abyss, I knew, but I couldn't help wondering who had been involved in the cauldron's creation, and if any of those people still existed. If there was any hope of its recreation, the Sidhe might be less inclined to smite the world when they learned of its destruction.

Her eyes flared with blue light. "He was bound. He was no longer a threat."

"And can you do the same again?"

"No." The hint of a snarl entered Lord Lyle's voice. "We will not make that mistake again."

"Mistake?" I echoed. "You stopped him from destroying the realms. I know there was a cost for it, but he'd have—" I broke off at the dangerous glint in his eyes.

"All who participated in the binding spell gave their lives," Lady Rive said softly. "Two humans tore the Huntsman's soul from his body while the Sidhe enacted the binding spell. All died as a consequence."

"I didn't know. I thought Fionn killed them." *Two humans?* She must mean necromancers, which fit with what I'd guessed about the direct witnesses all being killed.

"The spell required sacrifices," she said, "and the understanding was that it would never need to be repeated."

No wonder Lord Burdock had been so pissed off. I could only assume his wife had volunteered willingly, but they must surely have known the binding spell had always been a temporary measure. Only Fionn's permanent death would end this war.

"In any case," said Lady Rive, "we will fight only to defend our own realm. The Kingdom of Death is independent of the Winter Court, and if the Morrigan freely invited the Huntsman inside her territory, there is nothing we can do."

"She's enslaved to him," I said. "He has a chain around her ankle. Iron, I think."

"Then she will likely die when he does, or when he desires," she said dismissively. "And if her life is taken, she will be reborn at his side to be ensnared anew."

Shit. Until this moment, I hadn't realised I'd been holding onto the slightest thread of hope that the Morrigan could be persuaded to turn on her master or at least killed to weaken his influence. But if she was reborn, banshee-style, and immediately recaptured, killing her wouldn't do anything other than stall him temporarily.

An anguished cry rang out from the trees. I looked up, my spine prickling. Lord Lyle stiffened, scanning the bushes. "There should not be anyone here. Who did you bring here, human?"

"Nobody." *Uh-oh.* "I don't think the enemy's going to offer you any time to debate."

A familiar screech cut through the air, and the trees trembled in warning. *Furies.*

As I began to run, Lady Rive overtook me with ease, calling to her fellow Sidhe over her shoulder, "Tell the Queen at once."

Lord Lyle vanished between the bare-branched trees, which began to reach towards one another, forming a shield of interlocking branches. The effect spread, rapidly, and my instincts told me to get the hell out before I ended up trapped on the wrong side of the Winter Court's defences.

I continued down the path, at a jog, and a scream came from ahead, followed by a dazzling blue flash. I picked up speed, rounding a corner, and nearly threw up. Pieces of flesh scattered the ground, small enough that I couldn't begin to guess what they'd originally belonged to. Something with grey skin and a lot of it, anyway. Lady Rive stood in the centre of the carnage, surrounded by a halo of blue magic. Somehow, she'd managed not to get any blood on her pristine armour when she'd blasted whatever had attacked her into a thousand tiny pieces.

"You." She whirled on me. "You did this, human."

"It's Fionn, not me," I said. "I told you he wouldn't wait. I need to get out—"

The forest shook as a group of winged shapes soared overhead, sharp black and red wings visible above the branches. Furies, too many to count, flying straight at the heart of the Winter Court.

The trees began to shift once again, branches extended into viciously sharp points and rearing up to spear the enemy in midair. *Whoa.* The Winter Court had some serious defence mechanisms, but I wasn't convinced they'd hold up when the Morrigan showed her face. Or worse, Fionn himself.

Blood splattered my face as the spear-sharp branches impaled the furies and brought a wave of gore down upon the forest. I ran from the unpleasant downpour, my feet sliding through mud churned with fresh blood. Redcaps fell on the dead with glad cries, while a chorus of screams and yells came from elsewhere in the forest. The smell of death rose, suffocating, as I ran out of the maze of trees and followed the curve of the path to the area where the routes to Seelie and Unseelie converged.

In the space between stood a dozen ogres wielding blunt clubs. I halted, my heart sinking. Quentin was somewhere

here, and it'd be a dick move to leave him behind, but fighting a dozen ogres simultaneously was beyond me. Why were they standing so still? None of them moved an inch as I crept up behind them, holding my breath at a foul stench that made my eyes sting and bile burn my throat. The smell of the dead.

Oh. The *ogres* were undead. Their green skin had turned, clinging to bone and sagging muscle, and their blank eyes stared sightlessly ahead. What were they doing, waiting for orders as to which Court to attack? Silently I crept along, hoping Quentin was hidden in a bush nearby so I could grab him and get the hell out.

The ogres turned as one as a hellhound sprang out from among the trees, followed by another. Two more hellhounds joined them, springing out of the bushes and positioning themselves around me.

I'd thought all the hellhounds had disappeared after I broke the cauldron, but some must have come back to Winter. When one of them padded towards me, I said, "Listen—if you want to help, stay here and fight. I need to get out and warn my friends before the dead realise I'm…"

A large ogre rotated towards me, raising its club. *Too late.*

20

I cut down the oncoming ogre, its rotting flesh parting beneath my blade. The ogres' clubs swung, even clumsier than usual, and it was easy to dodge with my magic-enhanced speed and the hellhounds swarming amid their group. No signs of Quentin materialised, and when I neared the clearing where I'd left him, I slowed, gagging on the foul stench of rotting corpses.

The clearing was filled with undead. Huge ogres and trolls, tiny redcaps and imps, and everything in between. Someone had slaughtered them and raised them from death, but I didn't see the perpetrator, and from the way the dead had spread out, Fionn intended to have them attack both Courts at once.

Worse, I could only imagine how many more dead existed beyond Winter's boundaries, ready to be raised to fight on his side. The quickest way to dispose of undead was salt, but I didn't have enough on me to take out an army and I doubted the Sidhe's first instinct was to use salt as a weapon, either. Necromancy didn't exist here the way it did in the mortal realm. None of them had likely ever seen a ghost, let alone encountered undead before. Not in the land where everyone lived forever or got eaten alive.

The sound of metal biting into flesh rang out from the path into Winter. Beyond the hellhounds, I glimpsed Lady Rive slicing through an advancing ogre, her mouth twisted in revulsion. Hoping their defences held, I created a magical shield around myself and ran to join her.

My blade sliced through another undead ogre as I ran, severing its legs at the knees. "I see you've met your first undead."

Lady Rive cut me a glare. "You are familiar with these monstrosities, human?"

"Unfortunately." I sliced off the ogre's hands for good measure. "You might've noticed they don't stop moving unless you take them apart. They're usually summoned by a necromancer, but if the realm of the dead gets screwed up badly enough, they're capable of rising of their own accord. These guys seem to be taking orders from someone, though."

Another ogre swung its club at me. My blade severed its arm and sent it spinning away into the bushes. Lady Rive watched with horror as the beast kept on lumbering towards us until I brought down my sword and sliced its body clean in two.

"As you might have gathered, they don't feel any pain." I kicked the ogre's rotting corpse aside. "They also can't die, for obvious reasons, unless you burn them or douse them in salt. Your magic might be able to blow them into enough pieces to stop them from rising again, but there's a whole army over there."

I gestured towards the clearing, and then spied a hellhound making a beeline for me. *Not again.*

"They aren't his," I added quickly to Lady Rive. "The hellhounds are on our side."

Another undead ogre interrupted her reply. Its giant club

swung at her head, and in a flash of light, the beast exploded. Chunks of rotting flesh flew everywhere, except on Lady Rive herself.

I gagged and spat. "Yeah, just do that to all of them."

I moved towards the clearing again, hoping Quentin had managed to get away. Reaching into my pocket, I pulled out a canister of salt and hurled it into the thick of the army. The dead fell into one another in a slow, clumsy effort to avoid the salt eating through their flesh, while others fell under the hellhounds' teeth and more still were taken out by Lady Rive's magic. The dead were the least of Fionn's army, though.

This is a distraction. Where is he?

A pack of redcaps swept upon me, disintegrating flesh hanging from their bones. I threw magic at them, sending them scattering amid the trees, and glimpsed Lord Lyle sprinting over to join Lady Rive.

"What in—?" He halted, staring at the undead ogre lumbering towards him. The salt had burned through one of its legs, reducing it to bone and sinew, but the damn thing kept going.

I ran in behind and sliced its other leg off at the knee. "Now do you get it?" I called to Lord Lyle. "He can raise the dead, probably as a result of taking over the Morrigan's home. How many people have died on this territory?"

Lord Lyle made a choked noise. "Too many to count. The Huntsman used to come for the dead, but that was an honour reserved only for the Sidhe."

So only the Sidhe were reborn. The rest... damn. That meant every faerie who died on either territory might be waiting ready for Fionn to drag them out of Death and into life again. When you added the fact that there hadn't been a Huntsman at all for over twenty years and nobody had handled the dead in the interim, the Sidhe were in for a hell of a nasty surprise.

The only way to stop the army was to cut off the attack at its source—the Death Kingdom—but the Sidhe would be preoccupied defending their own Courts, and going in alone was out of the question when Fionn might be waiting for me to do exactly that.

The trees shook, and another undead ogre lumbered through. I blasted a hole through its chest before it reached us.

Lord Lyle's blade finished the job. "How did you learn to use our magic, human?"

"Trial and error," I said, cutting off a troll's arm. Its decomposing hand continued to flop around, trying to latch onto my ankle. "Same as fighting these things. You have to cut them to pieces otherwise they'll just keep coming back."

Revulsion rippled across his face. "*What?*"

I stomped on the troll's twitching hand. "It's necromancy. Human death magic. Pretty unpopular even in our realm, but Fionn seems to like it. Isn't it what goes on in your Death Kingdom?"

"The Death Kingdom was created for the souls of those waiting to be reborn, not for these monstrosities."

"So when you die, you go to the Death Kingdom?"

"We don't die."

"Clearly, you do." I indicated the fallen ogres. "I know the Huntsman's job was to collect your people's souls and take them to be reborn. He seems to have missed a few."

"The Huntsman's job was solely to take *Sidhe* to be reborn," he corrected. "The others are not of consequence."

"How delightful." I kicked a dead redcap that had attempted to sneak up on me. "Well, it looks as though you're about to get invaded by every non-Sidhe you refused to offer immortality to."

If you asked me, it served them right. As more dead emerged from the trees, Lord Lyle lifted a palm and sent a rippling current of Winter magic towards them. The undead froze—literally—as a coating of ice slid over their rotting bodies and halted their lumbering steps. Redcaps slipped around them, only to fall beneath the trampling feet of a hellhound. The beast slowed in front of me and lowered its head. This, I was fairly sure, was the same hellhound I'd hitched a ride with on the way to stop Fionn using the cauldron to create an immortal army.

"Where'd you come from?" I trod around the ogre's twitching corpse to the hellhound's side. "Have you been waiting on the Ley Line the whole time?"

Likely yes. The hellhounds had fled from the cauldron but hadn't had anywhere else to go. The Ley Line was the seam between Faerie and the Grey Vale, the place through which the Sidhe had exiled their gods.

Maybe the place where I could *find* their gods.

I clambered onto the hellhound's back, awkwardly, tightening my legs around its neck when it rose upright. The last time, I'd ridden without a physical body, not to mention a sword. My balance was a lot more precarious now, and I nearly fell off when the hellhound launched into motion, swerving to avoid an undead ogre's club.

"Whoa." I hung on tight and yelped when the hellhound took a particularly sharp turn down a path that I was positive hadn't been there beforehand. Greyness wreathed the trees and made it impossible to see what lay ahead. "Hey! Hang on. You aren't taking me to the Death Kingdom, are you?"

The hellhound growled. I bloody hoped it meant no, because a sole human riding a hellhound was no match for an army. The grey smoke thickened, and the sounds of fighting faded into the background with each lumbering step.

"Where are we?" My voice echoed with an odd quality, as though we were inside a tunnel. "Are we in *Death*?"

I scanned the smoke, expecting apparitions to appear at every step, but they didn't. As we bounded along, the fog lifted, revealing a familiar path lined with silvery leaves. The Vale.

"I didn't know the Courts had a direct route here." It made sense that they did, though, given that the Sidhe had created the place, and Fionn had discovered its crevices long before he'd ever stolen the title of Huntsman.

We came to a halt at a cliff's edge. Smoke coiled upward, but I couldn't see what lay below.

"What the devil are you doing here, Ivy?"

I jumped violently and damn near fell into the pit. Twisting around on the hellhound's back, I spied Frank the necromancer hovering behind me, his ghostly feet skimming the leafy path.

"I thought you'd gone," I said. "Ah. Thanks for sending Gerry to find me. Is this where you've been, since Death's totally locked off in the mortal realm?"

He scowled. "Yes. I was forced to leave the Gate, so I came here, hoping to find the source at the place where Death and the Vale are bound."

"It is?" I glanced back at the steep drop, seeing nothing but smoke. "I didn't intend to come here. I was in Faerie—the real Faerie—and Fionn has sent undead to attack the Courts."

Frank's ghostly face twisted in horror. "That's what caused the disturbance in the veil?"

"Apparently." I pushed on. "I don't know how long he's been doing it for, but I imagine it didn't help when he bound the Morrigan and took over the Death Kingdom. That's where the Sidhe send their dead before they're reborn—oh, and it turns out that little exclusive club only included their fellow Sidhe. Any other fae was left to rot, and Fionn has revived them all to fight on his side using the power of the Death Kingdom."

As Frank's face went through planes of deepening terror and disgust, I paused to let my words sink in.

"He must be stopped," Frank finally murmured. "For all our sakes."

"That was the plan." I held up my talisman. "The Sidhe filled this sword with the power of one of their gods, and if its owner is still out there, they might be able to help. Do you know where to find them?"

"What?" He recoiled. "You can't speak to the gods, Ivy. It's impossible."

"How do you know that?" I asked. "You were the one who told me how the Sidhe created the Vale, Frank. You must know they're here somewhere."

"I'm not an expert, Ivy. I only know as much as I do because of my position on the Council of Twelve. I was informed of how the Vale was created, but I certainly wasn't told where to *find* the gods. I would imagine they're long gone."

"There's one sleeping in my house. Well, Isabel's," I amended. "Never mind. Just tell me—"

A flash of blue light dazzled my eyes momentarily, and when I opened them, ice coated the path, creeping up the trees. *Shit.* The army was already here.

And the Grey Vale was one step away from the mortal realm.

"I have to go." I nudged the hellhound with my leg. "Take me back through the Ley Line. Take me home."

Frank shouted after me as the hellhound bounded away, leaving him in the dust. I held on tight, braced myself, but the crossing was as smooth as sliding downhill. The Vale slipped away, and I rode out into a crowd of shifters.

"Oh." I'd forgotten that slight problem. "Don't mind me."

The shifters reared back, shouting in alarm. What did they think I was, a Horseman of the Apocalypse come to declare judgement upon them? Quite possibly yes. Some had already begun to transform into their animal forms.

"There's an invasion coming through the Ley Line any second now," I told them. "Don't say I didn't warn you."

At my prompting, the hellhound rode eastward, following the line, dodging any shifter who tried to grab us. I ignored their outraged yells and repeated my warning to anyone within hearing distance. I could only assume something had drawn them to the line, or else they'd taken the warnings of an attack seriously after all, but I hoped the mages and witches were ready to fight, too.

"The invasion is coming!" I shouted at the top of my lungs. "Anyone who can't fight, move away from the Ley Line. Bring salt and iron. The undead are coming out of Faerie!"

Speaking of salt, I'd used up my only canister already, but I didn't have time to go home and get more. Already my vision flickered, showing me the dead awaiting on the other side.

"Take me back through," I urged the hellhound.

We rode back through the Ley Line and met the dead coming the other way. I swung my blade, calling to the other hellhounds. "Hold the line between here and the mortal realm. Protect us!"

The hellhounds fell on the undead army, teeth ripping and tearing. I cut down an ogre, slicing its head clean off, but the dead outnumbered the hellhounds and were already vanishing through the Ley Line and into the mortal realm.

Someone was commanding them, but who? Fionn wasn't here and I didn't see any living people to speak of, unless you counted a few hazy patches of distorted air that might have been ghosts or wraiths.

I took aim and fired magic into the army, blasting a hole in an undead's chest. At my prompting, the hellhound veered close enough to one of the dark patches for me to identify it as a wraith, albeit one that didn't look remotely like a human *or* fae. More like a malevolent concentration of blue-white death energy that extended grasping tendrils towards me.

I dodged, noting the way the undead moved around the wraith, as though its tendrils were nudging them in the right direction. *Is it commanding them?*

A number of undead waited behind the wraith, dead hands lifting clubs, axes, daggers. *That's a yes, then.*

"Ride towards it," I urged the hellhound, which growled its displeasure but obeyed. As we picked up speed, I swung Helena in an arc. Magic burst outward from both sides of my blade and engulfed the wraith, and its wrenching scream rang in my ears as its spirit exploded into dust.

Now I knew what to look for, I scanned the confusion of battle for more bright patches that indicated a wraith's presence. Destroying them wouldn't get rid of the undead but would slow the army's advance and sow confusion.

"Over there!" I directed the hellhound to ride towards a second wraith. Like the first, it was comprised of Winter magic, vibrant blue, and when I lifted my blade, sudden pressure seized my skull and nearly made me lose my grip. *Is it trying to possess me?*

"Cut that out!" I brought the sword down, and the sensation loosened as the wraith flew back. A second blast of magic finished it off. Gasping, I clutched my forehead with my free hand. My skull pounded with echoes of the wraith's presence, sending an ice-cold shudder throughout my entire body.

That's no normal spirit. No… these weren't human ghosts, or even half-bloods. They were Sidhe who'd perished here in the Grey Vale, now reduced to shells to fight in Fionn's army.

Their exile didn't just strip them of their magic, but it condemned them to a literal eternity of pain. Fionn had taken advantage of their entrapment, and while I didn't feel sorry for the wraiths in the least, I'd have a hell of a job taking down centuries of exiled ghosts on my own.

Another wraith flew straight *through* the hellhound I rode on. The beast reared up on its hind legs with a howl and I tumbled off its back.

Before I hit the ground, an undead ogre grabbed my foot and tried to use me as a golf club. I swung my blade into its ankle, which gave way, sending both of us toppling into a heap of undead flesh. Gagging, I sliced off the ogre's other foot and then blasted the offending wraith to smithereens.

Fuck this. I'd slowed the army enough to make a difference, but nothing would end the war short of Fionn's death. I kicked the ogre's remains off my boots and returned to the hellhound, and it bent its head to let me climb onto its back again.

"Take me somewhere on the Ley Line which isn't covered with undead," I told the hellhound. "We're going to find the lost god whose power lives in my talisman."

21

The hellhound obeyed. In a few bounds, we left the confusion of battle behind and were once again flanked by the Vale's silvery trees. No matter how far we moved, the distant sounds of fighting were audible, suggesting the battle must have spread deeply through the Vale. The Ley Line would soon be swarmed, but I had little doubt that the path to the lost god lay here, near the nexus from which the Sidhe had split the worlds asunder.

I held my talisman in my right hand, my gaze following the glyphs shimmering along its edge. "I hope one of these is your name."

In Faerie, names had power, and that went doubly so for beings whose very language contained strength enough to reshape the world. Though I no longer had access to the parchment on which the Invocations had been listed, I could still wrap my tongue around the language, still tap into that raw power.

I spoke to the Vale. "Take me to the god. Take me to my talisman's source."

The path warped and twisted, the swiftness of the

response making me wonder if the Vale—or my talisman—had been waiting for me to ask. Clouds swept in, masking the ground, and forming a bridge in front of me. The hellhound reeled back from the edge, and I hastily jumped down before it dislodged me out of fear. My steed vanished into the mist and left me alone, facing the bridge that I was pretty sure was the same place I'd fought the Lady of the Tree. And where she'd woken the dragon shifter. Having another god with me might have offered me more reassurance, but for all I knew, the pair of them were bitter enemies. Besides, the dragon shifter was in no fit state to travel between realms.

Here we go. I held up the talisman and studied the swirling glyphs. The symbols rippled and solidified into a single line across the talisman's edge. Recognition seized me. I was almost certain that Invocation that kept trying to nudge me into speaking it aloud every time I looked at the parchment now shone from my blade.

The first word of the Invocation sprang to my lips, cold as metal dipped in ice. This time, I made no attempt to resist. I opened my mouth and spoke. Each syllable resounded, its echo lingering the air like the fog swirling around me. My ears popped. My tongue burned with cold. My skin tingled. Even the bridge beneath my feet trembled as the last word left my mouth.

And then there wasn't anything beneath my feet at all.

In slow motion, I fell, down, down. Vibrant blue magic formed a shield around me, but its presence didn't break my fall. The blue light encased my body as my descent continued, slow enough to be more floating than falling. Ten seconds passed, then twenty. My brief panic leaked away but didn't disappear entirely; the dense fog concealed the drop and made it impossible to see how far I had to fall I hit the ground, or whatever else awaited below.

"Take me back," I whispered to the Vale. "Put me back on the bridge."

I hadn't expected a response and didn't get one, but at least a minute had passed by now and the flicker of fear stirred inside me again. The Vale was hardly a place of logic and sense, but now I had to wonder if I'd genuinely fallen off the edge of the world. For all I knew, I'd keep falling forever, tumbling into a void that marked the edge of the prison the Sidhe had created.

I pushed away my panic and tried to feel my way into the mortal realm, but even *that* didn't work. All that existed was the endless fog, and the sense of having reached an ending. *The* ending, perhaps. The place where everything, all of existence, ceased to be.

Then came the sudden incomprehensible certainty that I wasn't alone. My head lifted and I scanned the grey in search of whatever had tripped my instincts, but all I saw was grey, darkening to black in some areas. One particular spot of blackness resembled a giant pit in midair, like some kind of hellish wormhole. Looking into the pit brought a shiver to my skin, an inexplicable reminder of when I'd looked directly into the void of nothingness in which that beast slept on in the Hemlock Coven's forest.

The void *blinked.* A shutter came down, briefly masking the pit and the haze of white surrounding it, and horrified comprehension crashed over me. It wasn't a pit but a giant *eye.* Bigger than me. Bigger than anything I'd seen.

Oh, holy fucking shit...

The fall stopped as abruptly as it had started as I landed sprawling on a cloudlike mass in front of the dark pit. I lay on my front, gasping, icy terror filling my soul. Primal instinct told me to flee, but aside from the cloud I'd landed on, nothing was here except for that giant staring eye, and its owner, hidden amid the smoke.

A blue glow shone in front of me. My sword had fallen from my grip as I'd landed, and its brightly burning glyphs reminded me of how I'd got here. My hand closed around the hilt and I rose upward, extending the sword so that it faced the giant eye. Given its size, I could only imagine how big the rest of the creature was. I was nothing more than an ant by comparison, but the god should be able to sense its own magic burning within the blade. I had no idea whether showing the beast the talisman would help, given that the Sidhe had stripped away some of its power without permission, but the god should be able to tell I wasn't one the person responsible. Right?

Not a sound came from the beast. I shivered, my hand trembling on the blade. This creature was undeniably cut from the same cloth as the creature imprisoned beneath the Hemlock Coven's forest, but no binding spells held it in sleep, no glyphs contained its formidable power. Raw fear quaked through my bones as that giant eye raked over me, its pupil and iris merging into a swirling pit of darkness, its sclera a shimmering greyish haze.

Oh, god. The beast wasn't hiding in the fog… the fog was part of the creature itself. The shifting clouds formed the outline of the creature's head, the mass below might be its body, and its incorporeal form resembled an impossibly giant version of a wraith. *It's… it's dead.*

Someone had killed this god a long time ago, but its presence had lingered, for who knew how many centuries. A whimper escaped my mouth. I took a step back and fetched up against a solid surface that suggested a cliff. Was I still in the Vale? I must be, despite feeling as though I'd tumbled off the edge of the world. My fingers dug into the solid rock, and I sought to clear my muddled thoughts.

I'd come here for a reason, and I had a job to do. There was a war at home. People were counting on me. Yes, the god was fucking terrifying, but I held a piece of its power in my own hands and had claimed it as my own.

For the second time, I extended the blade towards the smoky eye to display its shimmering glyphs. "I'm Ivy. I really, really need your help."

A sharp voice spoke from within the smoke. "Who comes here?"

The words hit me like a hammer to the skull. I blinked, stunned for several seconds, then managed to croak out, "I— I'm Ivy. I'm human. Not Sidhe."

"Then you have come here to die."

A roaring wind kicked up, but my magic reacted before the attack hit. A shimmering blue shield formed between me and its master's rage. I staggered back against the cliff and raised my voice. "All the realms will be destroyed if you kill me. Stop!"

The roaring grew louder, and my shield brightened as my magic fought to hold off the god's wrath. The beast didn't care if the realms were destroyed. Why would an entity that had existed before the creation of the Courts have any care for the rest of us?

My shield began to falter. My sword started to slide out of my hand, and I fought the sudden urge to let go, to give the power up to the beast to whom it rightfully belonged. Who was I to think I was equal to the gods? I'd claimed the talisman, but its power had been stolen from another source, and that wouldn't change even now I wanted—no, needed— to use it to defeat a greater evil.

Nothing else can beat Fionn. I held onto that thought, drew on the pain and despair of my own futile quest, and the vibrant blue glow brightened. "Your magic *chose* me. We've fought together for years. Can't you sense it?"

A moment passed before the rumbling voice spoke again. "You are not the person who last held that weapon."

"Avalin? No. I'm not." The wind's roar had quietened, but my voice still sounded small, insignificant, in the face of a deity's wrath. "Avalin's dead. I killed him and tricked him into giving up his power to me, but I—I didn't know where his power came from."

"You speak true." The wind ceased to gust, and some of the tension eased out of me.

I released a breath but didn't drop my shield. Didn't dare hope that the god's rational words indicated its wrath had quietened. "I need to defeat someone who's immune to your magic."

"You fight the one who took my life."

"Fionn *killed* you?"

Was *that* why my magic reacted the way it did? Yes, Fionn had betrayed Avalin and had given my talisman good reason to project its wrath at the culprit, but the intensity of its anger went much deeper than that, and the only explanation…

…was that Fionn had slaughtered a god.

"Many of your lifetimes ago," said the rumbling voice. "The rash fool had intended to steal my power, but he was thwarted. When he took my life, my very essence declared itself against him, so he threw the talisman away."

"And… Avalin picked it up." Neither had known it at the time, but Fionn's actions had inadvertently put the talisman in my own hands. Part of me wanted to ask *how* Fionn had killed him, but I resisted. "You want to destroy Fionn and so does my talisman, so why can't I harm him?"

"I would assume that is because he still carries the nullifier."

"The what?" I said blankly. "Do you mean the ring? Summer's ring?"

Oh. That must be how Fionn had triumphed over the god. The ring had done so much more than ensure his victory in the invasion and nearly bring about the destruction of our realm—but that didn't answer my question. The ring was gone.

The wind roared again. I grabbed the cliff with my free hand to keep from being thrown sideways and bellowed, "The ring has gone! I threw it into the… into the place where the other god is sleeping."

The roaring ceased. "Did you, human?"

I caught my balance, my shield rippling. "Yes. The ring has been destroyed. How is it that I still can't use magic against him?"

"You are not his equal."

"But… nobody *is* his equal." Except maybe the other god, the dragon shifter, but he was out of commission.

"Truly you are a fool," rumbled the voice. "You already stole from the one who previously held that weapon you carry. Why not enact the same trickery on him?"

"Trickery?" I echoed. "What, a vow?"

Impossible. There was zero chance Fionn would acquiesce to the same bargain, and it wasn't like I could beat him in outright combat anyway. What did the god mean?

The realisation slid into me. Wasn't trickery exactly how Fionn had achieved all his goals? Sure, he *pretended* to play fair, but he stole and manipulated and had even gone as far as to perform a role that had fooled every Sidhe in the Courts into believing he was the true Huntsman.

As for the Sidhe themselves? They'd killed or exiled their gods, and stolen their magic and bound it into talismans, and they'd done so without ever uttering a lie.

Why couldn't I do the same to Fionn? As a mortal, I *could* lie. I could deceive. And I could snatch Fionn's victory from his fingertips and steal away the revenge he'd been willing to burn worlds down to achieve.

"Thank you." I didn't yet know *how* I would win, but my

hope bloomed anew, and even the god's terrifying presence didn't dampen the flame of determination within my heart. "You helped me. Really."

"Be careful, human," rumbled the deity. "There are others like me that are not so benign. We all remember how the Sidhe took our power for their own use, Seelie and Unseelie both."

"Yeah. I thought you would."

The ancient Sidhe had been real bastards. Killing the gods, stealing their power, and storing that power in artefacts created by harming their fellow faeries. Honestly, I almost felt sorry for the Lady of the Tree.

"Erm… how do I get out of here?"

Air buffeted against my shield, driving me backwards against the solid wall. Getting the message, I turned around. The cliff wasn't as sheer as I'd first thought, and there were dents I could use as handholds. After sheathing my blade, I began to climb, bolstered by the magic flooding my veins and resonating from the sword at my waist.

In seemingly no time, I reached the top and found myself on the bridge from which I'd fallen into the beast's lair. The edge of the Vale. There might be other gods down there for all I knew, other mysteries known only to the Vale, and to those who'd been exiled here.

I took in a shaky breath. Exhaled.

And then I stepped back into the mortal realm.

22

On the other side of the Ley Line, chaos reigned. The misty field was awash in carnage as the shifters tore into undead fae and ripped them to shreds. I'd lost my shield as I'd crossed realms and there was no clear path through the battlefield. I sidestepped, narrowly avoiding a fatal strike to the head from an ogre's weapon.

"Whoa." I drew my sword from its sheath and cut the ogre down, observing that the blue glow was more noticeable than before. Hoping that was a good sign, I lifted the blade and ran through the melee, dodging undead and shifters alike. The fighting didn't cease when I reached the field's end but extended into the road and beyond. Given the extent of the Ley Line, similar scenes would be occurring all over the city. No—the country.

I have to stop this. I veered down the country lane and spied a gleaming ward marking the road into the city. More wards were spaced at intervals, along with columns of undead, forming an unbroken line preventing the undead from getting past. Someone had been busy.

Further down the road, I found two mages—Rod and

Bailey—setting down another ward alongside a cloaked necromancer. Colby flipped his hood down and gasped when he saw me.

"Hey." I ran to a halt, initially confused by their alarmed expressions before I remembered I was covered in blood and gore and god knew what else. At least my sword was distinguishable enough to identify me. "Sorry I got tied up in Faerie. This is happening all over the city?"

"Yes." Colby's voice trembled. "The… the mages suggested we split into groups and put salt and wards in the roads to slow them down."

"Good thinking." I looked at Bailey, who crouched down, expertly drawing a glyph I didn't recognise. "What's that for?"

"It's a repelling ward, a complex one. Should slow anything down that isn't Sidhe."

Or Fionn. "Where's—?"

"The Mage Lord?" Rod guessed. "He'll probably be here any second now. He's been roaming up and down the Ley Line and helping anyone who needs it."

"Speaking of." Bailey lifted a hand in greeting as Vance appeared at my side.

With scarcely a pause, Vance took my hand, whisking us both away. We landed in the hallway of Francine's house. "What—"

He cut my words off with a kiss. "I was hoping you'd come back soon. I have a team of mages ready to cross into Faerie as soon as Quentin gives us permission."

"What—Quentin's okay?" A rush of guilt hit me. "I hoped he was hiding. I looked for him, but there were undead everywhere."

"He managed to escape before most of the army arrived," he said. "He also brought some Summer Sidhe to speak to you. They're waiting here for your instructions."

"They're waiting for *me*?" I asked. "As opposed to helping their Court?"

"They haven't been here long," he said. "Did you manage to convince anyone from Winter to help, too?"

"They were attacked first," I explained. "The army showed up before I could convince them. I guess Fionn ran out of patience."

"Yes," he said darkly. "It's lucky we were prepared. I have some of my people working with the necromancers to set up defences, and the witches are supplying everyone with spells."

"Isabel?"

"She's been running back and forth from the Ley Line handing out spells and defending anyone who needs it."

"Good." That was everyone accounted for. "I know we don't have a lot of time, but you should probably know that I talked to the god whose power is inside my talisman. The god said Fionn doesn't have an inherent immunity to my magic. I'm just not strong enough, but I can win by trickery. I'm not a hundred percent sure how to go about doing that, but the god told me so, and I should probably take the advice."

Vance stared at me. "What? You spoke to—Ivy, we're going to have words later."

"Yes, we are. When we survive this." I kissed him fiercely. "Let's go."

We ran into the main downstairs room. Every inch of floor space was covered in chalk circles, stacks of spells and ingredients, and containers of salt. Witches ran in and out, grabbing spells or stopping to reset the circles, and a few of the younger coven members were busy sorting wards into piles.

"Help yourself." Isabel waved us over to a pile of salt-shakers in the corner. "Both of you. We have other hubs at

Shana's house and the main hall so anyone can come in and grab what they need."

"Cheers." I grabbed as many salt containers as I could cram into my pockets.

Erwin flew overhead and grabbed one, too. "Dead not hurt Ivy!"

"Damn right," I said. "I'm guessing Larsen crawled back into his lair?"

"Some of the mercs have dropped by to get supplies," Isabel said. "They don't really have a choice. There's nowhere in town that's free from the dead. They're coming out of the Ley Line all over the city."

I zipped my pockets. "Where are the Summer faeries?"

"Back garden."

I trod carefully amid the piles of spells, picking up a few and selecting some iron daggers from a heap in the corner as well. When I was well-stocked, I walked through the door into the small kitchen that led to the back door. The dazzling green glow outside pointed to the Summer contingent. Lord Raivan and two more Sidhe sat on horseback near the Chief and a few other half-faeries, including Killian and the former guards of half-blood territory. The latter were dressed in their imitations of real faerie armour and all of them carried containers of salt in addition to their usual weapons. So did Quentin.

"Glad you made it out," I said to him, then addressed the others. "What the hell have you been doing out here, having a picnic while everyone else goes to war?"

The Chief recoiled when he saw me. "You look horrific."

"You've seen better days yourself." Sure, presenting myself to the Sidhe with bits of intestine hanging out of my hair was hardly the best impression, but this was war. "There's a contingent of undead invading through the Ley Line. Did none of you notice?"

"We have been waiting for you," said Lord Raivan haughtily. "The brownie promised that you would bring assistance."

"Isabel already did." I gestured to the house. "The mages, necromancers, witches, and shifters are prepared to defend their realm. I can't promise they'll come into Faerie, mostly because they aren't allowed to, as you've made quite clear. The half-faeries, too."

The Chief made an indistinct noise. It didn't escape my attention that he kept shooting Lord Raivan and the other Sidhe furtive looks, as though trying to work up the nerve to speak to them.

"Yes?" I said to the Chief. "Something wrong?"

"I want my magic back," said the Chief. "That is why I will fight alongside you."

"And I intend to defend Summer," added Lord Raivan. "It was my understanding that you sought a way to destroy the Huntsman."

"I did," I confirmed. "He can be killed by iron, or magic from someone stronger than him, but the real problem is that his wraith will endure beyond this death. That's how he came back the last time, and now that he has the Morrigan on his side, permanently finishing him off is going to be hard, if not outright impossible."

A ripple of horror and disgust travelled among both the Sidhe and half-faeries alike. The Chief sagged against the garden fence, while a couple of the other half-bloods fled the garden outright.

I sighed inwardly. "This is why I wanted help from both Courts and the cooperation of the supernaturals *before* the situation escalated to outright war between realms. We're up against someone whose very nature makes him almost invincible."

"He stole that power from another," said Lord Raivan.

"And I want to steal it back," I told him. "That's my strategy. Unfortunately, I have no idea whatsoever how to do that, but it seems like stripping away the Huntsman's magic will also remove all his advantages."

"Strip out his magic?" said one of the other Sidhe. "That's impossible."

"Is it?" I held up my blade. "I'm accusing nobody's ancestors of being foolish enough to tear magic from a god while it was still alive, but that power didn't get in here by accident. And don't say only Winter does it. Your Court created Summer's ring."

A stunned silence followed my words.

"Now that we're on the same page," I added, before anyone could start yelling at me, "I think you should open the way into Faerie and let us help you fight. Oh, and if you see any hellhounds, don't attack them. They're on our side. They know Fionn isn't the real Huntsman."

Lord Raivan uttered a strangled noise. "We cannot let mortals…"

"Then die." I spoke harshly. "Let everyone who wants to help come to Faerie. Half-blood, human, whatever. We're not invading. That's Fionn. And you know he's counting on you being too stubborn to let us help you."

All the fight seeped out of him. I could have sworn some of the vibrant green glow that made the Sidhe look so much more alive faded away as he studied me through narrowed eyes. Then he spoke. "Very well. You may fight at our side."

"Good choice there."

The half-bloods would get a magical boost from being in Faerie, though there was a strong chance they'd also go to their deaths. At least they'd be fighting on the right side this time around.

The Chief cleared his throat. Lord Raivan swivelled to him, and the Chief made a couple of indistinct noises then blurted out, "If we help the Courts win this fight, I expect compensation."

"Compensation?" Lord Raivan's tone rang with derision. "You will be lucky if your thin mortal blood survives the fight."

"No need for that." *Ah, screw it.* "Lord Raivan, these people are risking their lives for your Court, even though you have shown them nothing but contempt. I can't pretend I understand why, but if you have a shred of decency in you, you'll at least allow them free passage to visit Faerie in the future."

"You have the audacity..." Lord Raivan trailed off. "We shall revisit the matter later, human."

"Yes, we will." Seeing the Chief staring at me, I edged over to him and whispered, "What is it?"

"I—thank you." His alabaster skin had turned even paler than usual. "I won't forget this. I will owe you if we—if we survive."

"I'll try to negotiate on your behalf." Survive? Debateable. He was about to face down an army with nothing but a fake talisman and a canister of salt, but he hadn't run, and I had to admit to holding a smidgeon of respect for that. "In the meantime, look on the bright side. You get to lead an army into battle. Even some Sidhe lords don't get to do that."

Lord Raivan raised a hand. A flash of green light folded around our group, and the path to the Summer Court opened. A wall of noise hit us, and the half-faeries flinched away from the sight of the undead army. They far outnumbered the few Sidhe who'd shown up to fight, and despite their proximity, there was a clear division between Summer and Winter's forces. More hellhounds had arrived in the time I'd been gone, but the Sidhe weren't attacking them. They must have worked out that the beasts were on their side.

Amid the sea of undead, ghosts popped up, hurling magic at any living person they encountered. Furies, too, swooped above the ruined trees strewn across the battlefield. They'd wrecked half the forest in a short time, though at least Faerie could rebuild itself in seconds. The mortal realm might not be so lucky.

No sign of Fionn, though. Is he waiting for us to come to him?

"We're being overrun!" A Summer Sidhe ran past, shouting at Lord Raivan. "I thought you were bringing help from the mortal realm."

"We're right here." It took a moment for me to recognise Lord Kerien, who was now dressed in heavy-looking golden armour and wielding a gleaming talisman. "Also, there'd be more of us if we were allowed into your realm, but the connection on the Ley Line only goes one way, so we get your nasty dead monsters and nothing else."

"She wants us to open the way to the mortal realm." Lord Raivan brought down his sword through an oncoming undead ogre, and it fell beneath the hooves of his mount. "It's out of the question."

"I don't much care if you do, but I bet your Erlking does." I sank my blade into another undead ogre and sliced off its foot. "It's your choice."

A shimmering arose in the air, and my vision doubled. No, trebled. The winding silver-lit path of the Vale appeared and then so did the hillside upon which the shifters fought. Then a street lined with houses where teams of witches fought oncoming furies. A ruined high street. An empty field. A—

"Ivy." Vance caught my arm and pulled me away from a descending fury's claws; his blade severed the fury's spine in midair. "What's wrong?"

"You can't see…" I trailed off, my head pounding, and glared at Lord Raivan. "What *was* that?"

"I opened the way through," he said coldly. "As you requested."

Oh. "The Sidhe opened the Ley Line. The entire mortal realm only overlaps with this one part of Faerie, so I can see the Line up and down the country."

My head gave a throb as my vision flickered from street to beach to forest. A thousand overlapping scenes was not a sight designed to be injected into a regular human's eyes, let alone in the middle of a battle.

"Maybe it'll be less intense if you aren't standing on top of the line." Vance held my shoulder and steered me backwards, stopping to cut down an undead troll in the process.

I finished it off with my sword, squinting my eyes so that the effect of the colliding realms wasn't quite as intense. As we backed into the trees, my headache lifted enough for my focus to return.

"Thanks," I said to Vance. "I don't want to get myself brained. Or wander out of the Ley Line by accident and end up stranded in the middle of the ocean."

"Is that possible?"

"You'd think not, but neither is that." I gestured to the half-faeries fighting side by side with Sidhe, all covered in so much blood and viscera it was difficult at a distance to tell the difference between the half-bloods and the true fae. The humans put up a valiant fight of their own, too. I could see enough of the mortal realm on the other side of the line to glimpse witches hurling spells at the divide between realms, aiming so that they caught the dead just as they were crossing over.

I glimpsed Isabel at the front and felt a rush of worry for her, but every time a dead fae tried to grab her, the glyphs on her skin would ignite a blast that took them to pieces. Nearby, the mages formed their own contingent, conjuring a thunderous storm accompanied by bolts of fire and ice. Vance fought, too, blades flashing, displacing the air to knock enemies into one another.

I ran to check on Isabel, easily sliding between Faerie and the road in which she fought. The rest of the coven spread out around her, forming a deadly attack squad armed with explosives and other spells.

"Hey, Ivy." She waved at me with one hand and hurled an explosive with the other, blasting two undead to pieces mid-crossing. "You know, I've almost got used to your habit of appearing out of thin air, but this… is new." She gestured at the shimmering haze that marked the newly opened Ley Line.

"I know. We actually got the Sidhe to open the doors to Faerie."

I sheathed my sword in another undead and Isabel stepped in with an explosive spell to finish it off. The blast took out the ogre's kneecaps but the damn thing *still* kept pawing at my feet.

"Now I know why the Sidhe don't have necromancers," I muttered, severing one of its hands and stamping on the other. "How's Rick doing, do you know?"

"The necromancers are mostly working on defences," she replied. "Since, you know, they can't reach Death."

A fury flew out of the Ley Line, but the glyphs on Isabel's arms appeared in a golden haze and repelled the beast's claws before they could make contact. Other witches fought, too, wielding salt and iron and spells as they stood side by side with the mages.

A familiar chilling screech rang out from within the Ley Line. *The Morrigan.* I'd been wondering when she'd finally show her face.

"I'm going back in." I waved at Isabel and ran through the division into Faerie. Above the forest, a large shadow blanketed the trees as the colossal bird flew overhead.

There she is. The Morrigan soared above, her huge wings

splayed above the forest. A few arrows flew upward but made no impact upon her feathery hide.

"You're betraying your position, Morrigan," shouted Lord Lyle. "The entire Death Kingdom will suffer the wrath of the Unseelie Court."

"She's enslaved!" I yelled at him. "Declaring war on her Court doesn't matter. Kicking Fionn out is more important."

Fire burst over my head, setting a bank of trees and undead ablaze. I scrambled away from a dead ogre's flopping arm, unable to see where the flames had come from. Not the mages.

A second winged shadow fell overhead, almost as large as the Morrigan. *Eraenar.* He was back in his dragon shifter form, and a plume of fire burst from his mouth, igniting the trees and the dead all at once.

"Holy shit," I breathed. "He's awake."

I looked for Vance, but he'd disappeared in the chaos of the fighting and my allies had scattered throughout the forest and the realm on the other side of the dividing line.

The dragon uttered a roar. Charred branches rained down upon the battleground, and through the new gap in the canopy, I saw the Morrigan veering away from the dragon's flames. *Whoa.* The dragon had actually hit her, though she didn't seem to have suffered any physical damage.

Blue light burst across my vision. I threw up a shield to block the sudden onslaught of Winter magic, but the current still lifted me off my feet and slammed me onto my back. Ice formed beneath, and I slid, uncontrolled, until my back fetched up against an equally frozen tree. Icicles formed on its branches. My chest burned with cold, each breath searing my lungs. The only warmth I felt was the blood, mine and others', soaking into the frosted ground.

I lifted my head. Broken tree trunks surrounded me. The entire area had been levelled, and I gagged at the sight of the corpses impaled on shards of frozen branch. Even the undead hadn't been spared. The person who'd thrown the attack hadn't cared about hitting their allies.

I stumbled upright on numb feet, dread clutching my chest as I scanned the bodies. Undead, mostly, but the fighting on the other side of the line was no longer visible. I couldn't see the mortal realm.

The path between realms had closed. Whether the Sidhe themselves had slammed the door or it had been forced shut, my friends and allies were on the other side. I was alone in Faerie. Everyone else here was dead.

23

I lifted my gaze. Not only had the battle temporarily slowed, but I was no longer able to see the Morrigan and the dragon shifter grappling above. They hadn't gone into the mortal realm, had they? The silence was jarring, and the icy carnage could only have one source.

"Come out, Fionn." I raised my voice. "I know you're here."

There he was, as though the whole world had shifted aside to let him pass. He sat on horseback amid the wrecked forest, regarding me with an expression of profound, exaggerated disappointment, as though I'd failed him in some fundamental way.

"This is where you choose to die?" asked Fionn. "Not defending your own realm?"

"I'm defending my realm with every second I spend facing you. Don't doubt that for a minute." I held my blade up. "Ready to do this?"

The shock of the explosion had reduced my nerves to a minimum, but my heart began to beat faster again. With my allies gone, I had nothing but my wits and a vague idea of how to win that seemed less distinct by the minute.

Fionn sighed. "Kneel."

My knees hit the icy ground, shredding my jeans. My healing power kicked in instantly, but my hands refused to lift my talisman to strike him, and my iron weapons remained out of reach.

A loud screech was my only warning before the Morrigan's claws pierced my shoulders, lifting me into the air. My legs flailed, kicking out, as we rose above the husks of burned trees and the corpses of dead fae. Amid the ruined trees stood armoured horsemen, awaiting their master's command.

I twisted in the Morrigan's claws, gripping my sword's hilt. It was pretty much impossible to swing accurately at this angle, but I drove the sword sideways and managed to hit her leg, slicing into flesh and feathers. She screamed in rage, writhing so violently she almost dislodged me, but her claws remained locked into my skin. My shoulders tingled as my magic tried to heal the open wounds. *Fuck,* that hurt.

The pain fed into my magic, bolstering my talisman as I swiped again, my blade wedging into the Morrigan's claw. I stabbed, and she screeched as the sharp edge bit through feathers and flesh alike.

Her claw released me. I tumbled downward, hurtling towards the ground. As the air rushed past, my fall came to an abrupt halt when I landed in Vance's arms. Had he displaced me in midair?

"Thanks," I gasped as he placed my feet on the ground. "That would have hurt."

The Morrigan shrieked and dived. Leaping up, Vance struck, his claws sinking into her injured leg. I yelled a warning as her other claw aimed at his face, but Vance disappeared before the blow landed. He reappeared on her back, his claws slicing at her wings. I angled my blade and stabbed her as she fell, my blade sinking deep into her chest.

A horrible ripping sounded as Vance's claws released her ruined wings. I yanked my blade free of her chest, trusting him to finish the job.

Now for Fionn. A flurry of activity drew my eyes to the boundary, where Sidhe once again fought the dead alongside humans and the Chief's half-bloods. Someone had opened the doorway, and the battle was back in full swing. Fionn himself remained in the ruins of the forest, directing the action from his horse. He hadn't unleashed his beast form yet. Waiting for the opportune moment, I assumed. That and it was easier for him to fling taunts at me while in his humanoid guise. When our gazes connected, he shot me a smirk, daring me to come closer.

Bring it. I made my way towards him, my blade cutting down any enemy that crossed my path. The area around him was clear, but the mangled body of a Sidhe lay pinned beneath his horse's hooves.

"How's revenge going for you?" I called to him. "Is it everything you hoped for?"

Another horseman blocked my path, dressed in the same armour as the others. His face was hidden—I only assumed he was male at all because he was a bloody giant—and his blade swung with precision. I lifted my sword and caught the blow, staggering sideways with the weight.

"What're *you* getting out of this?" I asked the masked man. "He'll destroy you too, in the end. You're just puppets. Also, he's not actually the Huntsman."

"They serve the one who possesses the Huntsman's magic," said Fionn. "That happens to be me. They're more loyal than hellhounds."

Our swords broke apart. The horseman made to deal another blow and I blasted him with magic, drawing on the residual pain and anger from the battlefield and putting all my power behind the blow. His sword reared, and I launched a second attack that flung him sideways off his horse into the bushes, where I lost sight of him amid the rampaging dead.

I ran onward, keeping both eyes on Fionn so he didn't slip away. "What're you hiding in the woods for? Too scared to take part in your own battle, or are you already bored of fighting?"

"You forced my hand, Ivy." He smiled, a razor-edged grin more dangerous than a snarl. "You and your mage cheated me, and for that, you will suffer a truly spectacular death."

"Sure." I offered him an eye-roll. "We know how that turned out last time. I know you don't want to hear it, but you lost the second you decided to imitate the Sidhe you hate so much. You're too fucking predictable."

"Wrong," he said. "My army is limitless."

"No such thing," I retaliated. "Have you learned nothing from your past failures? Nobody is going to bow to you. We don't want you, Fionn. The gods themselves would rise up and smite you if you hadn't *killed* them."

His sharp smile turned into an equally cutting frown. "You know…?"

"I spoke to the one whose life you took. The same god who fights alongside me today." My blade gleamed, resonating with the hum of battle and suffused with the anger and pain of those who'd been slaughtered. As I neared him, my magic writhed, eager to strike him down.

"What did the god tell you?" Fionn demanded.

"Wouldn't you like to know." *Trickery.* I kept the god's words in mind. What would fool Fionn into giving up his power? He'd originally wanted *this* magic, but he'd made the mistake of trying to take it by force. Was that the key?

"I would very much like to know," said Fionn. "I'll pry

every word out of you, one at a time, as you scream for mercy."

He leapt from his horse and transformed. Wings sprouted from his shoulders, black and jagged, and scales coated his body as he grew into his monstrous form.

Fionn dived at me with deadly talons splayed, and I retaliated by firing magic directly into his eyes. My attack had no effect, but the bright flash offered me the chance to duck under his claw and drive my blade upward into the joint.

A gory mess exploded over the talisman, but his severed claw began regenerating the second I pulled my sword free. His other claw caught me in the chest. I twisted and caught the blow side-on, avoiding direct stab wounds, but the impact sent me flying. Winded, I rolled over, deflecting a blast of icy magic. My shield held up, but his own magic was stronger, and I'd never beat him in outright combat. I scrambled in my pocket for an iron knife, but the odds of getting in close enough to use it without the ring were not in my favour.

Nearby, the battle raged on, horsemen clashing with Sidhe, undead with mages and half-bloods, but the area around the pair of us had cleared, containing nothing but the scorched husks of ruined trees. Even the horseman I'd kicked aside had gone. This was as close to a fair fight as I'd get.

Not that I had any intention of fighting fair.

Fionn dived at me. I jumped to meet him, sinking my blade into his leg. He used the momentum to lift *me* off the ground; I wrenched my way free and landed in a roll. I came upright and sliced into his oncoming talon, and again he healed before I'd pulled the blade free. I needed to deal a more debilitating blow, but his thick shapeshifter body was hard to inflict any kind of damage on.

He dove again. I leapt, my sword slicing at his wing from behind and cutting deep into the membrane. As he lost height, I drove the blade deeper until he snarled and shook himself, trying to dislodge me. My blade came free, and he hit out, his claw slicing straight through my shield and sending me sprawling. Blood dampened my face and numbness filtered in, the sort of numb that preceded terrible pain.

Another roar sounded, this one much louder. The entire forest trembled as the dragon shifter came soaring into view. Fionn lifted his head, momentarily distracted. The pain hit then, my vision doubling as I writhed and gasped, willing my healing power to kick in. As blue light flared, the whole forest shook with the force of the two gods colliding in mid-flight.

The two shapeshifters clawed at one another, vicious and relentless, opening deep wounds. Their blood rained down in a fine mist, yet neither slowed. Both had healing powers, and both fought as though if they stopped, they'd cease to exist. I leapt aside when the pair of shifters slammed into the ground. Fionn held the other dragon pinned by the neck. Eraenar struggled, unable to free himself.

"No!"

A loud snap reverberated, and the talisman in my hands vibrated, too. There came a dazzling flash of green light and the fighting momentarily ceased while everyone shielded their eyes.

When the light faded, the dragon shifter lay still. Unmoving.

Eraenar.

The shifter god was dead, his neck cleanly snapped.

Fionn released him, and I stared numbly, unable to speak or move. Unable to take my eyes off Eraenar, not even when Fionn returned to his human form. He was soaked in blood from head to toe, his armour a mangled ruin, but he let out a guttural laugh of triumph as he stood over the dead god.

"No more miracles, Ivy." He spat blood onto the snow.

"Yes, I know it was he who saved you from my palace. And now you see that the gods themselves are no match for me."

More blood dripped from Fionn's mouth, indicating the dragon shifter had inflicted some kind of internal injury on him that was slower to heal. I wouldn't have a better chance than this. Pushing aside my shock, I leapt at Fionn and swung my blade at his neck.

My sword sank in at the same instant as his claws pierced my chest. A thick mass of scales and feathers formed on his neck, blocking my blade halfway, and I struggled to keep hold of my blade as blood poured from my chest and pain ripped through my core. The wounds tingled as my healing power tried to kick in, but my whitening vision warned that it wouldn't be enough.

I tried to pull my blade out of his neck, but it was too deeply lodged in. With a curse, I let go, staggering back, and Fionn's claws slid free from my chest.

He reached for my sword and pulled it free from his neck in a spray of blood. Then he hurled it at me.

Fast. Too fast to process. I didn't have time to blink, much less take in the sight of my own sword spinning towards me until it sank to the hilt in my chest.

Fionn smiled at me. "Please tell me how it feels to die. I'm curious."

Honestly... not like much at all. I didn't know if I was in shock or the adrenaline of the battle was delaying the response, but the sword... didn't hurt. Blue light flared out of the blade, and magic swirled around me in thick circles. A tingling came from my chest, but no pain.

I grabbed the hilt. Tugged the blade free. Blood sprayed out, but the healing buzz of my magic dampened the pain before it started.

Fionn took a step back, anger and disbelief flashing in his eyes. "What is this? No talisman cannot harm the owner. If that had been the case, the ring would have had no effect on me."

"No?" I smiled back. "Maybe it's because I actually tried to negotiate with my blade's original owner rather than stabbing them in the back. And the god and I aren't done with you yet."

As he gaped at me, I thrust my blade into his ribs. My magic buzzed furiously, itching to take his head off, but the wound sealed even with the blade still inside him. He laughed, half amused and half livid. The trees shook. Frost coated the air, burning against my skin.

With my free hand, I reached for my iron dagger, and I drove the weapon into his throat. Hard scales blocked me, but grey lines fanned out where the iron touched him. I pushed harder, and he coughed and snarled, transforming into his bird-form as I dug the blade in as deep as it would go.

Releasing the dagger, I yanked my sword free of his chest and finished decapitating him. His neck gave way and his hideous half-bird head fell to the ground, uttering a laugh as it did so. *Okay, that's creepy as fuck.*

"That won't work," he whispered, the voice appearing to come from his severed head. "I'm undying."

"Only as long as you host the Huntsman's magic," I said. "And I claim it as mine."

"We didn't make a deal."

"I don't give a shit, Fionn. You just take what you want anyway. I can do the same."

When I'd killed Avalin, his magic had rushed from his body and flooded me, obeying the terms of the bet we'd made. I didn't know what would happen with Fionn's, but already a current of silver-blue rose upward from the half-feathered thing that had once been his body.

"I will not die," the wraith whispered. "I am the Huntsman."

"No," I said. "The Huntsman is a title, not a person, and the magic you stole can be taken back. Even by a human."

Light wreathed his wraith form, clinging to him like a thick, many-layered net. His magic was woven into his very spirit, his essence, but I refused to believe it couldn't be pulled out.

"Kneel!" His shout rang through me, forced my body downward.

Even in death his vow remained active, but I was ready. Before my knees hit the ground, I left my body and flew towards his wraith-form.

The threads of magic were easier to see as a ghost, layers of green overlaid with blue. Remnants of the magic he'd stolen, including the most recent. He'd stolen a Winter Sidhe's power not long ago, and as I grabbed his wraith-form in my ghostly hands, coldness racked me, the sensation of a thousand knives stabbing me all over.

I held on tight, searching through the threads for the right one. My transparent fingers snagged on a thread amid the tapestry that made up Fionn's raging spirit, feeling a buzz of resistance as I connected with the one that my magic reacted to with a furious hum. *There.*

I dug in my fingers, hard, and pulled on that thread. Pulled, hard, until the thread began to unravel.

Fionn screamed, a wordless howl, and shoved me off him. I flew back, reeling with the icy shock, but his magic was already unspooling. Already coming undone. I slid back into my body and felt his command lift as I rose to my feet.

I lifted my blade, driving it through the heart of the thing that had once been Fionn.

His despairing scream froze the leaves on branches, made

frost spring up on my skin and then melt an instant later as another thread of magic unravelled. Wisps of blue and green light drifted away, perhaps remnants of other talismans he'd stolen in decades past, of others he'd murdered for their power.

The Huntsman's own magic became more and more distinct amid the others. Rather than dispersing, its snakelike tendrils reached in all directions as though searching for something to grab onto. A new host. *There must always be a Huntsman,* the Winter Sidhe had said.

I expected the moment when the tendrils found me, coiled around me, snaked up my wrists. Thoughts of riding on horseback through an endless night nudged into my mind's eye. The image conjured promised freedom, but I knew that the Huntsman's job was the precise opposite of that. I had absolutely no intention of spending eternity ferrying faeries' souls to Death.

Besides, the Sidhe had no need for a Huntsman, not with the cauldron gone. Their spirits would naturally move on, as it should be.

"I bind you." I opened my mouth and spoke the same words I'd said when I'd sealed Calder's magic, and the glyphs igniting along my talisman reflected my command.

The brightness spread, encompassing the tendrils climbing up my arms. Each thread disappeared, each fragment of the Huntsman's power dissipating along with the other magic Fionn had stolen.

The last word of the spell left my mouth. My body swayed, greyness encroaching on my vision, but an arm steadied me. Vance. I held onto him and didn't look away until the last remnant of Fionn's spirit disintegrated, blown away on the wind.

24

I*t's over*. The truth rippled through the battlefield. Fionn's warrior horsemen ceased fighting, his wraiths disappeared, and the undead stopped—well, dead. With nobody to control them, they were nothing but empty shells. Second by second, the fighters realised the battle was over.

Fionn was dead. For real, this time. The Huntsman would never come back.

A weight lifted from me, too large to comprehend. Fionn himself had haunted me ever since he'd first awoken, but before him, my thoughts had always been dogged by the Sidhe. The impossibly beautiful, deadly monsters who'd seemed invincible, unknowable. Even killing Avalin had felt like a dream, a fluke.

Until I'd accepted my magic as both a part of me, as an ally, and as a force I would use to defend my home.

The aftermath of the battle would linger for a while, but Fionn would never spread terror through our realm again. Shock and relief flooded me in equal measures as Vance and I moved among the battlefield, looking for any mages who'd remained behind. Not many had; they'd been better equipped to fight the enemy on the other side of the Ley Line, and the same went for the witches. I hoped that the undead attacking the city had also ceased their assault, but Isabel and the others would be more than equipped to take out any stragglers.

The Sidhe had already started to sneak away. I ran to waylay Lord Raivan near the path into Summer. "Hey—wait a minute."

"The battle is won," he said without turning around.

A thank-you would have been nice. "We need to make sure nothing like this ever happens again."

"We will send an envoy," said Lord Raivan.

"Not good enough." Out of the corner of my eye, I saw the Winter Sidhe melting into the surrounding trees, too. I sprinted after Lady Rive, calling, "Hey! Let me talk to you."

Lady Rive swivelled around, looking coolly at me. "What is it, human? I need to report to the Unseelie Queen."

"Yeah, I know. But what I said to you, about cooperation with the mortal realm... I reckon it's something to consider."

"We intend to undo the damage that the Huntsman did," said Lady Rive. "There must also be a new Huntsman as soon as possible."

Yeah, that's not happening. "I'm not sure you need a new Huntsman as much as you need to deal with the exiles in the Grey Vale," I said to her. "There are still plenty of them out there. We won one war, but this has been going on for generations."

"Winter started it," said Lord Raivan, who'd seemingly changed his mind about staying behind once he'd seen me talking to one of the Unseelie.

"Excuse me?" said Lady Rive. "It was the theft of your talisman that enabled the false Huntsman to gain the power he did."

"Hey!" I glared at both of them. "This is the time to cooperate, not point fingers at one another. We have our own problems to sort out in the mortal realm, but someone here needs to take responsibility, too."

"There is no place for us in your realm," said Lady Rive. "And no room for you in ours."

"So what?" I asked. "That didn't stop the old Council of Twelve, and there's no reason we can't set up a meeting with representatives of Summer, Winter, and the supernaturals of the mortal realm, to talk about our future. You might have the freedom to close your eyes to the rest of us, but we have to deal with the consequences of the last war every day. And the Grey Vale, which you created, isn't going anywhere."

"We will elect to discuss the matter of the Grey Vale," said Lady Rive. "On the basis that it presents a very real threat to all the realms and has not been fully mapped by the Winter Court."

"Summer will be involved, too," said Lord Raivan. "We will also take inventory of our talismans and ensure that none of them will fall into the wrong hands again. However, the notion of meeting with humans…"

"It won't kill you," I said. "You're talking to two of them right now."

"The Mage Lords would like to formally extend an invitation to join us at our next summit," Vance added. "Quentin, who is employed by Summer, will gladly serve as our emissary. If Winter would like to be involved as well, then you may send word via the same route or pick your own ambassador."

The Sidhe immediately focused their attention on him. No surprise. Even covered in blood and with his clothes torn, Vance was closer to the manners of a Court Sidhe than I'd ever be. Given his experience dealing with the mage council, he certainly stood a stronger chance of persuading them to cooperate, which was more than fine by me. I didn't want to spearhead any meetings between bickering faerie nobles and the other supernaturals. A link between the mortal and faerie worlds wouldn't solve all our problems, but it'd stop us from being taken by surprise if anyone else tried to do what Fionn had.

Already, ideas had begun to spin to life in my head. The Sidhe would know the names of all their exiles. We'd be able to prevent more Sidhe like Avalin taking innocent humans captive. And that, I was sure, would just be the beginning.

"Fine," said Lord Raivan, after listening to Vance's pitch. "I will endeavour to see what I can do to attend this meeting. Mortal timekeeping does not fit with ours."

"Then get a clock," I said. "Or just ask Quentin. It's really not hard to check. You're the ones with the ability to cross realms whenever you feel like it."

"Our responsibilities run deep, and our own Courts come first."

"Obviously." I suppressed the urge to roll my eyes. "Oh, and you should reward the half-faeries who fought in the war, too."

"What are they to you?" Lady Rive looked askance at me. "You're human."

"Every single one of them has been rejected by the faerie realm, and it's because of that that Fionn was able to be resurrected. He tricked the half-bloods into helping him because they had nowhere else to go. If you want to avoid a repeat of those events, then I suggest putting some kind of system in place where half-bloods can find their faerie parents."

"Why?" asked Lord Raivan. "This sounds like an impossibly complicated endeavour. No half-blood has ever come to our Court."

"For a start," I said, "it's not fun being a changeling,

yanked out of the world you think you belong in and thrown into another. I should know. Besides, dozens of half-bloods appeared in our realm twenty years ago, just after the invasion. If not hundreds. Funny how that happened, isn't it?"

Lord Raivan's eyes narrowed. "I don't know what you're implying, Ivy Lane, but I have never consorted with a mortal."

"But has anyone else from your Court? Hundreds of half-bloods don't fall out of the sky. Seems pretty suspect to me. Also, people like the Chief over there are technically descended from noble Sidhe lineage. You can't shut them out entirely. You created this mess."

"Fine," said Lord Raivan. "I will permit the nobles of the Seelie Court to vote on a decision about the half-bloods."

"And I will do the same for the Unseelie Court," added Lady Rive.

"Good." Someone would have to make sure they kept their word, but the half-bloods would finally have a shot at reaching the realm that had cruelly shut them out. I suspected it wouldn't be the haven they thought it would be, but the battle had doubtless removed some of those illusions already. The Chief was lucky to be alive, considering his weak magic. I saw him standing with Killian and the other half-faeries, and Roseanne was with them, too.

She looked utterly dejected, and when I approached her, she shrank in on herself, her shoulders hunching. "You… you killed her."

"Temporarily," I said, guessing she meant the Morrigan. "She'll be back, but I doubt she'll come after you. She was following Fionn's orders."

"How do you know?" Her voice trembled. "What if she tries to claim me again?"

"Pretty sure I'm first on her shit list," I commented. "And Vance. We'll keep her away from you."

"I can't come with you." Her face crumpled. "I don't belong in the mortal realm. I… I killed him. My father."

I winced. "Fionn forced you. He *and* the Morrigan have his blood on their hands, not you. You're free, and you don't have to live in exile."

"I do," she mumbled. "I fucked everything up."

"I've done that plenty of times myself," I pointed out. "If anything, that proves you're human."

Roseanne wouldn't have an easy time of it, but I'd been in her shoes at one time, with nothing behind me but mistakes and nothing ahead but uncertainty. In time, the wounds would heal, and without Fionn's hands around her throat, she'd finally have the chance to decide her own fate. To make something of her life.

She let out a sob. "Why would you care what I do?"

"Because I do." I mimicked the belligerent tone she'd used on me when we'd first met. "It's up to you. Come back, and I'll see if we can find you somewhere to live that isn't a rat-infested hole."

"I *like* my home," she said defensively.

"Better than the manor?" Vance strode over to join us. "I can't promise to offer you permanent accommodation there, but we won't leave you out in the cold."

"I like the cold."

"Sure you do." I rolled my eyes at her, though it was a relief to see her acting like a normal teenager again. "Hey, Vance. Ready to go?"

"Of course." He took my hand and turned towards home.

After a moment's hesitation, Roseanne did, too.

———

"Ivy." Frank the necromancer appeared in the middle of the summoning circle in the mausoleum. He was accompanied by Lord Evander this time, and the necromancers' former leader did not look thrilled to see me in the slightest.

"Hey," I said. "Thought I'd come and check the veil's back to normal."

"It is," Frank confirmed. "I thought you came to extend an offer to join your new council."

"What new council?" asked Lord Evander.

"We haven't really started setting it up yet," I said. "We've been too busy cleaning up the city. Also, we can't invite any necromancers to join until the living ones choose a new leader."

"Isn't that what they're doing right now?" Lord Evander said. "You didn't answer my question."

"You'd know what the council is if you paid attention to anyone other than the dead," I retaliated. "The council is going to be a union of all the supernaturals formed in conjunction with the faerie Courts to ensure nothing like this war ever happens again."

"The necromancers will not be involved with the faeries." Lord Evander scowled. "Nobody will ever agree to this."

"Have you learned nothing at all from this debacle?" asked Frank. "We might not occupy the mortal realm in the way that we did, but we have a responsibility towards the supernatural community."

"Yeah, you do," I said. "One you've neglected for too long. This council will be out in the open, not hidden in secrecy like the old one. Oh, and it'll extend further across the country. Hence why it's taking a while to set up."

"I expect so." An expression of contemplation travelled over Frank's face. "I understand the mistakes we made in the past. It used to be that if ever a human became aware of the faeries, it was an inevitable death sentence, and we could not even speak their names without inviting retribution. Now…"

"Now, we're better off without them," snapped Lord

Evander. "This *alliance* is out of the question. It's impossible to get every supernatural on the same page."

"So is killing a god, and I managed that. Work it out."

I left the mausoleum and closed the door on Lord Evander's shout of *You did what?* He'd escaped lightly, if you asked me. Hardly any ghosts were left on this side of the veil, but we'd still had a new spate of undead rising up to make a nuisance of themselves. I swore the past week had been an endless string of meetings punctuated by fights with stragglers from the battle who'd been left behind.

At the gate, I found Isabel waiting for me. "That was fast."

"There was slightly less yelling than usual, so it was an improvement," I said. "How're the living necromancers doing?"

"Much better since reinforcements showed up."

"Good." Someone had proposed the ingenious idea of rebuilding the necromancers' scattered ranks by inviting in those from outside of the city, similarly to how the mages had had representatives from other regions step in to offer a hand. Granted, Lady Granville was the last person anyone needed around in a crisis, but it turned out the necromancers in other cities had had no idea how bad the situation was here until the war with Fionn had erupted across the Ley Line up and down the country. Within days, a whole host of necromancers from Edinburgh and London—the biggest branches—had shown up to help. I didn't know if the new leader would be chosen from among the newcomers or if one of our own locals would get the spot, but it was a welcome change from their usual inefficiency.

"I'm not sure if they've chosen a leader yet," Isabel added. "I put in word for Rick, but you know, I'm biased."

"I mean, yeah." The guy was decent. Maybe not leader material, but an empty shoebox would be a better leader than Lord Evander. "It'll be good when we have people from all the supernatural groups ready to join the new council, too."

Isabel and I walked across the road to the safe house where half the city's mages were still based. While the manor had reopened, a fair few people had refused to go back, and the lingering outside visitors needed somewhere to stay until they finally buggered off, too. I knocked on the door, and Vance greeted me with a kiss.

"Take it your meeting with the shifters went okay?" I asked him.

"Better than the last."

"Did you tell them… about the dragon shifter?" We hadn't been sure where to bury him, and in the end, we'd opted to reuse the same hole on shifter territory in which he'd originally been imprisoned. It was likely the closest he'd get to his former home and none of the shifters had objected. I'd found no traces of him in the spirit realm, so I assumed he'd moved on to wherever the gods, or faeries, went after they died. Since the shifters had refused to set foot near the Ley Line since the battle, I didn't know how much they really knew about the being they'd once worshipped as a god..

Vance shook his head. "I tried, but they refused to believe he was any relation of theirs. I'm not convinced he was the origin of the entirety of the shifter population either. There were many gods, and many of them came to this realm and mingled with humans. It's not my place to force them to accept a truth they'll have to come to terms with on their own."

"What about Wyatt?"

"I did tell him. He said I was speaking complete nonsense and never to bother his family again."

I snorted. "Sure. Faerie invasions, undead running amok all over town, but dragon shifter gods are too much for some people to believe in."

"Sometimes I wonder if he's channelling non-supernatural instead of shifter ancestry."

"Hey, we boring normal humans aren't too bad." I winked at him.

"You're the opposite of normal, Ivy."

"And boring," added Isabel. "Frankly, I'd be worried if you ever wanted to give up running into trouble."

"Not happening, don't worry. Not as long as I have this." I tapped the talisman at my side. If I'd wanted to, I could have given the sword and its power back to the god. It carried memories, and not all good ones. But the sword was mine, and it represented what I'd struggled through, and what I'd survived. For that, the magic would be a part of me as long as I lived.

"Good," said Vance. "I decided to wait until things have calmed down a little to explain to Wyatt that I'll be obliged to come and visit if Anabel shows any signs of her mage ability. Which, if she develops the gift early like most people in my family have, might be sometime within the next year."

"You're joking." A grin spread across my face. "Please say there's a good chance she ends up with the same ability as you have."

"It's unlikely, but I wouldn't rule anything out at this point."

"Nope." I hoped she did. It'd serve Wyatt right. "And she'll be your apprentice?"

"If she wants."

"Obviously she will." I nudged him in the arm. "She worships you despite how much of a dickhead her dad is. Anyway, how's it going with the other mages? Lady Granville still hanging around making a nuisance of herself?"

I peered past him into the safe house, but I didn't see any curious onlookers. Except for Wanda, who waved from the doorway to the main room when she saw me watching.

"Hey, Ivy," she said. "Sorry for listening in. I was wondering if you heard from my grandmother."

"She didn't go running off into the forest again, did she?"

"Apparently so." Her mouth turned down at the corners. "I don't know what she and the Hemlocks are planning."

"Mischief, no doubt," I said. "You ought to come back to the manor. It's got to be more pleasant than staying here."

"Oh, I'm waiting for the necromancers' elections to finish," she said. "Now the necromancers from out of town are here, I'm hoping to run into a friend or two of mine from up in Edinburgh."

"Really?" I frowned. "Then was it you who suggested getting in touch with them?"

"I wish I'd called them sooner, but I had no idea that the other necromancers didn't know how bad it was here," she said. "My friend Jas and I hadn't spoken in years, but you know, those attacks from the Ley Line hit all across the country and all kinds of connections are reopening."

"That includes the mages," Vance added. "That was what I was going to tell you, Ivy. The other mages left earlier today."

"All of them?" I asked. "Even Lady Granville? What changed?"

"I believe it had to do with a hundred necromancers showing up outside the safe house in the early hours of the morning," Vance said.

"Or maybe my grandmother getting mad at her for disturbing her nap," added Wanda.

I bit back a laugh. "Seriously?"

"Yes, and as I reminded her, she has a responsibility to help her new council fix the damage caused by the incident on the Ley Line," Vance said. "Our own interim council is more than capable of handling things here, as Lady Granville saw for herself."

"Absolutely." Lady Penrose's death had likely shaken her,

and while the other mages would never forget the losses they'd suffered, I was glad that they'd be able to establish their new ranks without interference.

As we parted ways with Wanda and left the mages' safe house behind, a cool breeze blew over us, a reminder that winter was on the way, but the normal kind of winter, not the result of faerie magic running amok.

"I hope Lady Granville stays away while we're setting up the Council of Twelve, or whatever we end up calling it," I remarked to Vance. "We almost have a full set now. If not actual volunteers, we've at least spoken to the shifters, the necromancers, and the witches. The half-bloods are on hold for now. I think the Chief's waiting until we've wrangled a proper commitment out of the Courts."

"They'll come around," Vance said. "The Sidhe, too."

"Yeah, but the Sidhe like you."

Quentin had invited some of them to speak with the mages a couple of days ago and discuss their future relationship with the mortal realm. Everyone had been rendered speechless when they'd shown up at the manor, except Vance, who acted like they were ordinary guests who'd shown up unexpectedly. Lady Granville had nearly passed out in the council room, and I was pretty sure that had also contributed to her decision to leave early. Even Lady Harper respected the Sidhe, though they treated *her* with a level of politeness that I'd never have expected of them. When I'd asked if her mind-breaking power worked on Sidhe, she'd given such an evil laugh that I'd abandoned that line of questioning outright.

The Sidhe would probably never like *me*, but the same could be said of the Chief, and he'd made the altogether surprising and mildly mortifying decision to drag me to his official re-instatement ceremony in which he'd been re-elected as Chief and had then told everyone present that I was to be treated as an honorary fae and allowed to come and go as I pleased without being attacked. Time would tell if the other half-faeries kept their word, but it helped that their magic was functioning again and that they'd been able to repair the damage the banshee had inflicted when she'd bulldozed half the territory.

I didn't think the pure-blooded faeries would ever truly warm to the half-bloods, but whatever decision the Sidhe made would be dissatisfying to someone, and just having the choice was enough for most of the half-bloods. Now they'd seen the real Faerie, I doubted they'd be tempted by the Vale again.

"The Sidhe aren't as difficult to deal with as I expected," Vance said.

"It won't last. They'll have their own ulterior motives for deciding to involve themselves with humans."

"Probably," said Isabel. "At least they've stopped bringing up that bloody ring."

"Don't even." We'd got through the last meeting without anyone mentioning it at all, which seemed a minor miracle. "And if anything else gets stolen from the Erlking, they'd better keep me out of it. I'm done with faerie drama."

"Sure you are." Isabel grinned at me. "Weren't you dealing with a troll just this morning?"

"It wandered into the Hemlock witches' forest. I decided it was better not to piss them off."

"Did you speak to them?" asked Isabel.

"Briefly," I said. "I'm getting the impression Cordelia wants to talk to the Sidhe, but I doubt I can persuade any of them to go into the forest."

"I think the Sidhe would be a little disarmed by how much the witches know about their realm," Vance said.

"True." Thanks to the forest's ability to read memories,

the witches already knew pretty much all their recent history.

Of course, there was just one *tiny* issue I hadn't brought up with the Sidhe yet, and one that made me glad they hadn't gone near the forest yet. Without immortality, the Sidhe would have to embrace the change they so rigorously tried to avoid. I didn't envy them the bumpy road ahead, but I wouldn't be the one to steer them along. I'd been blessed—or cursed—with faerie magic, but that didn't mean I was single-handedly responsible for solving all their problems.

"Where do you want to go?" Vance asked.

"Drop us off at the office." I nodded to Isabel. "Unless you want to ride the bus like a regular person."

"Not with the state the roads are in at the moment," Isabel said. "I sometimes wish there was a spell that could handle large-scale cleanup."

"Hey, if anyone can invent one, it's you."

Vance transported us from necromancer territory to the witches' part of town. All the shops were open, buses and cars rumbled past, and few signs remained of the furies that had been terrorising the streets only a few short days ago. I revelled in the sheer ordinariness of it all and grinned at a passing mercenary. "Hey, Gregor."

Gregor yelped and ran to the other side of the road, holding his hands over his head as if to avoid a dive-bombing fury. The mercs had mostly stayed out of the battle, though Larsen had taken to being absurdly polite to me in a blatantly false way whenever we'd run into one another. Apparently, he was always available to give me advice on running my own business. Considering I'd grasped two concepts he hadn't—don't treat your employees like shit, and don't gamble other people's money away—I was leagues ahead of him already.

As we reached the road leading to our office, Erwin came

flying to greet us. I was pretty sure he didn't have much of a clue what was going on, but he seemed glad that we'd mostly returned to our usual routines.

Isabel unlocked the front door. "Coming in? Or do you two have somewhere else to be?"

"Not at the moment." I looked at Vance, who smiled. "Now our unwanted mage guests have left town, we have the afternoon free."

"I'm sure someone will start a fight soon enough." Isabel opened the door and walked in. "Or show up asking us to evict a nest of piskies from their house."

"Better piskies than furies." I followed her. "At least there's never a dull moment."

"Even more if you're going to be an emissary between the Courts and the mortal realm."

I nearly tripped over the doorstep. "Who told you that?"

"I kind of… assumed," Isabel said. "I mean, someone has to do it, and who else is qualified?"

Ah. I should have known the topic would come up eventually.

"Someone is," I hedged. "There's something I haven't mentioned to you guys yet. Since you know, we had bigger issues to deal with."

Isabel and Vance exchanged glances but neither pushed me to speak.

"There's this family," I began. "The Lynns. Gerry told me about them—I ran into his ghost in the Vale, and he said that my surname is similar enough that he wondered if we might be distantly related. Anyway, this Lynn family has supposedly been connected with the Summer and Winter Courts for generations."

Isabel's eyes rounded. "And they're human?"

"Yes, as far as I know," I said. "Gerry didn't know how that came about, but I figure that if they *are* involved with the

Courts, they're probably entangled in a dozen faerie vows to stop them from spilling the beans. Anyway, he said they're peacekeepers, and I figured I should probably let them know about the cauldron."

"Are they trustworthy?" Vance queried. "Being tied to the Sidhe?"

"Haven't a clue," I said. "They're also way up in Scotland, or they were the last time Gerry knew of them, so finding them is probably a long shot. I just figured I might as well tell you. It's not every day you find out you might have distant relatives who can use faerie magic."

Isabel gaped at me. "They can?"

"Either trickery runs in the family or the Sidhe are just worse at keeping humans from swiping their talismans than they like to pretend." I shrugged. "I mean, I don't know if a talisman is involved, but mine is completely unrelated to this family. I'm a hundred percent human."

"And if you *do* find them?" asked Isabel. "Are you sure we should tell anyone about the cauldron at all? If even the Sidhe haven't worked it out yet…"

"They will," I said. "Next time one of them gets stabbed over a minor infraction. I don't know if it's possible for them to replace the cauldron, but these Lynns are supposed to be peacekeepers. I reckon we'll need some of those to handle the inevitable shitstorm."

"I feel sorry for them already," Isabel remarked. "I was worried you'd run back to Faerie at the first opportunity."

"Hell, no. I'm staying here." I took Vance's hand. "You'd have to pry me away."

Vance smiled at me. "Good. I'd hate to have to borrow one of our new Sidhe friends to come after you."

"Ha. Don't worry, I still can't cross over to the Courts by myself. I already told them all our meetings would take place on *our* territory, until they learn to stop randomly turning people into trees."

"Drake did kind of deserve it, though," said Isabel.

"Yeah, he did," I added. "Lucky it was in this realm, otherwise it might've been permanent."

"And he was in a good mood." Isabel's gaze caught the ring on my finger. She'd screamed when she saw it, though the news hadn't surprised her, and Drake had also been delighted. Lady Harper had sulked for a day, but I didn't particularly care what she thought. "Have you two made any plans yet...?"

"Oh god, no," I said. "Like we've had a moment's peace since we got back."

"Ivy doesn't want to make a big deal of it." Vance put an arm around my shoulder.

"Nope. Definitely not." The wedding, when it came, would be a private, simple affair. Out of the spotlight, the way I liked it. "I'd prefer to keep a low profile for a while."

"Give it a week or two," said Vance.

"He's right," said Isabel. "You can't stay away from trouble."

"Suppose I can't." I smiled at both of them. My family. Faerie had taken away my old life, but I'd chosen to build a new one. To find a home. And right now, I was exactly where I wanted to be.

ABOUT THE AUTHOR

Emma is the New York Times and USA Today Bestselling author of the Changeling Chronicles urban fantasy series.

Emma spent her childhood creating imaginary worlds to compensate for a disappointingly average reality, so it was probably inevitable that she ended up writing fantasy novels. When she's not immersed in her own fictional universes, Emma can be found with her head in a book or wandering around the world in search of adventure.

Find out more about Emma's books at www.emmaladams.com.

www.ingramcontent.com/pod-product-compliance
Lightning Source LLC
Chambersburg PA
CBHW020748190726
48285CB00006B/1929